THE INCOMPARABLE

Serena gave him hope. Being dubbed the Incomparable implied that a girl was not only beautiful and accomplished, but also that she was the epitome of all that a man of the *ton* could want in a bride. Every debutante would aspire to be like her; every gentleman would clamor after her. No one would ever expect that there might be a real person under that lovely exterior. Except that she had, in the few hours of their acquaintance, proved herself to be very much an individual, indeed.

Lady Serena, Charles corrected himself. It was not only the intensity of their situation that made him feel as if he'd known her longer than he had. In truth, he knew nothing about her, except that she kept a cool head when faced with danger. He doubted that many of society's hothouse roses would have behaved as she had, eluding her captors and then fighting so valiantly in her own defense. He doubted that many people realized she had such depths. She might not even have known it herself.

<u>BOOK YOUR PLACE ON OUR WEBSITE</u> AND MAKE THE <u>READING CONNECTION!</u>

We've created a customized website just for our very special readers, where you can get the inside scoop on everything that's going on with Zebra, Pinnacle and Kensington books.

When you come online, you'll have the exciting opportunity to:

- View covers of upcoming books
- Read sample chapters
- Learn about our future publishing schedule (listed by publication month *and author*)
- Find out when your favorite authors will be visiting a city near you
- Search for and order backlist books from our online catalog
- Check out author bios and background information
- Send e-mail to your favorite authors
- Meet the Kensington staff online
- Join us in weekly chats with authors, readers and other guests
- Get writing guidelines
- AND MUCH MORE!

Visit our website at
http://www.kensingtonbooks.com

THE RELUCTANT HERO

MARY KINGSLEY

ZEBRA BOOKS
Kensington Publishing Corp.
http://www.kensingtonbooks.com

To the Regency Tea New England, for the food, tea, conversation, and far too many books. Let us forever meet on quarter days.

Lady Mary of New Beige

A NOTE ON PORTUGUESE PRONUNCIATION

Portuguese is unlike most of the other Romance languages. Due to the sometimes-nasal vowels and the aspirated consonants, it often has a harsher sound. Because I didn't want my readers to have to pronounce the characters' names each time they encountered them, I was very careful in selecting them. "Joaquim" is relatively easy; the "ei" in Texeira, the family name, is pronounced as a short "e," and the "z" in the female name "Luz" is pronounced as in English.

I fell in love with "Luz" the first time I heard it, and knew that it was perfect for this book. Using "Joaquim" was a more difficult decision. Be glad I chose it. I could have named Luz's brother "João."

ONE

Charles Kirk, late of His Majesty's army on the Iberian Peninsula, felt his tension ease as the soft summer breeze drifted across his face. The air was not particularly fresh, not in London, but it was English air, and the view was of the garden outside the drawing room of Sherbourne House. Lounging on the window seat, apart from the others who sat in the drawing room, he felt curiously detached from their casual talk of *ton* events, of discussions of marriages and betrothals and other *on-dits*. He hadn't expected this, not any of it, to feel the hollowness on seeing the happiness of his brother Geoffrey, Viscount Sherbourne, with his wife, Ariel, and, more surprisingly, of Lord Adam Burnet. He had married his Elizabeth only a few weeks previously, though everyone considered him too lazy to do anything. "I never expected to return home to find all this," Charles burst out, drawing the attention of everyone in the room. "Everyone's married. You, Geoffrey, Adam, even Lyndon. What has possessed everyone?"

Geoffrey and Ariel exchanged a look. "I'd wager you could guess," he said, making Ariel give him another look.

"Lud, dear boy," Adam said from his lounging position on a sofa. "Love, don't you know."

"Something you should consider, Charles," Geoffrey remarked.

Charles glanced away, wishing he'd never brought up the topic. Marriage seemed to have tamed Geoffrey, who had been something of a rake before Charles had gone to war. Yet now he seemed content in a way he never had before. Charles well knew that feeling would never be for him. "I suppose you'd see me leg-shackled to this year's Incomparable. Or the Diamond of the First Water, or some such."

"Of course not." Ariel looked up from her knitting and smiled. "I was certainly no such thing. Neither was Lyndon's wife, but when we saw them on their country estate they seemed perfectly happy."

"Who are this year's Diamonds, by the by?" he asked, in an effort to appear interested.

Geoffrey, settled in a high-backed chair with curving, polished wooden arms, gave him a look that said he knew perfectly well why Charles had asked. "The Diamond, as you call her, is a Miss Watson. A quite beautiful widgeon."

"Perfect for Charles, don't you think?" Adam said in languid tones.

Charles gave a mock shudder. "Lord save me. And the Incomparable?" he asked. "Or is there one?"

Geoffrey and Ariel looked at each other again. "The Incomparable seems to have disappeared," Adam said.

"Disappeared? Gone home, you mean?"

"No. Disappeared, yesterday. No one knows where she is. Her father's tried to hush it up, of course, but servants always seem to know everything."

For the first time, the conversation intrigued Charles. "How could someone possibly do something like that? Especially an heiress? I take it she is an heiress, or she wouldn't be so sought after."

"That's terribly cynical of you," Ariel protested.

"But true, I imagine. It was such when I left. Who is her father?"

"The Earl of Harlow."

Charles gave a low whistle. "Lady—who is she now? I know there was a Lady Anne Fairchild."

"Her sister. This one is Lady Serena."

"Then she does have expectations. Does anyone know why she left?"

"No." Ariel frowned down at her knitting. "Oh, dear, I seem to have dropped a stitch."

Charles glanced at her work, something small and white and fluffy. He was, so he'd been told, going to be an uncle. Not a father. Never a father. "It's rather strange."

"Lud, so it is," Adam said. "It's become one of the scandals of the Season."

"Adam," Elizabeth reprimanded him softly. "That's not kind."

"But true."

"No one knows what happened," Ariel put in. "She seemed to be enjoying herself. Certainly she had suitors aplenty."

"For her fortune, you mean."

Ariel's answer was slower in coming this time. "Perhaps."

"I wonder what they would do, were she poor."

"Harlow's been patient with her," Adam put in. "I hear she rejected a number of suitors."

"Perry Faraday, for one. He's only one and twenty, but I do believe he's in love with her."

"Calf love. His mama mustn't be pleased about it."

"No, I gather she's not, especially now," Adam said. "Then there's Ronald Gaskin, definitely a fortune hunter. Harlow sent him to the roundabout."

"Adam," Elizabeth said, reproving him on his language. He merely grinned at her.

"George Duncan," Ariel pressed on. "I do think he really cares about her, even now."

"Mayhap," Adam said. "And then there's Sir Osbert Hyatt."

"That round little dandy?" Geoffrey said in disdain.

"Everyone knows he's always pockets to let," Adam said.

"I wonder if he has something to do with her disappearance," Charles said, entering the conversation for the first time in a while.

Adam gave him a long look. "I doubt that, dear boy. He's more concerned with his clothes." His smile faded. "In any event, no one will want her now."

"Poor girl," Charles said softly.

Adam gave Charles another searching look, making him uncomfortable. "Yes. Do you go to Lady Hathaway's rout tonight?" he asked, and the conversation became general. It was still about *ton* events, though, so that Charles drifted away, content simply to be in this room, in this house. There were arranged marriages aplenty, he heard, some marriages of convenience, even some love matches. It meant little to him. He would never marry, there was no doubt of that. Nor would he ever fit into *ton* life again. He had, once. He had been a dashing young officer wearing the green uniform of the 95th Rifles, pretending to be self-deprecating that his uniform wasn't scarlet, to all the pretty girls who were making their come-outs. There was a reason, though, why he'd bought his colors in that particular regiment. He was deadly with any firearm, shotgun or pistol or rifle, and he knew his services were needed. That was something the pretty young debutantes didn't know. That the uniform didn't protect a man was something only another soldier would understand.

Someone was watching him. Charles's instinct for danger, for sensing a possible enemy, had been finely honed in Spain and Portugal. Casually looking up, he saw Geoffrey assessing him from across the room. Charles returned the look with a sardonic smile. Geoffrey, he suspected, was about to act, not only as the head of the Kirk family, but as an older brother. There was irony in that. As boys growing up, they had not been close.

Their guests had made their farewells before Geoffrey approached him. "Come to the library with me for a drink."

Ariel looked up from her knitting. "Geoffrey, do you intend to play the heavy-handed viscount again?"

"'Tis what I am." His face softened as he looked down at his wife, as he briefly touched her shoulder before moving away. So there *was* love in the world, Charles thought, feeling that familiar ache inside him. It simply wasn't for him.

Wordlessly, Geoffrey walked into the library, ignoring the footman who opened the door for them. He glanced inquiringly at the decanters of drinks, which were on a table that had straight, carved legs. Charles shook his head, and they settled into club chairs of well-padded, glove-soft leather. He had forgotten how beautiful this room was, with its glass-fronted bookcases and the large mahogany library table. Sunlight streamed across the Turkey carpet, making its colors glow. It was a comfortable room, a welcoming room, and Charles wished to the devil he were somewhere else. He no longer belonged here.

He leaned back, his legs crossed. If Geoffrey wanted to talk, then let him begin. This had not been his idea. Yet the silence stretched on, yawning between them.

"You look like hell," Geoffrey said abruptly.

Charles inclined his head. "Thank you. I appreciate the compliment."

"What happened to you?"

"War happened to me."

"No." Geoffrey's eyes searched his face. "There's something more."

"Oh, for God's sake, Geoffrey," he said, shifting in his chair to find a comfortable position. There were days when his arm hurt like the devil, though he hoped no one noticed. "Ariel was right. You are being particularly heavy-handed."

"I care about you."

Charles gave a bitter laugh. "When did that occur?"

"A very long time ago."

"Ha. As I recall, the person whose affections you wanted was Father."

Geoffrey stiffened. "What passed between him and me has nothing to say to this matter."

"Doesn't it? It rather left me out."

"It did, didn't it?" Geoffrey said after a moment. "I owe you an apology for that."

Charles waved him off. "It's of little moment now."

"Not to me." Geoffrey leaned forward. "Charles, what *happened* to you? I don't mean just your wound."

Charles looked bleakly at him, as bleak as he felt. "War," he said again. "Shall I describe it for you?"

"I read the newspapers."

"Ha." His laugh was mirthless. "The newspapers."

"I am your brother, Charles. Whether you wish to acknowledge that or not, it's true."

Charles shook his head. "I do, but I fail to see how that can help me this late."

Geoffrey leaned back, his legs crossed, too, his eyes shrewd. "I'm giving you the management of Oakhurst," he said.

"The devil! One of your properties?"

"A smaller one, in Sussex. It needs a good manager."

"I know nothing about farming, Geoffrey."

"You'll learn in time. It's well enough now," he went

on, forestalling Charles's next protest. "I didn't know anything about it until I came into the title."

"Until you married, is what I heard."

Geoffrey smiled. "Yes, from Ariel. She ran her father's estate for years."

Charles blinked. "Ariel?" He tried to reconcile that image with the laughing, seemingly carefree woman Geoffrey had married. "That comes as a surprise."

"To me, too, at first. She saw things at Oakhurst I might otherwise have missed." His grin was wry. "Of course, she noted everything down."

"Is there anything left there for me to do?" Charles burst out.

"Yes," Geoffrey said seriously. "It needs a master's touch. All properties do. And you"—he took a deep breath—"need it."

Charles looked at him sharply. "Charity, Geoffrey?"

"No," he said quietly. "Concern and affection."

Affection. It was a long time since someone had offered him that. It was something he couldn't fight. "Oh, very well," he said, his capitulation obviously something that came sooner than Geoffrey anticipated. He nearly laughed at the look of ludicrous surprise on his brother's face. "It will give me something to do, any roads."

Geoffrey nodded. "You're not made for London."

"Not now," Charles agreed promptly. "Perhaps once, a long time ago."

Again Geoffrey nodded, as if he understood, and then rose. "I'll see to it that all the necessary papers are sent to you."

"Thank you." Charles looked at his brother across that abyss again, and then impulsively held out his hand. It wasn't just a handshake, but a bond between brothers that Charles hadn't even known was there. " 'Twill be good to have something to do, at least. Perhaps I should visit my tailor." He looked down at his buff pantaloons and his jacket of dark green merino. Why had he chosen green, of all colors? "I haven't the ensembles for a stay in the country, and one must be prepared for all eventualities," he said, in the languid tones of a bored dandy.

Geoffrey grinned. "One must," he agreed.

"Then I'd best get started, curse it. I feel like a man-milliner already.

Geoffrey walked to the door with him, his hand upon Charles's good shoulder. "Oakhurst is worthy of a well-dressed manager."

"We must see to it that it has one, then," he said, grinning.

"You'll do," Geoffrey said, opening the door, his voice relieved. "You'll do, indeed."

"I believe I will," he said, as they went into the hall.

"Yes." Geoffrey stayed back a few paces, waving off the footman who stepped forward to close the library door. He spoke so softly that Charles was never quite certain he'd heard him aright. "And perhaps it might heal you."

Thus it was that, a few days later, Charles's horse picked its way along the narrow lane which branched off the main road from Mayfield, under a spread of leaves that let through the occasional ray of sun, past a wild-flower meadow to his left, past a green, green field stretching to his right. It all still felt a little unreal to Charles. Two years on the Peninsula had accustomed him to a different landscape, a different view, of merciless sun and dusty plains, of ruined towns and wary, frightened people. Not so here. In high summer, England was in glorious bloom, and all the foliage was lush. More importantly, the towns and villages he'd passed through were prosperous and bustling, and the people were, for the most part, busy and cheerful. It was very hard to remember that there was war raging someplace.

It was hard to remember that, not long ago, he'd been part of that war.

In an odd way, Charles, dressed in a tweed coat and sueded leather buff breeches, as befitted the manager of a country estate, regretted that he was no longer in the army. He'd felt important there in a way he never had at home. Oakhurst, he'd no doubt, was no more in need of an estate manager than he was of an estate. Geoffrey, for all his former rackety ways, would have seen to that. No, he'd likely been given the management of the estate simply as a way to keep him busy. He didn't know whether he resented such largesse, or welcomed it.

Oakhurst was just ahead, perhaps a mile or so along the lane. Though he'd been here only a few times when he was younger, already he recognized landmarks. Over there, long felled by a lightning bolt, lay one of the oaks that gave the estate its name; here was the stream, which cut deeply enough in its banks to require a plank bridge, rather than a ford. Samson's hooves rang hollow as he crossed it, the sound so homey that insensibly, Charles felt his spirits lifting. He breathed deeply of the smell of damp earth, listened more intently than he ever had to the counterpoint of birdsong and the buzz of cicadas, and rejoiced in the view of fields as devoid of threats as they were of people. If he'd been put out to pasture, as it were, he could think of worse fates, and worse places. He would grow roses, he decided, and let peace again seep into his soul.

From the corner of his eyes he caught just the merest flicker of motion, so small that he wasn't sure he'd seen it. It was enough, however, for him to stand in the saddle, scanning the field. Nothing. It was likely just a bird, he thought, triggering a response to danger honed too well on the Peninsula. That, more than anything else, was an indicator of the state his nerves had been reduced to.

No, there it was again, a flash of blue through the

trees edging the field, neither fast enough nor small enough to be a bird, after all. He tightened one hand on the reins, reaching his other hand down to his saddlebag, where he kept his pistol, primed and ready. Damn, but he'd not expected to face possible danger, not in England. Not on this peaceful, restful lane.

Again the blue flashed, closer this time. He aimed the pistol, his arm steadier now than it had been since his return. Closer now, and closer—and the blue flicker resolved itself into a woman's skirts. She held them almost to her knees as she ran, throwing quick, frightened glances over her shoulder. For a moment he relaxed his posture. There certainly was something amiss, but it wasn't likely dangerous. Not here on . . .

Behind the woman—a girl, he realized, likely not much older than his sister—lumbered a rough-looking character, a man who shouted at her in words he couldn't quite make out. Their tone was clear, though, and so was the long, deadly pistol in his hand. He was followed by another man, not quite so rough in appearance, but as deadly, judging by the pistol he held.

"Oh, help me, sir!" the woman cried, swerving and running toward him. "Help me!"

Through Charles's mind flashed another time, another place, and a scene that was still part of his nightmares. His stomach churned. He didn't want to be involved in anything like this, he truly didn't, and yet this time he knew enough to react more quickly. Jabbing his spurs into Samson's side to intercept her, he held down his hand. "Take hold," he called.

"Oh, thank you!" She grasped his hand, and, not knowing quite how he did it, he pulled her up behind him, though fierce pain rocketed up from his wounded shoulder to almost behind his teeth. "Oh, thank you! I didn't know what I would do—"

Abruptly a pistol barked. The shot flew harmlessly by;

it, too, was a reminder of another time, and of a peril he'd not thought to encounter again. The first man might have discharged his shot, but the other hadn't, and both were pounding too near for his comfort. Holding his arm absolutely steady, as he had countless times during battles, he fired, and the first man fell.

"Oh, capital!" the woman said, perhaps the most bizarre moment of this entire bizarre incident. There was no time to consider that, though, not with one of the enemy still standing. Retreat was clearly in order. Wheeling Samson around, he dug his spurs in again. They took off at a gallop, pounding down the lane. A pistol sounded behind them again, but they were safely out of reach. For now.

"Oh, thank you! I—"

"Do they have horses?" he demanded at the same time.

"No. Yes, of course they do. They brought me here in a closed carriage, but they could use the horses for riding, couldn't they?"

Overhead arched the same leafy trees as before; to his right, now, was the wildflower meadow. What was different was that he had somehow managed to saddle himself with a totty-headed female. "Quite," he said, his voice clipped.

Surprisingly, she chuckled. "I do beg your pardon. That was an extremely ridiculous thing for me to say, wasn't it? I do hope they don't catch us up."

"On Samson? Highly unlikely."

"So I'd think. Arabian, is he not?"

"Yes," he said, startled.

"And very nicely mannered, considering all he's been through the last few moments. Very nice horseflesh, sir."

"Thank you," he said, the conversation only adding

to his feeling of unreality. "Excuse me, miss, but who are you?"

She gurgled with laughter, strange in someone who had been in dire peril not five minutes hence. "Of course. We've not been properly introduced, have we?"

Charles smiled in spite of himself. One would think they were in a London drawing room, from the way she talked. She had bottom, this young lady. And a lady she was, he had no doubt, in spite of her disordered hair and crumpled gown. "My apologies. I am Major Charles Kirk, late of His Majesty's army." Now why the devil had he introduced himself like that?

"Oh, so that is why you reacted as quickly as you did, and thank heavens for me."

"Yes. May I ask who you are? I do like to know the names of the damsels in distress I rescue."

She laughed again, a low, seductive, and yet innocent sound, and he felt a shiver go up his spine. "Of course. I am Serena Fairchild, Sir Knight."

Bedamned! "Lady Serena? The Incomparable?"

"Yes, sir," she said, startled. "Though I very much doubt I am incomparable, no matter what others might think."

"What the devil are you doing here?"

"I was abducted."

"Bedamned! My apologies. Why?"

She was quiet a moment. "Now that, sir, is something I would like to know. I imagine, though, that my disappearance has caused any number of rumors in Town."

"Quite," he said again, more concerned about her present situation than any damage, real or imagined, to her reputation. For the moment, though, they seemed to be safe. He eased Samson to a canter. "My estate is near here. Once I find a different way to it, you'll be safe."

"Thank God," she said, so fervently that for the first

time he realized that she wasn't so nonchalant as she had appeared. With the danger behind them, he could feel her trembling, a reaction he knew too well, from the aftermath of battle. He was also uncomfortably aware of her body, so close to him, and of her breasts pressing into his back. "Mayhap I could have a bath."

He smiled to himself again. "I believe that can be arranged. Oakhurst has—"

"Oakhurst?" she said sharply.

"Yes."

"That is the name of your estate?"

"My brother's, actually, but yes."

"Oh, no," she moaned.

For the first time she sounded so dispirited that he wanted to turn and comfort her. "What is it?"

"I heard them say that was where they were taking me."

TWO

"Bedamned!" Charles swore. "Are you sure?"

"Yes. 'Twas unmistakable. The carriage stopped on the way, so I presume they were lost. I heard them arguing about a crossroad, with Mayfield in one direction and Maresfield in the other. One said Oakhurst quite distinctly."

"Bedamned," he swore again as he came to a stop. She relaxed her grip at last. Thank God he'd come along when he had, else she wasn't certain what would have happened to her. Of course, she'd been uncertain of that for the last four days, but yesterday both of her captors had begun looking at her in a different, speculative way. She shuddered, in little doubt of what that look meant. "I don't know where to take you."

"Surely there are any number of houses about here?"

"Certainly, but I'm not known at any of them."

"People must know your name."

"Yes. Your reputation will be ruined, though."

"Oh, hang my reputation! I just want to go home."

"I realize that, but if it becomes known you've spent any time in my presence, people will believe we were together the entire time."

She sucked in her breath. "But you've only just arrived from London!"

"Nevertheless, there are always those who think the worst. I did not go about in company much."

Would her father be one of those who believed ill of her? she wondered, with a lost, sick feeling. Sometimes it was so hard to tell what he thought. She couldn't bear his disapproval. " 'Tis my reputation, Mr. Kirk, and my life," she said, coming to a decision. Just now it didn't matter what anyone thought. "I believe my safety is far more important. Or are you afraid of the consequences to yourself should it be considered that you have compromised me?"

"Don't be foolish," he snapped. He took up the reins again. "The problem is, this lane leads only to Oakhurst. I don't know the lay of the land enough to go cross-country."

"Aren't you familiar with your own estate, sir?"

"My brother's estate," he corrected her. "I've not been here in years." He was quiet a moment, letting his horse amble along the lane. "I don't imagine you can shoot."

"Yes," she said, startled. "That is, I've handled a rifle."

"An unusual skill in a woman."

"I'm country-bred, sir."

"Have you ever used a pistol?"

Her lips pursed. "No, but I daresay I could, should I need to." She paused. "Will I need to?"

" 'Tis possible. There's an extra one in my saddlebag. Even I cannot shoot two at once."

If that were meant to make her smile, it succeeded. "Give it me, then, sir, so I can have it at the ready." She paused. "Why are you doing this?"

Charles, rummaging in the bag, came out with a lethal-looking pistol and some shot. "It seems the thing to do." He handed her the pistol. "Can you load it?"

"Of course," she said, hefting the pistol in her hand. It was lighter than any gun she'd ever handled, though she doubted she'd be able to hold it in one hand as he'd done. Why was he doing this? she repeated to herself. He didn't even know her.

"Good." He had loaded his pistol quickly, which spoke of long experience. Too long, judging by the bleak look in his eyes. "Will you be able to load it on the fly?"

"I don't know," she said testily. For all her apparent steadiness, the thought of being chased again, of being caught again, terrified her. They had not been particularly gentle, her captors, not when they'd first abducted her, not when they'd held her captive. They'd be less so if they recaptured her. "I am not a soldier."

He was silent so long she thought he wouldn't answer. "Quite," he said, his voice cold, his entire demeanor stiff. "There's a manor house to the east, I believe. We'll have to be careful getting there."

"Do you really fear my abductors will be ahead of us? I thought you winged one of them."

"I did, but 'tis possible, if they went for the horses. I wonder why they chose Oakhurst, of all places." She could almost sense his mind weighing all possibilities. She was lucky that she'd fallen in with a soldier. "How is it that one of them was dressed so well?" he asked. "I'd swear that coat came from Stultz."

In spite of the seriousness of the situation, Serena grinned. "You could tell that from a distance, sir?"

"His boots were from Hoby," he went on. "As for his neckcloth—"

"Oh, he spent considerable time tying that each day. He even had freshly starched ones with him."

"Hmph." Again he fell quiet, so that she wondered what he was thinking. "Did they use their names in front of you?"

"No, just one of them, the rougher-looking one, Alf. Why do you ask?"

"'Tis curious, that's all."

"'Tis not good, you mean."

"Did I say so?"

"I can tell from your voice."

"And do you know me so well after so short an acquaintance, Lady Serena?"

"Rather an intense one, would you not agree?"

"Rather," he said, and stiffened. "Have your pistol ready. There's a bend in the lane ahead."

"Perfect for an ambush," she murmured, understanding him at once.

"Shh." He reached forward to pat his horse on the flank, and then, to her surprise, transferred his pistol to his left hand. "Hold yours on the right."

She nodded, understanding now. Her mouth had gone dry; her heart was pounding. *Oh, please,* she prayed incoherently. *Please.*

With the horse at a slow walk, their approach to the bend was nearly soundless. Major Kirk's body, under her encircling arm, was taut with tension, while her own hand was steady. That was something she would never have expected back in London, when she'd danced at Almack's or Vauxhall or at *ton* balls. Incomparable, he'd called her. No, *the* Incomparable, and therein lay a world of difference. She wondered why she felt so depressed at the thought.

Something rustled in the undergrowth to the side of the lane, just at the bend, waking her from her memories. In front of her, Charles raised his gun and cocked it, the click loud in the hush of the lane. Following suit, heart hammering in her chest, she raised her own pistol. Major Kirk looked back at her quickly, set his teeth, and walked Samson forward.

At the bend now, around it with nothing in sight, but with the rustling growing louder. Suddenly the undergrowth parted. As one, both Charles and Serena aimed their pistols, just as a hedgehog waddled across the lane.

Serena stifled a hysterical giggle and collapsed against Charles. She hadn't realized she was quite so tense. Now that the danger was past, she could relax. Major Kirk hadn't, though, she realized suddenly. His back was as tight as it had been before the ridiculous animal had crossed their path. The sense of their danger returned, and the reminder that he retained his soldier's instincts. Yet he'd left war behind. Considering that he had been on his way to Oakhurst, she must be a dreadful nuisance to him. Why was he helping her?

"There's no one about," she said.

"No," he agreed. "The animals would be quiet if there were. Still, we must be on guard."

She bit her lips, a habit she thought she'd outgrown. "I know."

"There are quite a few dips and bends in the lane, and in the road. We're in the South Downs, remember."

"Are we? I'd no idea."

"Mayfield is in Sussex." He turned suddenly in the saddle. "Have you any relatives near?"

"Why?" she asked, surprised. "Could I not simply return to London?"

"Probably, but 'tis best to have a second choice. We can't trust Oakhurst." His voice was grim. "I don't know why they chose it as a hiding place."

"I've an aunt in Ardingly, near the Brighton road."

"Northwest of here," he said after a moment.

"Do you have a map?"

"In my head," he said absently. With the dangerous curve behind them, he set Samson into an easy canter. "It isn't quite as far as London, I believe."

"I don't know." She had lowered her pistol, but still she kept it ready. She was not, she knew with acute awareness, out of danger yet. "Why do you think I might need to go there rather than London?"

"That's what they'd expect. You were taken there,

weren't you?" He turned in the saddle to look at her. "How were you taken, by the way?"

"I like to walk in the park of a morning," she said. "Of course, I have my maid with me. On this particular day—three days ago?" She counted in her head. "No, four. They made me drink such vile-tasting stuff. It gave me such nasty dreams, that first night."

"Laudanum, most likely."

"That morning there was a carriage there. I didn't think anything of it, really. Then the man you mentioned, the one with the coat from Stultz—"

"It could have been from Weston," he interrupted,

She smiled at the unexpected humor. "Possibly. His boots had quite a gloss. In any event, he stepped in front of me and spoke to me. I was surprised that he would accost me." Her smile faded, and she tightened her grip around Major Kirk's waist. "I don't really know what happened next, 'tis so hazy. From the laudanum, I expect. Something was thrown over my head." Her nose wrinkled. "A horse blanket, from the way it smelled. I do wish they had chosen something cleaner."

"Thoughtless of them."

"Very. Something hit me over the head, and the next thing I knew I was in the carriage, and that stuff was being forced down my throat. And that," she concluded, "was that."

His voice, when he spoke, was tight. "What of your maid?"

"What of her?"

"Do you think she was harmed, too?"

"Daisy?" She frowned. "I do hope not. I don't remember her screaming."

"She may not have been. Has it occurred to you that she might be in league with them?"

"Oh, surely not!"

"They knew where to find you."

"But I walked there nearly every day," she argued. "Anyone could have watched me, and know that. I doubt Daisy had a thing to do with it."

"Such things have happened."

"Not to me."

"Yes, ma'am. To you."

"I do wish you wouldn't call me 'ma'am' in that odious way. It makes me sound quite ancient."

"Very well, miss. Or would you prefer 'my lady'?"

"Now you are laughing at me."

"Devil a bit. Would I do that?"

"Yes," she stated, though she could not have said how she knew.

"So I might," he said, and though she couldn't see him, she thought she heard a smile in his voice.

"Is it your habit to do so, then?"

"It entirely depends on the lady."

"I believe I've just been insulted."

"Oh, not a bit of it," he assured her, enjoying himself hugely in spite of the situation. He had not bantered with a woman in such a way since before he'd gone off to war. He'd never had a woman up behind him on a horse, either. It was a disconcertingly pleasant experience.

Ahead, the road came into sight, with shrubbery to either side where the land ended. He might have been more concerned about an ambush again, except for the small stream that turned the land marshy on either side. Samson's hooves splashed as they forded the stream and turned onto the road, heading northeast. Soon he would leave Lady Serena in safety at the nearest house, and this particular adventure, so reminiscent of others in the Peninsula, would be over. The thought shouldn't have been depressing, but it was.

A farmer, passing by on a hay wain, gave them a startled look as they turned onto the road, and then raised a hand to the brim of his cap. Charles nodded in reply as they rode by. "I must look a sight," Serena said wryly, after a few minutes. "I have worn this gown for so many days."

"But still it looks lovely," he said, rising to the occasion.

"Liar." She spoke almost absently. "I wonder what they'll think of me at this house. Do you know the people?"

He shook his head. "No. As I said, I've rarely been to this part of the world. I shouldn't worry." He turned down another lane; as he'd told her, he carried a map in his head, and he was persuaded that a substantial manor house was nearby. "They'll understand, once you explain."

"I'm not sure I would, and it happened to me."

"It is odd." Idly he glanced down at her hands. "You've marks on your wrists," he said, and leaned closer. A raw, red line ran across her wrist. "Bedamned. Rope burns?"

"Yes."

"You were bound?"

"Just my hands, except when they brought me here. Of course, they had my ankles bound, too—"

"Bedamned!"

"But since then, just my wrists." Held humiliatingly out to either side, with the ropes fastened to bolts, with one of them awake all the time, watching her, watching her. With both of them watching her in a different way this past day. She shuddered again.

"But you were safe?" he said urgently, as if he'd read her thoughts.

"As safe as the situation allowed."

"That was foolish of me," he remarked. "Did they harm you?"

"No. Only when they took me."

His back was tense again. "How did you get free?"

"They didn't tie my hand quite tightly enough this noon, after I ate."

"They trusted you enough to untie you?" he said incredulously.

"I was always watched. Also, they made it clear what would happen if I tried to fight."

"What was that?"

"That they'd tie my ankles the same way they had my wrists." She swallowed. "Out to each side."

"The bastards," he said, with surprising heat for someone who had met her just an hour or so ago.

"But they didn't have to." Her voice was falsely bright. "I behaved myself. But when I realized my wrist was tied loosely, I knew I had a chance. You see, I've this ability to fold my hand very small." She held out her arm and pulled her thumb and fingers together so that her hand seemed half the size. "When one went out to use—well, when one went out, and the other paid me little mind, I pulled my hand out and loosened the other knot. Then it was simply a matter of waiting for the right opportunity."

"Quite simple," he agreed ironically. "I presume when there was only one watching again?"

"Yes, Alf. He fell asleep." In spite of the circumstances, she smiled wryly. "He seemed to be able to sleep at any time. I moved very quietly, and I was out the door before he noticed."

"And the other one?"

She grimaced. "He's the one who saw me. I had a start, but my skirts held me back. If you hadn't come along—Major Kirk!"

"What?" he said, instantly alert,

"I hear their voices! Ahead of us."

He bit back an oath, and without thought swerved into the trees. Serena hunched close behind him, but she gave no other sign of distress. Brave girl, he thought, to have undergone such an ordeal and yet still have so much spirit. And he, without saying so to her, had been concerned about compromising her. Compromising! This was not a London ballroom. This was, as much as the Peninsula had been, a battlefield.

Samson was a sorrel and so would blend into the trees. He was also well trained enough to stand still and stolid, head down, not making a sound. Charles slid off quickly and just as quickly pulled Serena down, dropping with her so that they both lay on their stomachs. He looked cautiously up, awaiting their foes' approach. Barely thinking about it, he slipped his arm about her, and she huddled against him, trembling. He wouldn't let harm come to her, he vowed. Never again would he allow a woman under his protection to be harmed.

"Eh, Guv, that's put pyed to them," a rough voice said, still a few yards distant, above the clopping of hooves. The accent was distinctly that of London's East End.

" 'Tis 'paid,' not 'pyed,'" a more cultured, urbane voice said tiredly, "as I've told you many times. And, yes, we may hope we have. Naturally, the more places we stop at, the better. We shall have to go farther afield, of course."

"They can't miss 'em, Guv, the gentry mort and 'im—who is 'e, Guv? I'd loikes to get me 'ands on 'im, I would. Damned arm hurts," he added, putting his hand up to his arm, where a rough bandage was tied. Good, Charles thought. So he had got one of them, after all.

"I've no idea. We must soon find out, however, else all will go wrong."

"Eh, I don't like to think of what 'e'll do when 'e learns of this."

Into Charles's view came two broad-chested horses. His eyes narrowed. Good horses for large carriages, he thought, just as one nickered and stepped toward the trees where he and Serena hid. He could not see the rider, but the quality of his clothes—his boots did, indeed, have a high gloss—proved him to be the more cultured of the two.

"Back, you," he said now, and Charles could tell from the way the horse sidled that his reins had been pulled hard. "Indeed, no. We must control this situation before he hears of it, else 'twill go hard on us."

"Don't trust 'im a bit, all's said and done. 'E'd see us floatin' in the river."

"Indeed." The man called Guv sounded thoughtful. "What would you suggest, then, Alf?"

"Think we thinks how to take care o' ourselves."

"Indeed," Guv said. The rest of his answer was indistinct as the horse passed farther along the road, and then faded.

Only when the road was absolutely peaceful did Serena raise her head. "They're gone?" she whispered.

"Yes. Who the hell are they?" Charles said, and abruptly realized that he'd been swearing since meeting Lady Serena, for all the world as if he were still with his troops. But then, in some ways, this was like being in the army.

"I don't know."

"And who is this 'he' they keep talking about? No, don't get up yet," he added, as she began to rise, and again realized something. He had been holding her close to his side since they'd gone to ground. She felt absolutely right there, and that was so disconcerting that he almost wanted to push her away. She was under his protection, he reminded himself, and not in the sense that gentlemen usually used that word, for their mistresses. He had to keep her safe.

"When Guv's horse came toward us—"

"Odd."

"What?"

"I named him 'Guv', too."

For a moment they gazed at each other, and then she

looked away. "Not so very strange, really," she went on. "'Tis the only thing Alf ever calls him, to my knowledge."

"Hm. One man was protected, and one wasn't." One man was more important to the plot, whatever it was, than the other. Yet both seemed to feel they were in danger. Men in danger, it was his experience, tended to do dangerous things. What worried him was what they had been doing along here. How could they have known of their quarry's presence?

He rose and held his hand down to her. "The sooner you're got to safety, the better," he said. "We don't know what they have planned."

Serena strode toward Samson once she was on her feet. "Well?" she said impatiently. "Will you help me up?"

Annoyance surged through him, replacing his concern. "It would be my pleasure, princess," he said sarcastically.

She raised her chin and somehow managed to look down her nose at him, a remarkable feat, since he was nearly a head taller than she. "You needn't speak in such a way. Shall we be on our way, or not?"

He glared at her and then stalked toward Samson. His bad arm ached like the devil from pulling her on behind him earlier, but he reached down to do so again.

"And how am I to ride?" she demanded, again appearing to look down her nose at him, though he was so much farther above her.

He held back the choice words he longed to hurl at her. She could at least show some gratitude to him. He had just saved her from danger, from being abducted again, or perhaps something worse. Much worse.

His anger faded. She had known exactly what would be in store for her, should her captors decide to use the remaining ropes on her. He'd felt it in the increased tension of her body against his, in the way she'd clutched his waist. What else would have happened to her, he wondered, had she not escaped as she had?

"Never mind, princess," he said more gently, and held his arms down to her. Uncertainty flickered in her eyes before she grasped his hands and let him pull her up. This time he settled her before him, and the feel of her as she leaned back against his chest brought an odd sensation to his throat. Steeling himself against it, he took up the reins, his arms encircling her. "Are you comfortable?"

"Yes." Her voice was softer now, filled with that same uncertainty he'd seen in her eyes.

"Hold on, then, at least until we're back on the road."

"Do you think they're truly gone?"

"Yes."

She sighed, and he felt some of the tension leave her. "Thank God. I so feared we'd be seen." She patted Samson's neck as they emerged from the woods onto the road. "I am surprised at how well your horse behaved."

"Samson is an old campaigner," he said. "Never flinched or bolted, even at Corunna."

She turned her head to look at him. "You were at Corunna?"

"Yes," he said shortly.

"I'm sure you fought well."

He looked down at her in surprise. Most people reacted with horror or prurient interest on the rare occasions when he spoke of his experiences. "Not well enough."

"You're hard on yourself." She faced forward again. "Whatever happened could not have been your fault."

Perhaps not, but he was to blame for other things. "Thank you," he said shortly. "I must apologize to you. My language has been intolerable."

"Your language!" she exclaimed, and burst out

laughing. "All that has happened, and you're concerned about that?"

A reluctant smile tugged at his lips. "It seems the thing to do."

"Do you always do what is expected of you?" she asked as they turned down a lane.

"Usually."

"So do I," she said after a moment, all merriment gone from her voice.

Now what, he wondered, was that about? He cleared his throat. "I am surprised we've not come to the house yet."

"Are you certain we're on the right lane?"

"I believe so. Ah." He nodded. I see a break in the trees."

"Yes." She sounded regretful.

"Yes," he said, his words oddly regretful as well. In the last few hours, he'd lived intensely, felt as intensely as ever he had. He had met the Incomparable in a way he had never expected.

"I imagine they'll send word to my father. I can't imagine what he's thinking."

Charles thought quickly of what he knew of the Earl of Harlow, a proud, autocratic man. "I'd think he's out of all reason worried about you."

"Mm." She nestled back against him. She felt fragile against him, and a wave of protectiveness swept over him. No one would hurt her, not if he had anything to say to it.

"I'll see you back to London, if you'd like," he offered gruffly.

She raised startled eyes to his, and he realized for the first time how pretty she was, even with smudges of dirt on her nose and cheeks. Her features were as delicate as her bone structure, and her eyes were a clear green under finely arched brows. "You needn't do that."

"It would be best, I believe."

"You'd be expected to marry me, you realize."

He gritted his teeth, already regretting his offer. "You're the one who's in danger of that, princess." It was as well that she would soon no longer be his concern, he thought, trying to convince himself. She could be deucedly sharp-tongued and forward, attributes he didn't like in a lady at all.

"I am sorry," she said after a moment. "That was uncalled for, after what you've done for me."

"It was the least I could do," he said gruffly, touched again.

"Don't be foolish. I have this habit." She stopped, and then drew in her breath. "Oh, well, you may as well know the worst. I can be terribly snappish at times."

"I hadn't noticed."

Again she turned to him, this time grinning. "Only when I feel challenged or afraid, though."

"Afraid? Of me?" he said, startled.

"No. Challenged, of course." Her eyes twinkled. "You're not like any man I've met in London."

"Then you've met the wrong men."

"I'm not so sure of that."

He nearly groaned. Lord help him if she began to develop feelings for him, even if only admiration. He didn't want any female to care for him again. Soon, though, she would no longer be his responsibility, he thought with mingled relief and regret. Strange. All he asked from life now was peace, was it not?

Both were quiet for the remainder of the ride to the house, a half-timbered manor whose diamond-paned windows glowed golden in the early evening sun. Edged about it were flowers, and an emerald green lawn. A groom ran up to take Samson's reins. Charles dismounted and raised his arms to help Serena down. Her waist was so small that he was almost tempted to span it, to see if his fingers would meet. Then she stepped back and he released her, though the imprint of her remained.

His hand at her back, Charles escorted her up the few stairs to the door, glad of the respite after their adventures. His arm ached like the very devil. Though he was fit enough now, his body still needed time to rest and heal. It was rather a bother.

A wooden-faced butler opened the door to them, bowed, took their names, and, before either could say a word, ushered them into a parlor, quite as if they had been expected. It made them glance at each other in surprise; it made unease prickle down his spine.

The parlor, however, dispelled some of that discomfort. In spite of the warmth of the day, a fire burned merrily in the wide, paneled fireplace. It was reflected on the board floor, gleaming with the patina of wax applied over many years, and glowed on the white plaster walls, crossed by dark beams and hung with cheerful, amateurish paintings. A huge mastiff unfolded himself from the worn, but fine, Turkey carpet, giving out one "woof," though his tail wagged furiously. "Oh, do be quiet, Toby," a woman said from a sofa upholstered in a rose-patterned chintz, as she stabbed her needle into her tapestry work. She was so pleasant, so welcoming in her sturdy, somewhat outmoded gown of twilled cotton, that the last of Charles's discomfort faded. They were safe at last.

"Oh, my dear." The woman bustled toward them, her hands outstretched to Serena, with only one quick, disparaging look thrown at Charles. It made him draw back as if he'd been slapped, and he frowned. Something was not right. "Such an ordeal as you have had," she continued. "But come, sit down and have some tea, and we'll soon make things right."

"Thank you." Serena threw a glance at Charles, apparently as puzzled as he was. "I am Lady Serena Fairchild—"

"Yes, my dear, I know who you are."

And how was that? Charles wondered, suddenly tense. The butler hadn't announced them. "Mrs.—I'm sorry, I didn't catch your name," he began.

She gave him another quick, cold look, and sniffed. "Mrs. Holmes. Now, my dear—"

"My brother has spoken of you," he said, relieved. Mrs. Holmes was a widow, an amiable if not overly intelligent, woman. "I am Mr.—"

"Yes, I know who you are, too," she broke in, her eyes colder than before.

He straightened. "How can you, ma'am, when you've not let me introduce myself?" he said in his best parade-ground voice.

Mrs. Holmes ignored him. "Now, my dear, you may be certain you are perfectly safe here."

Serena's brow had puckered. Whatever else one might say about her, her understanding was quick. "I can only be grateful to you, ma'am. If you only knew what I've been through—"

"But I do know," Mrs. Holmes interrupted yet again. "Your brother told me."

Serena and Charles exchanged startled looks. "My brother? But I don't have—"

"He has been so worried about you. Why, he has been going to every house looking for you. But there, when he returns, you'll be here all nice and safe."

"Ma'am?" Serena set down her tea. "What did this—brother—tell you?"

This time Mrs. Holmes did look at Charles. "Why, that you'd eloped with a fortune hunter, of course."

THREE

"What!" Serena exclaimed, as Charles let out a laugh. "It isn't funny." She rounded furiously on him. "Who do you think this supposed brother is?"

His face had grown serious. "Mrs. Holmes, my brother is Viscount—"

"I don't care two pins who your brother is!" Mrs. Holmes glared at him. "You are a villain, sir, to treat an innocent young girl as you have."

"Yes, ma'am," he said with such meekness that Serena looked at him suspiciously, to see his eyes still gleaming with humor.

"Yes, he is wicked," she agreed, and saw him start in surprise. "Although not as you might expect. Please, ma'am, if you will let me explain—"

"Your brother explained all to me, my dear."

"He's not my brother." She looked at Charles. "It must be Guv, don't you think?"

"Of course it's Guv," he said crisply.

"Nonsense." Mrs. Holmes set down her cup with a thump. "It was Mr. Fairchild who came here."

"Ma'am, there is no Mr. Fairchild," Serena interrupted. "All you need do is look at Debrett's to know that."

"Of course there is." Mrs. Holmes's expression was mulish. "Wasn't he just here, saying he'd return tonight?"

Serena jumped to her feet. "What?" she said in unison with Charles, and turned to him in appeal. "Oh, please. I cannot let myself be caught again."

He strode across the room and grasped her hand. "I won't let you be. Come."

"You don't mean to leave," Mrs. Holmes exclaimed in alarm as she rose.

"Yes," Charles said grimly as he continued out of the room. Serena was grateful for the grip of his hand, a veritable lifeline, on hers.

"You cannot. Oh, Potter." She looked past him to the butler. "They must be stopped."

Not by a blink of an eye did Potter, aged and stooped though he was, show any surprise. "Of course, madam," he said, and stepped in front of them.

Charles's eyes flicked at the butler, toward the open door, and then back. "Sorry, old man," he murmured, and pushed the man firmly to the side. Mrs. Holmes cried out as the man staggered, and Charles, in the confusion, ran past them both, out into the golden, mellow sunshine.

Caught off guard, Serena stumbled behind him. "What are you doing?" she cried, as they continued running down the drive. "We'll be caught."

He flashed a smile back at her. "Don't worry. I have a plan."

"But we're on foot! They'll catch us up."

"No, they won't," he said, and, not ten feet from the end of the drive, dove into the woods, dragging her behind him.

Serena gasped as she fell to the ground. "Are you mad? They'll know we've left the lane."

Charles was busy bending back any branches they'd dislodged in their fall. "Don't worry. I'm rather good at this."

"But—"

"Would you just be a good girl and do as I say?"

"I have no control over my life anymore—what are you doing?" she protested, as he started to throw twigs and decaying leaves over her.

"Be quiet!" He continued tossing up leaves as quickly as she shed them. "I am trying to cover your gown so it won't show and give us away."

She stared at him for a moment before comprehension struck. Of course. His brown coat would blend with the forest floor, but her own sky blue walking gown would be a sure sign of their presence. She, too, went to work, digging as much of the leaf mould as she could and ducking her head when he began to spread it over her. "Can you breathe?" he hissed, just as the first pursuers pounded by on horseback.

"Yes," she hissed back. "But your breeches, and hair—"

"I'll manage."

Serena closed her eyes as she rested her head on her forearms. Oh, dear, what would she look like before this adventure was over? she wondered, and stifled a hysterical giggle. As to that, what would he? His pale fawn breeches would no longer be spotless, and his hair would certainly never shake free of leaves. Again she bit back the urge to giggle. To think she had once longed for adventure!

More people ran by on the lane, and though some prodded at the bushes that lined the road, Serena, almost relaxed, lay with her eyes closed. She was so tired. So much had happened to her lately. Who was the man next to her? Charles Kirk, brother to Viscount—Viscount Sherbourne? But who else could it be? Yes, she thought suddenly. She'd heard him spoken of just recently. Strange, how unalike he and his brother were. The viscount was dark, while this man's hair was blond. Tarnished gold, she thought dizzily. His face was lean, almost hawk-like; his features were chiseled, and his face unfashionably brown. There were lines at the corners of his eyes, deep-set and, she suspected, far-seeing gray eyes. The bleakness in their depths, though, troubled her. Old eyes, she thought, though he couldn't be above thirty.

At length she heard the men from the manor house returning. "We won't find them tonight. It's too dark," one of them said dispiritedly. "Who are they, anyway?"

"I don't know," the other answered, his voice fading as he walked away. "But that's a fine horse he's riding."

"A very fine horse," Serena whispered.

"Shh." Charles had not moved so much as a finger since they'd hidden. "There are several more still to come—there."

She closed her eyes again as those on horseback passed by. They, too, were complaining; they, too, were unaware of how close their quarry was. This time she didn't stir, and so was surprised when Charles rolled over beside her.

"That should be the lot of them," he said, his voice still low.

Serena sat up, stiff and aching. She was tired and hungry, and she wanted nothing so much as to go home. "Then we may go?"

"No. You've forgotten Guv."

She groaned. In the face of this latest threat she'd forgotten the greater one. "I'm so tired," she complained as she leaned against the tree.

"I imagine you are."

"And hungry, and I have to—well, never mind," she added hastily.

"I'd imagine so."

"Oh, dear." She pressed her hands to her eyes, embarrassed beyond measure. She'd had so little privacy these past days. Always a man had been nearby when she'd used the necessary, and though Charles was her rescuer, still her situation was mortifying. "I wouldn't know where to go—oh, dear. I mean, 'tis too dark here in the woods to stumble about."

"So it is," Charles said, with admirable composure, given her faux pas. "We'll manage something once we're certain Guv is gone."

She sighed. "I hope 'twill be soon."

"So do I. Here, move over." She shifted to let him rest his back against the tree, and then stiffened as his arm stole around her shoulder. Only for a moment, though. It felt so absolutely right, to be tucked up so closely to this man's side. He was so solid, so strong—dependable, but quick-thinking, too. "Are you truly Viscount Sherbourne's brother?"

He didn't answer right away. "Figured that out, did you?"

"Yes, after a bit. I had to connect your names first."

"I'd not been in London long before Geoffrey sent me to Oakhurst. I imagine my reputation here will be irredeemable."

"I cannot believe the way you pushed that poor old man."

"Sometimes one must do harsh things." He sounded regretful. "It was either that or hit him."

"Oh, my!" She pondered the ruthlessness of that. "What will you do now?"

"Once I see you safely to London? I don't know. I had hoped," he said wryly, "to find some peace."

"You needn't see me to London. Simply put me on a coach. I've surely disrupted your life enough."

"No." He shook his head. "London's far off, and you were taken there. I'd as soon see you safely to your father."

"But you'd not be in this situation if not for me."

"Should I have left you to the tender mercies of Guv and Alf? No, I don't believe I could have."

She shuddered. "I'm grateful you didn't." She leaned her head against his shoulder and closed her eyes. For a very long time she had been essentially alone, even when constantly surrounded by people. Being with this man made that aloneness fade just a bit, though she barely knew him. The thought made her chuckle.

"What is it?" he asked.

"You. Us. This." Her hands fluttered aimlessly before her. "And to think that I once longed for adventure."

"In London?"

"Yes."

"Not very comfortable, is it?"

"No, but they don't tell you that in storybooks. The handsome knight rides off with the beautiful princess, and they live happily ever after." She laughed again. "Amazing that a princess somehow stays beautiful during an adventure. Have you heard of one with leaf mould in her hair?"

His laugh was low and easy. "No, but I'm certain they'd be more distressed than you are."

"Oh, yes, all they ever have to face are fire-breathing dragons or wicked witches or ugly trolls."

"People can be far worse," he said after a pause, all traces of humor gone from his voice.

It was an unpleasant reminder of her situation, precarious at best. The only good thing to come out of it was meeting this man. Their acquaintance was already far more intense than it ever would have been in London, where they would have been hedged about by society's rules. She knew him, though, as a man who was chivalrous and honorable and quick-thinking. His actions today spoke volumes about him.

She began to ease herself free. "I think I—"

"Shh," he said at the same time, pulling her back. Faint in the distance came the sound of horses moving at a trot. It was the third time today she'd crouched in hiding, and suddenly it was too much. She wanted to jump up, to proclaim her presence, if only to put an end to the tension.

As if he sensed her intent, Charles tightened his arms around her, stilling her desire to struggle. Men, she thought bitterly. Always using their superior physical strength against one. Even those who claimed to care for her, those who'd proclaimed themselves to be suitors for her hand, had pressed unwelcome attentions upon her. At this moment, she was heartily sick of the lot of them.

The hoofbeats neared, and then slowed as the riders approached the drive. "Think she'll be here?" came Alf's voice, and in her hiding place, Serena squeezed her eyes shut.

"It's the last house." Guv sounded grim. "At least we've put paid to their chances at the inn."

Serena's body jerked. If they had told their tale at the inn, she'd be unable to catch the stage for London. She'd been counting on it so.

"I'll get you safely home, princess," Charles whispered into her hair under cover of the sounds of voices coming from the house, again as if he'd read her mind. Her resentment of this man faded. He'd risked his own life today. He had every right to ride off if he wished, leaving her to her own devices. The thought was so frightening that, in spite of herself, she burrowed as close to Charles as she could.

Charles settled in for a long wait, his head against the tree, his arm encircling this girl he'd known for so brief a time, but who felt so right in his embrace. Brave girl, he thought again. He knew she had to be exhausted, that her nerves had undergone a severe shock, and yet she refused to give in. He was tired, too, and the discomfort in his shoulder had grown from an ache to full pain. He ignored it, not just because of his training, but also because of Serena. She needed him too much.

Never mind, he thought. Somehow they'd be safely out of it soon, and he could get on with his life. Once they got past this most recent hurdle, that was. Though the situation was dire, his lips curved upward. He could imagine Guv's reaction when he learned that he and Serena—Lady Serena, he reminded himself—had been there, and were gone.

Could he still bring her to Oakhurst, even if she'd been held on the property? He considered that, and then rejected the idea. There were too many unknowns. Certainly he was Sherbourne's brother and could prove it, but he didn't know what was about at the estate. It was possible that someone there was in collusion with Guv and Alf, and that was dangerous. It would be best to consider something else.

A long time later, or so it seemed, voices from the direction of the house came clearly to them, followed again by hoofbeats. This time the riders walked their horses slowly by, puzzling Charles. Why not canter, since the moon was high and the lane was clear? It wasn't as if they were talking and had to be heard above the horses. No, there they went, he thought. He felt Serena relax as the sounds faded in the night.

She pulled away. "Can we—"

"Be quiet," he whispered harshly, tightening his hold again. Something wasn't right, though he wasn't quite sure what. Why hadn't Guv and Alf broken into a gallop yet? Surely he would have heard them.

That was it, he thought suddenly. The night was still. Sounds would carry clearly, and yet there was only silence. "It's a ruse," he said suddenly.

"What?" she whispered back.

"A ruse. To flush us out of hiding. They think that we'll believe they've gone, and will come out of hiding."

"How can you know that?"

"Shh." He patted her hand. "Be quiet now, like a good girl."

Serena stiffened beside him. "A good girl," she muttered, but she didn't attempt to move again.

Charles grinned in the darkness. So, she didn't take well to that kind of comment, did she? An independent puss, then. It might make this entire escapade more difficult, but it was also exhilarating. It was an odd sort of exhilaration, the total concentrated awareness of life he'd previously felt only in battle. Make no mistake about it, he thought. This was a battle, one that, perhaps because of what he'd fought on the Peninsula, he must win.

Serena's breathing was quick and shallow against his throat. He felt such sympathy for her, and yet he couldn't imagine sharing what she had called an adventure with anyone else. The señoritas and senhoras of the Peninsula had long ago ceased to interest him, and in London he'd felt nothing but boredom when he'd met yet another fresh-faced young miss. Come to think of it, he wasn't particularly interested in the older, more experienced matrons, either. They were all much of a piece to him—cultured, well gowned, bred to take the only role society allotted to them. He still didn't know how Geoffrey had found such a unique and special mate. He knew only that there could be no such woman for him.

Serena gave him hope. Being dubbed the Incomparable implied that a girl was not only beautiful and accomplished, but also that she was the epitome of all that a man of the *ton* could want in a bride. Every debutante would aspire to be like her; every gentleman would clamor after her. No one would ever expect that there might be a real person under that lovely exterior. Except that she had, in the few hours of their acquaintance, proved herself to be very much an individual, indeed.

Lady Serena, Charles corrected himself. It was only the intensity of their situation that made him feel as if he'd known her longer than he had. In truth, he knew nothing about her, except that she kept a cool head when faced with danger. He doubted that many of society's hothouse roses would have behaved as she had, eluding her captors and then fighting so valiantly in her own defense. He doubted that many people realized she had such depths. She might not even have known it herself.

Serena stirred briefly in his arms, drawing him out of his thoughts, returning him to awareness of her in a totally different, more fundamental way. In his embrace she was slender, though far more shapely than the word implied. Her hips next to his were rounded; her breasts, pressed against his chest, were soft and unexpectedly full. Their bodies fit together, he thought, and felt a stirring of unexpected, and not totally welcome, desire. It was almost painful. It shattered the dull, numbing comfort of feeling nothing, and left him prey to a variety of emotions he'd rather not feel. In spite of his family's compassion and assumptions, in spite of the pressure society would put on him, he didn't wish to marry, not now, perhaps not ever. Yet the people he cared most about would not understand what drove him. They did not understand that his real wounds weren't on the outside, or that they were still raw. Perhaps they always would be.

Not so very far away, the clop of horses' hooves began again, and voices carried back to them, in normal, if indistinct, tones. Serena pulled away. He hastily pressed a finger to her lips to forestall any speech. Oh, Lord, but they were as soft and desirable as the rest of her, those lips, awakening in him the fierce need to kiss her. Yet again it was both a relief and a temptation when she jerked her head back. Reluctantly he set her free.

"Quietly, now," he said in low tones. "We're not out of danger yet."

"Oh, so I am allowed to speak now?" she said waspishly.

He grinned. "Could I stop you?"

"I am not a fool, sir. I would not so endanger our lives."

"My gratitude, miss," he said gravely.

"You need not mock me," she said, and rolled to her knees.

His hand shot out and caught her wrist. "Where are you going?"

She turned back toward him. "To find a tree," she said, with what sounded like embarrassment.

"Not yet." He flipped over onto his stomach.

"Why? Is it another ruse?"

"No."

"Then how did you know it was one—what are you doing?" she asked in astonishment, as he began to crawl forward.

"I've used such a trick a time or two myself. As to what I'm doing." He looked back over his shoulder. "I'm going forward to reconnoiter."

Serena made a face at his back. "Do please find some food while you're gone," she said, and resigned herself to sitting back against the tree again. The sounds of a woods at night, the various small rustlings or occasional hoot of an owl, held no fears for her. She had been bred in the country; she knew all too well that the animal she had most to fear was man. Yet she'd fallen in with someone so completely opposite to her captors that it was nearly miraculous.

Her stomach growled, unexpectedly loud, and she

pressed her hands to it. It seemed petty to complain of hunger, when the danger she'd faced was so great, and yet the demands of her body were more immediate. And Charles—Mr. Kirk—had gone ahead to reconnoiter! Her annoyance faded. That he used such a word, that he clearly knew what to do, spoke volumes for his past experiences. She smiled. She doubted that any man she knew in the *ton* had such skills or could keep so cool a head in the face of the adventure she'd foisted upon him. He seemed to take it in stride. He was a soldier, through and through.

The feeling of something brushing her foot was Serena's first hint that he'd returned. "Oh!" She started as his face became visible as a dim blur in the darkness. "You gave me such a turn."

"My apologies," he said, in a tone that indicated he felt no remorse. "All seems quiet."

"Then we may go."

"No." Again he caught her wrist to prevent her rising. Try though she might, she couldn't break his grip, iron-firm and solid. "I told you, my girl, that we're not out of danger yet."

"But if Guv and Alf are gone—"

"Not so far, unless I miss my guess."

"At the inn," she said, feeling her stomach sink.

"At the inn," he agreed.

"Where the coach to London departs?"

"Most likely."

"Oh." She closed her eyes. "They'll alert every stop, won't they?"

"That's intelligent of you to think of such a thing."

"I am not light-minded simply because I'm the Incomparable," she said, surprising herself with her bitterness.

"I never said you were," he said with surprising gentleness.

"Thank you for that." She paused. "If they do, how will I get home?"

"By another road. We'll have to think on that one."

"They'll use that same faradiddle about an elopement, won't they? Oh, Mr. Kirk." Impulsively she laid her hand on his arm. "I am sorry for involving you in this."

"It's of no moment," he said gruffly. "I'm just doing what anyone would."

"I doubt that." Her stomach rumbled again. "Oh, dear. I fear I am hungry, sir."

"My apologies, princess." She could swear he was smiling. "I can tell a mushroom from a toadstool, but I doubt you'd wish me to do so in the dark."

"Hmph." She crossed her arms. "There are certain realities to be faced, sir, apart from your playing soldier."

"I beg your pardon?" he said coldly.

"Oh, my dear Mr. Kirk." Again she laid her hand on his arm. "I am so sorry I said that."

"One of those—realities—may be seen to behind a tree."

Heat surged into her face. "I am sorry I offended you."

He didn't answer right away. "We're both tired," he finally said. "And tense, and yes, I'm as hungry as you."

"I daresay we'll survive. We may even find that tree," she added, and had the satisfaction of hearing him chuckle.

"That's my girl." Briefly he placed his hand on her neck.

She started, both at the unexpected warmth of his touch, and at his words. Several hours ago she hadn't even known this man, and yet she felt closer to him than to anyone she'd ever met in town. "What do we do now?"

"We wait."

"Still?"

"Yes, until all is quiet. 'A horse, a horse, my kingdom for a horse.'"

"What?" she said in astonishment.

"Once we're certain all in the house are asleep," he went on, "we can do something."

"Such as?"

"We, my dear lady, are about to become horse thieves."

FOUR

Some hours later, Charles and Serena crept from their hiding place under the trees. The thin quarter moon had set some time ago, leaving the world in shadowy darkness. The house nearby slept, vastly to Charles's relief. What they were about to attempt was chancy, at best.

The stable block was, as he'd expected, at the back of the house. All was dark within, though not quiet; from the loft above came loud, grunting snores, presumably made by a groom. Samson, bless his sound heart and steadfast nature, did not betray Charles's presence by so much as a snort, though he tossed his head in something like a greeting. Charles rubbed the horse's nose and then crept to the tack room. His saddle, worn and comfortable, hung on a peg on the wall, as he had hoped. So, to his surprise, did his saddlebags. That they hadn't been removed to the house was an unlooked-for boon.

Quietly he slung the bags over his shoulder and crept out again. Only one of the horses in the loose boxes had shown any nervous activity at his presence, though it was hard to tell its true nature. He'd no idea of how accomplished a horsewoman Lady Serena was, but even on a placid horse they should be able to make decent time away from the neighborhood.

Once back in the trees, he rummaged about in a

saddlebag for the bread and cheese he'd placed there in what seemed like another life. They were to have been his luncheon, he reflected wryly as he broke each into two hunks, sharing them out with Serena. She ate with gusto, he noted with amusement; no delicate little bites for her. Oddly enough, his admiration rose a notch. Serena not only had courage and a sense of humor, but she was also obviously pragmatic. He could have a worse companion on such an adventure.

Now they were stealing their way into the stable, each of them carrying one of his pistols, which again surprisingly had been left in the saddlebags. The stable door creaked as they slipped within, making them go absolutely still. One or two of the horses nickered, but above them the snores went on. Leaving Serena near the door, should she need to escape quickly, he went again to the tack room, this time taking his saddle, harness, and reins. They had agreed that he would saddle Samson, the one horse they knew to be steady and reliable, first, again if they needed to escape.

With Samson saddled, he went in search of Serena, and was alarmed when he found her standing before the loose box of that one horse that had made any noise during his previous sortie. "Let us find a mount for you," he said in low tones.

"I have." Her voice, equally low, sent a familiar, if unexpected, sensation through him. "This one."

He frowned. "No. Much too spirited."

"Yes. I told you I am a bruising rider."

"I'd prefer you didn't try to prove it to me just yet."

"Oh, pooh. I feel comfortable with him, and he with me." She turned from the box and brushed past him to the tack room, so that he had to follow. He could not very well argue with her, not when the groom, still snoring above them, might hear.

"No," he said, when he found her lifting a sidesaddle.

"Yes. Here. Do you carry this, and I'll find a bridle."

"Serena, you will kindly allow me to make the decisions in this instance."

"No," she said, and turned away, stalking back into the main part of the stable. Curse the woman. Did she not realize she ran the risk of being discovered, if not worse?

"Wait." He put a staying hand on her arm as he reached her, just before she opened the door to the loose box. "At least let me let Samson out first."

She paused. "You've muffled his hooves?"

"Yes." He grinned to himself. Earlier Serena had, without hesitation, sacrificed her petticoat, tearing it into strips of cloth to be bound around the horses' hooves. "I will see to your mount."

"Yes, Mr. Kirk," she said with deceptive meekness, and Charles, smiling, crossed to Samson's box. He was enjoying this. There was enjoyment in what he was, and in Serena's presence. Not Lady Serena, he thought, remembering how he had used her name without the title a moment before. Simply Serena.

Charles left Samson standing on the cobbled floor, and then, taking a deep breath, paced to the loose box where Serena waited, with his arguments prepared. Before he could reach there, however, Serena had already drawn back the bolts, well-oiled and quiet, and was about to open the door. "Stop," he whispered, putting a staying hand on her arm.

"You're becoming rather tiresome, Mr. Kirk."

His fist clenched. "I? When you—"

"We've no time to waste," she said, and opened the door.

Curse it. "I'll go first," he said firmly. To his surprise, Serena stepped back. What had he got himself into? he wondered as he walked into the box.

The horse nickered and shied, as he had expected, and then, as he stroked his neck and whispered soft, crooning words, settled down. Knowing he might be kicked, Charles bent to muffle the horse's hooves, and then rose to place the saddle on his back. "He may not be used to a sidesaddle," he whispered.

"I realize that," Serena whispered back. Her voice was closer than he had expected, and he turned to see her standing behind him. He should have known, he thought with resignation. She was not one to allow others to do what she wished to do.

"Still," she went on as she checked the girth, "he seems placid enough. Of course, we won't know until I've mounted. We do still plan to lead them to the lane, do we not?"

"Unless we're discovered." He took up the reins and the horse balked. "Damn," he said, and this time, without argument, passed the reins to Serena. She said nothing, but he thought he sensed a certain smugness in her as she easily led the horse from the stable.

Outside all was quiet and dark. Dawn was still several hours away. By then, with any luck, they'd be long gone, with their direction unknown. He'd chosen the time well, he thought, when there came the unmistakable sound of metal being struck, and then rolling, rolling endlessly away.

"What the devil happened?" Charles demanded, as somewhere in the house a dog began to bark.

"I think we struck some kind of pail." Serena's voice was high and thin. For the first time that day, he heard panic in it. "We've alerted them, haven't we?"

"Damn." Looking back at the stables, he saw a light in the window of the loft overhead. "It woke the groom."

"Oh, no! Then we must be away."

"Keep your voice down," he hissed. "There's still a chance, if we stay in the shadows."

"But, don't you see? We must go. Oh, please help me up."

"No, and be quiet." He urged her toward an out-building. "If we stay still, they'll likely think it was some animal."

"If you won't help me up, I'll have to find a way myself," she said, pulling her horse away from him.

Curse it! Charles thought, stepping up his pace behind her. In the darkness Serena had managed to find a mounting block and was clambering onto the horse's back. He swore again as he swung himself onto Samson. Serena was already cantering away. His plan of moving stealthily had been completely shattered.

The dog barked again and was joined by others. In the house, one window glowed with light, and then another. Charles quickened Samson's pace, heedless of the noise he made, even with the horses' hooves muffled. There was no longer any time to be circumspect about this. Events had conspired against them.

He finally caught up with Serena at the turn to the lane. She did ride well, he noted, as he bent low over Samson's neck. When they reached the road they would slow down to keep from tiring their mounts too soon. For now, though, escape was the main priority. "They'll be after us soon," he said.

"I know," she said, her voice returned to normal. "But we still have some chance to gain some distance."

"Why the devil did you act as you did, when I had a plan?"

"Oh, you and your plans. They would have investigated the noise. You know they would."

"We could still have walked the horses to the woods."

"Well, we didn't," she said flatly. "I can't let myself be taken again. I simply can't."

"Don't be more foolish than you can help," he snapped. "I would simply have told them who I am."

"Would they have let you? Would they have believed you, for that matter?"

"I have my card case," he interrupted. "I carry it on my person, not in saddlebags."

"They would still have thought I was eloping with you. They would have held me there."

"They would have recognized me as Sherbourne's brother," he retorted. "I would have sent an express to London to verify it."

"They could have gotten word to Guv. They still will, if they can."

"And then tell him who I am. This way they'll know where we're going, until we reach the road." He frowned. "Where are we going?"

"To my aunt's, of course. I thought we'd decided that."

"Yes, but I've had no chance to discover the direction."

"Northwest. You said so yourself."

"What roads do we take? Do you know that?"

"I'm not sure."

"That should help us a great deal."

"You needn't be sarcastic. I don't know quite where I am."

"Near Mayfield."

"That helps me a great deal."

"You don't know where we're going, do you?"

"Of course I do. To Ardingly."

Charles gritted his teeth. "And just how do we get there?"

"I'll puzzle it out. I didn't ask to be smuggled to your estate."

Charles's anger faded. No, she hadn't wanted that. It was unfair of him to blame her for his anger and frustration and discomfort. "Have you any idea where Ardingly is?"

"We've always traveled the Brighton road to reach there."

"Brighton," he said thoughtfully.

"What are you thinking?"

"Nothing quite yet. Where do you turn off the road?"

"Staplefield, I believe."

"Ah." His anger evaporated. "West of us, about fifteen or twenty miles. I'd have to consult my map, but I believe we could make that in a night."

"A night?" She frowned. "Why not during the day?"

"Too dangerous. We'll sleep by day, travel by night."

"Dangerous because—oh, I see." She nodded. "Few will be about at night."

"Exactly. It's not easy to do if you're not used to it, but 'twill be only for one night."

"Believe me, Mr. Kirk, I've had to accustom myself to worse than that."

He glanced over at her. In the dimness, her face was set. Again he held back his words. He suspected she would not welcome sympathy from him just now. "We can't do much now, without knowing our direction. I'll have to find that out in the morning."

"At least you have something to guide us."

"Yes, in my head," he said absently.

"That should help."

"Princess," he said through gritted teeth, "I am in this adventure only because of you."

"I know," she said, her voice very small. "I do apologize."

"No, I deserved it. I—listen!"

"What?"

"Hoofbeats." He urged Samson faster. "They're chasing us."

"We expected it." She, too, bent low over her horse's neck, urging him on. "Our mounts will tire soon."

"Samson is an old campaigner." His voice was abstracted. "If I remember aright, there's a lane to the left soon."

"But shouldn't we keep to the road? Mayhap they won't keep up."

"A chance I'm not willing to take." He sounded grim. "If we go that way—ah."

Charles veered suddenly to the left, into a patch of darkness deeper than that of the trees. How did he know of these things? Serena wondered, wheeling her mount to follow. The horse, however, was not used to her ways, nor she to his. Faced with this new demand after everything he'd been expected to do, he simply balked.

"Charles!" she cried. "He won't move."

She heard Charles swear, but in a moment he was at her side, reaching for the horse's bridle. "Come on, old thing," he murmured, holding on when the horse reared his head and snorted. "A few more steps, and you can rest. There's water, and food. No oats, though, I fear."

At the sound of "oats," the horse tossed his head again, but this time he took a few tentative steps toward Charles. *Oh, please, oh, please,* Serena thought, fighting the impulse to tighten her hand on the reins. The hoofbeats behind them were louder now. Their pursuers were gaining on them.

"This way, boy. Come with me," Charles said softly, patiently, and, to Serena's immense surprise, the horse turned. "Good. Walk into the lane now, Serena. Quietly. I've found a good place for us to stop."

"Why?" she asked, as softly as he had.

"They'll think we're still on the road. Come."

"How do you know these things?" Her voice was peevish, though she reached down to pat her mount's flank in approval.

"Experience. Now, into the trees, here."

"Again?" she exclaimed. She was growing very tired of hiding among trees.

"They won't expect it," he said patiently, as if to a child.

"Oh, very well." She knew she still sounded pettish,

but she let him help her dismount. His hands at her waist were so strong, she thought, suddenly breathless. So strong, and his body was lean and hard, as she'd learned before. The thought, at this particular moment, was not particularly welcome.

Her horse chose that time to sidle toward them. Off balance, Charles staggered back. Instead of being set down with a proper pace or two between them, she slid down his body, her hands stroking his shoulders, his arms, her breasts brushing his chest. Lean, hard male, so different from the dandies and fops she knew in London, she thought again, and felt her face flame.

"I beg your pardon," he said, stepping away, his voice as stifled as hers had been a few moments ago.

"It wasn't your fault." Her breathlessness annoyed her out of all reason. She was tired, she told herself. Tired and frightened and hungry.

"We've no time to waste." His voice had returned to its normal note of command. "Here."

Sighing to herself, though she wasn't quite sure why, Serena stepped into the woods yet again, where he held back some branches. The horse nickered. *I sympathize with you,* she thought, following Charles, wondering where they were going. She was vastly surprised and relieved when they reached a small clearing, while all the time, the hoofbeats grew nearer.

"There's a stream over there," he whispered, pointing. "Loop his reins over a branch."

"Where are you going?" she whispered back, panic heavy in her stomach.

He turned to leave. "To fetch Samson. Now be quiet like a good girl, and find a place to rest."

A good girl, she thought, fuming, glad he'd gone. She might have given him a piece of her mind else. It would, she admitted, be terribly unfair of her. Folding her arms across her stomach, she looked around for a suitable place to rest, though she instinctively wanted to flee. The sounds of pursuit were growing louder now. What did he mean by this freakish start? Surely they'd have done better to stay on the road. The likelihood that they'd be found was terribly high.

A crackling in the woods made her tense. Suddenly frightened, she turned, and then her shoulders sagged in relief. It was only Charles, leading Samson in.

Without a word, without wasting any movements, he looped Samson's reins over a branch near the other horse. Then, with the same economy of movement, he strode over to her, taking her arm and guiding her to a rock she'd not noticed. Without any ceremony, he pulled her close. "Be very quiet, now," he murmured into her ear. "They're close."

Why? She wanted to ask. Why were they doing this? Yet she'd come to trust this man since her escape— could it only have been this afternoon? With all that had happened, she simply had no choice.

The hoofbeats were very near, and her stomach clenched with panic again. Closer and closer—and then they were past, fading into the distance. Serena slumped, letting out a breath she hadn't known she was holding. "Are they gone?"

"Yes." Charles was already rising. "We must be away. They'll search for us along the road for a time before they realize we've gone to ground again."

Serena was usually quick of thought, but the events of the past days, along with her exhaustion, conspired against her. It took her several minutes to understand his meaning. Of course. If they didn't take to the road again now, their pursuers were likely to search every lane and clearing they came across. "Oh." She took the reins of her horse from his hands. "I cannot fathom how you know these things."

"I was a soldier," he said briefly. "Come. We haven't much time before they return."

Silently she followed him back onto the lane, where he cupped his hands for her to step into, and threw her onto her horse. "Where now?"

"West. I recall a cross road a few miles back, before the turn for Oakhurst. We'll take that."

She sighed. She longed to rest. He was right, though. She took a quick look at his face as they turned onto the road again and urged their mounts on, though the light was dim and they were now moving at a gallop. His profile was chiseled, austere, almost cold, and yet she'd felt his unexpected warmth and concern as he'd held her, near the manor house. He was a puzzle: a soldier at heart, if not in fact, and something of a knight-errant. Perhaps the two were sometimes one and the same.

At the crossroads they turned left, not even stopping to read the signpost. Charles must be as burnt to the socket as she was, and perhaps hurt. She had noticed, more than once, that he tended to reach up to rub his left shoulder, as if to massage pain away. Guilt flooded her. He had used that hand to pull her up when he'd rescued her. What had she done to this man?

"Oakhurst is to the left," he said quietly as he slowed Samson to a walk. "If I remember aright, there's an old outbuilding along the boundary."

She looked sharply at him. "You don't think Guv and Alf are there, do you?"

"I don't know where they are. As well not to give them any sign that we're near."

Serena swallowed and looked away. She'd thought the nightmare was done. "I want to go home," she said, her voice trembling.

"Shh, princess." He laid his hand briefly on her arm. "I'll keep you safe."

She turned to study him again. She did feel safe with him. She wasn't sure why he'd gone to such lengths to rescue her, but she knew with absolute certainty that he would protect her against all comers.

At length they reached another crossroads. Charles stood in the stirrups to peer at the signpost, and then sat again, nodding. "Crawden is to the right, and Clayton to the left," he said quietly. "We've left Oakhurst land."

She closed her eyes in relief. The danger was behind her. "What do we do now?"

"Put as much space between Oakhurst and us as possible, and then find a place to rest." His teeth flashed in a smile, giving her the impression that he relished this.

Serena caught her breath. So absorbed had she been in her plight that she'd paid little heed to his appearance. The one impression she had gained was of his lean, ascetic face, but now she realized that she remembered more from when they'd ridden by day. That one smile set her pulse to pounding. His nose might be a trifle long, the planes of his cheeks a little angular, but that didn't matter. He was, by far, the most attractive man she had ever met. For the first time, she regretted the fact that they would soon go their separate ways.

It seemed that they rode for a very long time, passing villages long asleep, riding up the steep hills that marked the South Downs, and then back down. "Serena," Charles said softly. "Lady Serena?"

"Hm?" Serena came alert with a jerk that made her horse dance, to see dawn tinting the sky. "What?"

They had slowed their pace. "I believe 'tis time for us to find a place to put up for the day."

"Oh." She looked over at him, her brain still muzzy, though two things were clear. One was that he was smiling, and that the sight again took her breath away. The other was that they'd compromised each other, perhaps irredeemably. Her pulse began to pound again.

Perhaps they wouldn't have to part at the end of this adventure. "I think I fell asleep."

"I did so once or twice on the Peninsula." He looked straight ahead. "You're a brave girl, Lady Serena."

So they had returned to formality. "I'm not quite sure why, Mr. Kirk. I simply did what I had to do."

"The definition of valor. You didn't once succumb to the vapors," he added.

"Oh, I never have been vaporish, though I must tell you I came near it once or twice." She yawned, not daintily, but so widely her jaws cracked. "Do pray excuse me. I've had little sleep the last few days."

"Think nothing of it. I think that copse of trees might be a good place to stay," he said, pointing with his riding crop.

"More trees?" she exclaimed involuntarily.

He flashed a smile at her again. "Never mind. It won't be for long. If it were night, I'd chance finding a barn, but I don't want us to be discovered."

"Oh, very well," she said grumpily. "The copse it will be."

"But first," he said as he swung himself down from the saddle, "we'll have to set your horse loose."

She frowned as he reached up to lift her down. "Why?"

"Easy, there." His arm shot out to catch her as she swayed. "They'll be on the search for him."

He took his arm away too soon, too soon. "Won't they be looking for yours, too?"

"Oh, undoubtedly, but Samson is mine. Unlike this one." He slapped the horse she had been riding on its hindquarters. It merely turned to look at them.

Serena burst out laughing. "How very contrary of him."

"Indeed." Charles was smiling at her; she wondered why. "Go, you stupid thing," he said, slapping the horse again. "Damn." This as the horse refused to move yet again.

"Go!" Serena, her voice obscured by giggles, took off her hat and advanced toward the horse. Its only reaction was to step back a pace or two and stare curiously at them. "Oh, you great, dumb beast!" She waved her hands at him. "Go!"

That did it. Without a backward glance the horse took off, galloping back the way they had come. Perplexed, Serena and Charles stared at each other, and then she began to giggle again. "Of all the foolish things!" she exclaimed.

"I hope he's smart enough to find his home." Still smiling, Charles took her arm. "Come, madam. Your bower awaits."

The copse proved to be more impenetrable than any of their previous hiding places had been. The undergrowth was thick, especially near the banks of a stream running through it. "I believe I hate trees," Serena said conversationally, and knelt by the bank of the stream to take water into her cupped hands. She drank deeply and rinsed her face, and then reached for her handkerchief, fortunately still in her pocket. "Oh, that is heavenly." She smiled up at Charles to see him watching her, a peculiar look on his face. "What do you look at?"

"Nothing," he said briefly, and returned to rubbing Samson down with clumps of grass.

His economy of movement fascinated her, and she again noted that he favored his left arm. "May I help?"

"No. Thank you," he added. "I prefer to do this myself."

"Of course." She watched for a few moments more, before dipping her handkerchief in the water. Folding it into a neat square, she pressed it against the back of her neck. Her eyes closed with sheer pleasure. Why had she never realized how something so simple could feel so good, or that the tang of damp earth could surpass the fragrance of any food prepared by London's finest chef, or that the blue sky arching overhead was so beautiful that it made her heart ache? She had been spoiled. Having her life threatened had apparently sharpened her appreciation of simple things.

She glanced up at Charles again. He looked tired, she thought, and, on an impulse, rose to hand her handkerchief to him. "Here."

He looked at the cloth in surprise. "What is that for?"

"To wipe your face. Oh, go on, do," she said as he hesitated. "It will do you good."

There was an odd look on his face as he took it. "Thank you."

"You're welcome. Your arm is bothering you, isn't it?"

"'Tis nothing," he said curtly.

"Mm-hm." Bending, she pulled up clumps of grass and began rubbing down Samson, too. "Now, pray don't tell me I'm not to do this," she said as he opened his mouth to speak. "The work will go quicker if 'tis shared."

He gave her a level look, and then nodded. "Very well."

Well! There's gratitude for you, she thought, disgruntled, but she went to work. She was used to caring for horses, and usually the work gave her pleasure. Today, however, it was a chore. Her arms felt heavy, and her back ached, and her eyes had a disconcerting habit of closing of their own accord. Still, there was something soothing about the work, almost soporific, especially with such a big horse to lean against. Surely it wouldn't hurt if she closed her eyes for just a moment. . . .

Strong hands gripped her shoulders. With a gasp she started awake, throwing out her arms and twisting away. "No! Oh, no, please—"

"Serena. Easy, now. 'Tis just me."

Serena stared uncomprehendingly at the man who

faced her, his hair gilded by the rising sun. He was suddenly a frightening stranger, and there was no guessing what he would do.

Gasping, she whirled about in an attempt to run, and instead staggered as she lost her balance. Those same strong hands settled on her arms, awakening fresh panic within her. This time they held her too firmly for her to pull away. "Please," she begged, hating that she did so. She had been so strong throughout this entire ordeal. "Let me go."

"Are you able to stand?"

The question seemed so nonsensical that she looked at him over her shoulders. "Charles," she said in surprise.

"Yes." He let her go and then, as she turned back, took both her hands in his. This time she didn't even attempt to pull away. "Who did you think it was?"

"I—don't know."

"Come." He slipped his arm about her waist and led her toward the trees. "You're tired."

His arm felt solid and strong and right, though she knew she shouldn't allow him such familiarity. The thought made her want to giggle. Familiarity, when they'd been together all day? "No more so than you."

"To the contrary. You have had several difficult days. Here." They stopped at a place just within the edges of the copse. Without her knowing it, he had cleared away some underbrush, leaving a small rectangular space. It was covered with leaves from last year's foliage, while at the head of it lay a saddlebag. "I know you're not used to sleeping rough, but this is all I can contrive at the moment."

"It will do." In other circumstances Serena would have been horrified at having a man watch her lie down, but these were not normal times. Dropping to her knees, she crawled toward the saddlebag and rested her head on it. "Thank you," she said, and to her surprise gave a prodigious yawn. "Excuse me."

She thought he chuckled. "Don't regard it."

"Thank you." She shivered involuntarily in the damp, chilly air. Wrapping her arms about herself, she turned onto her side and curled up into a ball. A moment later, something warm and heavy settled about her, making her start. "What is that?"

Charles rose. "You'll need it."

Serena fingered the wool of whatever he'd placed on her, and then looked up to see him in shirtsleeves. "Your coat? But you'll be cold," she protested.

"I've faced worse. Go to sleep now, Serena."

Serena, she thought. They had returned to informality. She was glad. Gratitude for all he'd done for her settled within her. Snuggling into his coat, she fell asleep.

Sitting by her, Charles watched Serena for a time, surprised that she trusted him. He wished that it were brighter and he could see her, now that she slept and he could do so unobserved. Yet he must have taken serious notice of her yesterday. She was a beauty, he thought, even with her face shadowed by the terror she must have felt over the past days. Her hair was a deep chestnut that hinted of red. It wasn't styled in the crop that was fashionable, but instead looked impossibly thick and smooth and long. It was the perfect complement to her smooth, pale skin and the perfect oval of her face, with its classic features and strong chin. Her finely shaped brows arched over those amazingly deep blue eyes; her nose was straight and small, and her lips were full. Kissable lips, he thought, and sat back, almost appalled by the idea. He had no intention of becoming involved with any woman, not even with one known as the Incomparable. He would be a bad bargain as a suitor, let alone as a husband, not when he had yet to recover from his experiences on the Peninsula. Not when he still loved another woman.

Still, it would be marriage between them, he thought as he rose. They had been together unchaperoned for too long, a ludicrous idea under the circumstances. Never mind that he had rescued her from kidnappers who would eventually have done her great harm. Never mind that any of their touches had been chaste. In the eyes of the world he had compromised her irredeemably. There was no way to redeem her reputation, except through marriage.

Charles looked at her for a few more moments and then turned away. Serena was right. He was tired, and his shoulder did ache abominably. Odd that he was in much the same situation as he had been some months back, though this time only trees arched over him, rather than a solidly built house. No, he wouldn't think of that. It was in the past. It had to be.

Hands clenching into fists, he settled on the rock. *I won't fail this time, Luz,* he vowed, and settled down to keep vigil.

"So." Sir Osbert Hyatt, baronet, pursed his lips as he looked up from his polished rosewood desk at his two employees. It was the day after Serena's escape. His attempt to sound stern was, however, somewhat marred by his dandyish clothes, his balding head, and his fluting, plummy voice. "You let her go."

"I tied her right and tight, Guv," Alf protested, and then swallowed at a look from him. "I mean, Sir Osbert."

"Oh? Then how was it she managed to work herself free? And how," he said, turning to the other man, "is it that she managed to flee behind your back?"

Quigley Garnett, dubbed "Guv" by Charles and Serena, knew better than to try to defend himself. He didn't underestimate Hyatt, but he didn't fear him, either. "I don't believe they could have got very far, even on horseback."

"'They.'" Hyatt swiveled in his chair and gazed at the books lining his library walls as if looking for a particular title, though he'd bought them by the yard for appearance's sake. "'They,'" he repeated as he turned back, "Who is he, Garnett? Who is this man she met?"

Quigley gazed steadily back at him. There was no question but that this was a disaster. There had been no sign of their quarry, except for some indications that Lady Serena and her unknown rescuer had hidden in some trees near the manor house, and that they had stolen a horse. Neither had shown up at Oakhurst, or at any of the coaching inns. No one knew where they had gone, which was a true calamity.

"I don't know, Sir Osbert, but I imagine I can find out," Quigley said, some of his poise recovered.

"You had better. A military man," Hyatt mused. "How d-do you know that, Garnett?"

Quigley came instantly alert. By careful observation, he had learned that Hyatt stammered when he was scared or uncertain. "By his posture, sir, and the way he sat on his horse. By the way he acted."

"Hm. On the lane to Oakhurst. I wonder . . ." He tapped his fingers against his chin. "Oakhurst is Sherbourne land," he went on, as his employees remained silent. "I do wonder. Ah." His smile was humorless. "I believe he must be Charles Kirk."

"Kirk?" Quigley said, almost hissing the name.

"Yes, Kirk. I'd heard he'd been invalided out of the army." His gaze on Quigley was keen. "Do you know the man?"

"Yes, sir."

"What regiment were you in?"

"The Ninth, sir."

"The same as Kirk's?"

"No, sir. We were together at Corunna and Douro."

"Hmm." Hyatt tapped his teeth. "I want you to find them," he said decisively. "Use any means necessary. I want the girl unharmed. That means untouched, Connor."

Alf squirmed under the scrutiny of Hyatt's cold, dead eyes. "Yes, Guv—sir."

"Good. See to it, or it will go hard with you both."

"We'll have to get by Kirk first," Quigley said. "What shall we do about him?"

"Kirk. Hm." Hyatt's smile was humorless. "Why, kill him, of course."

And Quigley, though he still wanted to laugh at Hyatt's mannerisms, agreed with all his heart.

FIVE

The moon was rising high in the sky when Charles and Serena at last set out for Ardingly. According to Charles's copy of *Paterson's Roads,* the village wasn't important enough to be mentioned, or to have a coaching stop nearby. That had its advantages, as well as disadvantages. On the one hand, there was little chance they'd meet other travelers on a busy road. On the other, Charles had no clear route to follow. He would simply have to trust to his innate sense of direction, and hope that there would be signposts at each crossroads to guide him.

Behind him, Serena rode pillion on Samson, her arms about his waist, her head resting against his shoulder. Something about her relaxed stillness told him she was at least drowsing, if not asleep, though her hold on him was tight. Poor girl, he thought with an unexpected well of tenderness. If the past two days had been difficult for him, at least he was accustomed to similar situations. For a gently bred lady, however, who had spent four days in the hands of unknown captors, they must have been nightmarish. She had no reason to trust him. That she did spoke volumes for her need of a hero. *A hero. Bah.* If he were one, it was with the greatest reluctance. He knew better than anyone that a hero was the last thing he was.

Serena stirred at that moment, rescuing him from

the beginnings of the self-reproach he knew all too well. "Where are we?" she asked, her voice husky.

"Somewhere near Shipper's Hill, I believe."

"We've a way to go, then?"

"So it appears." He held the reins easily, in spite of the tension she aroused in him. "We knew it would be a long road."

"Yet I don't know where I'd be if—well, never mind." She snuggled her head against him, and his tension increased. "I don't know how to thank you, Mr. Kirk."

"Think nothing of it," he said crisply, hoping to ward off more of her gratitude. "Are you comfortable?"

"Comfortable enough," she said wryly. "At least I am not spending more time among trees."

"Come, Lady Serena, you must admit that 'twas cozy enough today, with enough leaves about you."

"Oh, yes, the accommodations were vastly luxurious. And the food so very delicious."

"Did you not enjoy the roasted rabbit?"

"And the potatoes you managed to find. Where did you find them, by the by?"

"Nowhere in particular," he said vaguely.

"At that barn we saw?"

"You have found me out, madam."

"And the eggs this morning. I am dining like a princess."

"I am only too glad to please you."

"How did you catch the rabbit? I admit I was quite surprised this evening."

"I set a snare."

"With what?"

"A bit of string." He stopped to peer at yet another signpost, considered for a moment, and then turned right. "A bit to the north here, I believe. I always keep some string handy."

"And then had your cook prepare what you caught, of course."

"Not quite. Cooking is a skill one learns on the march. Or retreat," he added, the words dragged out of him.

"At Corunna?"

"Unfortunately." He didn't care to remember that nightmarish time, or what followed.

"How terrible. Is that when you sold out?"

"No," he snapped, and felt her flinch. "I was invalided out."

"Oh, I am sorry. How terrible for you." She paused. "Where did it happen?" she asked hesitantly.

"In my arm and shoulder, rather badly," he answered, deliberately misunderstanding her.

"Yet you ride well enough."

"Mm." Another signpost loomed up, and he turned again, toward the west. With the circuitous route they were taking, they would be lucky to make Ardingly before daybreak. "You do realize you're getting rather a bad bargain."

"What do you mean?"

"With me. Surely you realize we must marry."

Abruptly she pulled back, and Samson, usually so steady, tossed up his head in reaction. "We never will."

"Why?" Oddly enough, he was offended. "Am I not good enough for the Incomparable?"

"That's not it," she shot back. "You know how grateful I am to you—"

"Stubble that," he said, as sharply as she had. "I don't wish to hear any more of that foolishness. We've compromised each other, Serena."

"No."

"No?"

"I will not marry you."

He sighed. "Let me explain matters to you, princess. We have been together for two nights—"

"You rescued me, Sir Knight."

"Which will count for nothing in the eyes of society."

"I care not for what others will say," she said, though the defiance in her voice sounded suspiciously hollow.

"Perhaps I do. Perhaps I don't wish to be known as someone who is less than honorable."

"Oh, stubble your honor!"

"Curse it, Serena! Do you really wish to see your name dragged through the mud?"

"I don't care a snap for what people will think!"

"But what of your father?"

That silenced her. "He's harder to predict."

"Why?"

"Oh, 'tis hard to explain. He can care so much about appearances sometimes, and at others they bother him not at all." She rested her head against him. "We're as like to find ourselves married as I am like to be banished to the country."

Charles brought Samson to a stop. "He wouldn't do that."

"He might. He'll be quite angry with me, especially since I won't now be able to make an advantageous match."

"Advantageous?" He frowned. "Does he not care for your happiness?"

"Of course he does, but sometimes our ideas of that differ."

Into Charles's mind flashed the image of his mother's face, so caring, so concerned, when he had returned home, still nursing his wounds. Never had she pressed any of her children to choose a path destined to lead to their future unhappiness, not even his sisters. Not even his brother, for all that he held the title. Grandmama was more autocratic, he admitted with a wry smile, but even she had a soft heart under her crusty exterior. "Who would your father have chosen for you?"

She sighed. "I don't know. Perhaps one of the four suitors I rejected, though I suspect he was testing me with them. To my mind, none was suitable."

"Hm. Are you one of those romantical ladies who wish to marry for love?"

Unexpectedly, she laughed. "Oh, no! There's no such thing."

He turned, frowning in perplexity. "You don't really believe that, do you?"

"Of course I do. Don't you?"

"I'd have agreed with you once," he said slowly.

"Oh, now really, Major."

"Yes, really. I've seen too many love matches of late. Of course," he added, "it's early days for all of them."

"You sound more cynical than I do, Major."

"Major?" he queried, turning to her again. "Why do you call me that?"

She shrugged, a movement he felt against his back, and that made a curious shock go through him. "'Tis appropriate."

It distanced them. For some reason, he didn't like that. "Why do you not believe in love?"

"I've seen too many love matches go wrong."

"Some succeed," he said, wondering why he was arguing with her.

"Most don't." Her tone was flat. "I may just have come out this year, but I'm not naïve. I've heard the *on-dits*." She paused. "I've seen too many girls—women, now, I suppose—unhappy while their husbands take mistresses. Yes, we do know about mistresses, though we're not supposed to," she went on, as if to forestall his speaking. "I've seen them find lovers, or appear to enjoy themselves at every ball or rout or soirée. But I've also seen their eyes.

They're unhappy." Again she paused. "And so are their husbands."

"Surely not every match ends that way," he protested. "No, but enough."

"Serena, that wouldn't be the reason for us to marry." He picked his words carefully. "I know you don't wish to be forced into anything. No, hear what I have to say," he went on, cutting off any protest. "If you'd let that happen, you'd have married any one of those four suitors." He paused. "Also, after what's happened to you, I don't imagine you'd want any man near you."

A shudder ran through her. For a moment he feared she would break down. She had been so incredibly strong, but he knew too well that the strongest were also likely to be the most devastated by what happened to them. "That's not true," she said in a small voice.

"I wouldn't force you to anything." Charles spoke as gently as possible. "But I could protect you, Serena."

This time Serena went still, and pressed her face against his back. "I don't know if anyone can protect me again."

Curse it. Two men had taken her sense of safety away. Curse him, for the fool that he was. How could he undertake to protect her, when something so common as a walk in the park had proved to be her undoing? More to the point, why did he want to? "At least I'll see you safely home, princess."

The moon had set long ago. Dawn had come in a swirling mist that was at last lifting. Charles stopped at yet another signpost. "Ardingly," he murmured in satisfaction.

At his back, Serena stirred. She had dozed on and off throughout the long night's journey, exhausted from the events of the previous days. Long experience, however, and the knowledge that he could survive through nearly anything, had kept Charles awake. That, and the nagging, aching pain in his shoulder.

Of course, neither one of them had slept particularly well the day before. Serena had never expected to sleep on a hard forest floor, in full daylight. It was different for him. He had learned to sleep when and where he could. To his surprise, however, keeping watch over Serena had proved to be more important than mere rest.

Now the danger was past, and he could return to the life he had planned. A peaceful life, without battles or someone shooting at one. A dull life. Quickly he suppressed that thought. More than anything, he needed, wanted, peace. He needed it to heal, not just his body, but his soul. He needed action as well, to forget the damage that had been done to that soul. Most of all, he needed absolution.

By now Geoffrey would know that he hadn't arrived at Oakhurst, Charles thought, and was likely growing concerned. Ardingly, however, was close enough to the main roads and their inns that he would be able to send letters—one to Geoffrey, and one, more importantly, to the Earl of Harlow. The earl needed to know that his daughter was safe. He needed, as well, to learn how badly she had been compromised, but that Charles intended to do the right thing. Once he saw Serena safely ensconced in her aunt's home, he would ride to Cuckfield, some miles away, and post the letters there. His hopes for a quiet, peaceful life had been dashed. Oddly enough, he wasn't as upset as he would have thought. Apparently, campaigning was in his blood.

Samson topped a small rise, and Charles drew in. There below him lay what he guessed was Ardingly, the small river that flowed through it glinting in the early morning sun. It was a hamlet more than a village, at an intersection of two roads, with a few houses clustered around a squarish church. Journey's end.

"Princess," he murmured, and felt Serena stir behind him. For a moment her breasts pressed more firmly against his back, making everything within him stiffen. "I believe we're there."

Serena peered around him. "So we are," she said, and sighed, a surprisingly melancholy sound. "My aunt's house is just past the church."

"There's no smoke coming from the chimney." Odd, that. All the other houses showed some signs of activity. "Are you certain she's at home?"

"I've no reason not to think so."

"Hm." He set Samson into motion down the hill. When all this was done, he would find a way to reward the horse for his yeoman service. "It will be good to have some real food for a change."

"And a bath. If you say that you've a plan one more time . . ."

"But I always did," Charles protested. "We never were caught."

"And I always got dirtier," she said. "Leaves in my hair, dirt on my gown—and to think it was once blue. With all the grass stains I'd swear 'twas green." She grimaced. "Oh, well. Mayhap I'll start a new fashion for color. Verdant blue."

Charles grinned as they turned onto the road that led through the village. That was his Serena, still able to tease in spite of everything. "I thought Incomparables cared only for clothing."

"Oh, la, sir, and for balls and being presented at court and such. Such a tedious life—I vow I am ready to sink under it."

"We'll be back in such tedium soon enough."

"Yes." Serena's tone was morose. "I suppose we will. Oh, dear."

"What?"

"Someone I know. Good morning, Mr. Wills."

The solid, substantial man, dressed in a worn tweed coat and leather breeches that strained over his ample girth, frowned and then bowed. "Lady Serena," he said in surprise. "What do you here?"

"I've come to visit my aunt."

"Hm." He looked from her to Charles, his gaze curious and skeptical. What he thought about seeing Serena with a strange man was all too clear. "Mrs. Wills, come and see who's here. Mrs. Wills?"

A middle-aged lady, as substantial as her husband, bustled out of the house. "George, surely you know this is my day for baking—Lady Serena!" she exclaimed. "How very nice to see you. Are you here to visit your aunt?"

"Good morning, Mrs. Wills. Yes, as it happens, I am."

"But surely you know she's not here."

"What!" Charles and Serena exclaimed in unison.

"Why, no. She's gone to Bath, to take the waters."

"Bath," Serena said, almost in a wail. "Oh, Charles—"

"Then we shall just have to return to London," Charles said grimly. There was no rescuing this situation now. By late afternoon all of London would know what had happened. Any efforts they might make to keep the affair quiet would be for naught.

Mr. Wills frowned. "And you are, sir?"

"Oh, dear, do forgive me," Serena said. "My manners have gone begging. Charles—Major Kirk—this is Mr. Wills and his wife. Major Kirk was good enough to rescue me."

"Rescue you?"

"Yes. 'Tis a very long story." She sighed. "I suppose it will have to be London, won't it?"

"I see no hope for it," Charles said. With a nod at Mr. Wills, he set Samson to a walk. At that precise moment, Guv and Alf stepped out from behind the church.

* * *

The previous day, after their interview with Hyatt, Quigley and Alf had set out from London, Quigley driving his curricle competently, if not with the dash exhibited by the whipsters of the *ton*. Nor could his team compete favorably with their showy horseflesh. He cared little about their appearance, though, singly or together. All that mattered was that they had both speed and endurance, qualities he would need to see this misadventure through. Qualities that now, along with his superior intelligence and Alf's superior strength, would be tested.

Quigley was no fool. Before undertaking this commission from Hyatt, something he now regretted despite his pressing need for money, he had thought carefully about where to keep Lady Serena for a few days. More than once, before his army years, he'd seen a perfectly good scheme ruined by poor planning. Or a battle, for that matter. Unfortunately, planning wasn't enough, not when the unforeseen and the unpredicted happened. And Major Charles bloody Kirk's presence was certainly unforeseen. So far as he'd known, Kirk was still in hospital in Portugal, probably with a limb missing.

That was his mistake, though he'd never admit it to either Hyatt or Alf. He'd chosen Oakhurst with gleeful malice, not just because it was within a day's ride of London, but because it was owned by the Kirk family. To his knowledge, confirmed by the bailiff, who believed naively that Quigley had come to visit an old army comrade, the viscount never visited the estate.

It was easy after that to find the ramshackle hut, perhaps once used by a shepherd or such, at the edge of the estate. It was easy to discover that it met all his requirements. After that, it remained only to abduct Lady Serena and bring her there, aided by one of Harlow's servants who knew of Lady Serena's habit of walking in the park in the mornings, and who was not averse to a bribe. It had even seemed, when several days had passed without any word from Hyatt, that he and Alf would be able to enjoy her at their leisure. Even now, the thought of her, at his mercy, was enough to make him break out in a sweat.

"You know that Hyatt's going to put paid to us," Alf said abruptly.

Quigley glanced briefly at him, and then flicked his whip at the off-leader. "Have you been thinking, Alf? How unusual."

"I gots something in my brain box, Guv. Gots some ideas, I do, and I says we got trouble."

"Don't strain yourself," Quigley said coolly. "I'll do the thinking for us. You use your muscles."

"Don't take much thinking to know what Hyatt's got planned," Alf persisted. "I grew up in Five Dials, Guv. Couldn't of survived, without learning a thing or two."

"You refine upon it too much. I've already considered what Hyatt will do."

"'E can't let us live, with us to speak up about what we did."

"I realize that."

"Wonder why's 'e want this gentry mort? Too thin a piece for me."

"Ah, but you'd have taken her if you could."

"O'course. What do you takes me for? A bloody eunuch?"

Quigley glanced at him, amused. "Wherever did you learn that word? Not in Five Dials, certainly."

"What's 'e want 'er for, Guv, a flash cove like 'im?"

"For the ready, I imagine." Quigley suppressed a sigh. He really wished Alf wouldn't try to think, or that he was not so stubborn about his ideas when he did. He was meant to supply muscle to this enterprise, not intelligence. No matter, though. Once he had Lady Serena in his grasp again, once he'd dealt with Kirk, he'd put paid to Alf. Hyatt, too. He'd deal directly with Harlow, who would no doubt be grateful to have his daughter returned to him. He'd no intention of sharing whatever reward Harlow chose to bestow with anyone. Or Lady Serena, for that matter.

For now, however, there was some unfinished business to see to, including, he hoped, a rendezvous at some benighted village named Ardingly. Oh, yes. He'd taken care to learn about Lady Serena, too, especially the location of her relatives, though at that time he'd not expected her to escape. Since she had an aunt living within a day's ride of Oakhurst, it was a reasonable assumption that she and Kirk would go there.

"I understand that Harlow turned Hyatt down for his daughter," he said now, not betraying by so much as a blink the direction of his thoughts.

Alf nodded in understanding. "Eh. That explains it."

"There are advantages to working with someone like myself, are there not?"

"Eh, some. Must be hard, seeing that much of the ready whistled down the wind."

"Indeed. I imagine it was."

"But if we cuts out Hyatt, afore 'e can cut us out," Alf said slowly, frowning in thought, "that money'll be for us."

"So it will," Quigley said. "So it will."

By day's end, after long, dusty hours on the road, the pair at last stopped at Staplefield. Ardingly was but a few miles away, but by mutual consent they decided to put up at the Jolly Tanner, much to the consternation of the innkeeper. It would be best, Quigley decided, to confront their quarry in the morning, when they were fresh, and Kirk, likely having traveled all night, was not. It was possible Kirk and Lady Serena were on their way to London, though Quigley doubted it. Kirk, as he recalled, was far-thinking, and he had probably guessed that along that road lay danger. Quigley had used that characteristic to his advantage in Portugal. He intended to do so again now.

In the meantime, he and Alf had stopped at every coaching inn along the way, where he had inquired, once again, in most solicitous tones about his sister, who had eloped with some bounder. Everyone had proved to be sympathetic; everyone had agreed to hold Lady Serena and her escort should they arrive at any of the inns, and send notice to Quigley at Staplefield. Unfortunately, there were several other routes heading out from London for the area, but Staplefield was the closest of their destinations. He felt it in his bones that this road would be the one they chose.

And so, very early in the morning, they arrived in Ardingly. A substantial man of middle years looked at them askance when they asked after Lady Serena's aunt. Perhaps because of his suspicion, he was ready enough to inform them that the woman was not at home. That the man stood by the road and watched them drive away gave Quigley some worry, though he dismissed it. So far he and Alf had proved themselves to be equal to nearly any situation. They would do so now.

"Might be she won't come here, Guv," Alf said.

"She'll come." Quigley pulled his curricle to a halt beside the church, out of sight of the road and close to the aunt's house. Now that they were here, he was certain of his reasoning. Kirk would want the woman off his hands as quickly as possible. Once he was gone, they would take her again. This time, perhaps he would do with her as he wished.

"I 'ears a 'orse, Guv," Alf said in a sudden, urgent whisper.

"Probably that village squire we passed," Quigley whispered back, but he peered around the corner of the church. "Ah. Good."

"It's them, Guv?"

"So it is." Major Kirk and the girl. He had his second chance.

With his hand upon his pistol, near to hand in his coat pocket, Quigley looked out again and frowned. Kirk had drawn to a stop, and the girl was talking to the older man he and Alf had seen earlier. Nothing for it but to wait, he thought, straining to hear their voices. At last, though, he heard the horse start again. He gave the signal to Alf, and with pistols drawn, they stepped out from the shelter of the church.

And Kirk abruptly wheeled his horse around.

SIX

"Damn!" Charles exclaimed as he spurred his horse back toward Mr. Wills.

"Charles!" Serena clutched at him. "It was they."

"Curse it, and your aunt's not here."

"They wouldn't dare shoot, would they?" she asked, even as she rooted in the saddlebag for the pistol. "Oh, Charles, look! Mr. Wills is still there."

Charles wheeled Samson again, and for the first time, they faced Serena's captors. Though she was safe behind Charles's broad back, though she held a pistol in a remarkably steady hand, still panic rose within her in a wave. Charles, too, had his pistol out, and Mr. Wills, bless him, had come to stand by their side, though he held no weapon. "If they shoot, we're at least prepared," she began,

Charles spoke at the same time. "Curse it!"

"What is it?"

"Captain Garnett."

"Who?" she asked, bewildered.

"Guv is Captain Garnett."

She peered cautiously past his shoulder. "Do you know him?"

"Yes, for my sins. Well, Garnett."

"Well, Kirk," Garnett mocked, his stance easy, his grip on his pistol firm. "You always have had a habit of sticking your nose in where it doesn't belong."

"They're two ugly customers," Mr. Wills said in a low voice beside Serena. "Wouldn't trust them far as I could throw them."

Serena didn't spare him so much as a glance. "You've spoken to them, then?"

"A little while ago, about your aunt. Who are they?"

She shook her head. "I'll try to explain later." She was aware of Mr. Wills eyeing her pistol, but she paid him little heed. Dear heavens, how were they to escape this?

"You may as well give up the girl, Kirk," Garnett was saying almost pleasantly. "My quarrel's not with you."

"Like hell it's not," Charles said. He held himself stiff, upright, and she wondered what the effort cost him. Increasingly he favored his left arm. Should it come to a fight, he would quickly be overpowered. The thought made her shudder. "It's always been between us."

"Not now." Again Garnett sounded falsely pleasant. "Give us the girl, and we will let you go."

Charles gave a bark of laughter that held little amusement. "You can't. I know too much."

"As do I," a voice unexpectedly said. She looked down to see Mr. Wills training a rifle upon Garnett and Alf.

Garnett's eyes barely flicked toward Mr. Wills. "Be off with you, old man. This fight's none of yours."

"I wouldn't move, if I were you." Mr. Will's voice was cool as he raised the rifle. "It's well oiled and loaded— thank you, Mother." He nodded at his wife, who stood at the gate, holding high, of all things, a carving knife. "Which would you prefer first? Be warned," he added quickly as Garnett took another step forward. "I served in America during their revolution."

Garnett laughed. "Thirty years ago, old man. Be gone with you, before *you* feel my barker."

Mr. Wills cocked the rifle. "Where would you like it? I'm a good shot, sir. Granted I use it only on deer nowadays, but that's deuced tricky." He paused. "As well as vermin."

Garnett ignored him, instead focusing on Serena and tossing her a mocking salute. "You've champions, Lady Serena. A soldier with a useless arm, and an old man."

"And me," another voice said, causing them all to glance in surprise at the house, where a brawny footman stood, holding another rifle.

"And us." From around the side of the house came the gardener, carrying a rake, along with a groom with a pitchfork.

"And be warned, sir," yet another voice said, and this time Serena didn't have to turn. The vicar had come out of the rectory, holding high what looked like an ancient blunderbuss. *Good heavens! Of all people.* "I may be a man of God, but you, sir, are condemned elsewhere."

"You hurt one hair on Lady Serena's head and you'll feel this," someone else said.

This time it was the Willses' cook, holding up a cast iron pan. Serena held back a hysterical giggle. "Oh, my."

"Indeed. Outflanked and outmaneuvered, Garnett," Charles called. "You may as well give in."

Garnett looked from one to the other of the group arrayed against him, and his face settled into hard lines. He must realize at last that too many people were witnesses to his actions, Serena thought. "Very well. For now. But I'm not finished with you, Kirk. And as for you." The look he gave Serena was so leering, so threatening, that she shivered. "We've unfinished business."

"So you say," she retorted.

"Oh, yes, my lady. Until then, I bid you adieu." With a slight bow, he turned and walked back toward the church. Alf followed, though not before glaring at them. A few moments later the curricle rattled away along the road to the west. Only then did Serena release her breath; only then did she sag against Charles's back. Thank God. They were gone.

By now more people, curious, had come out from their houses to see what was about. Serena glanced around at the faces and closed her eyes. Here, among those who'd known her for years, she at last admitted the truth of Charles's repeated assertion. Her reputation had been compromised beyond repair.

"Of course you'll stay here," Mr. Wills was saying, and Serena came to herself to realize that an argument was going on between him and Charles. "Those two won't have gone far."

"Besides, Lady Serena looks all done in," Mrs. Wills put in. "Come down, lamb. When did you last sleep?"

To Serena's surprise, tears started to her eyes. "I haven't the slightest idea."

Charles had turned in the saddle to look at her. "Brave girl," he said, and the warmth that went through her more than compensated for her exhaustion and her strange weepiness. "If you'll but wait until I can get down, I'll help you."

"I have her, Major." Mr. Wills held up his arms to her, and she slid gratefully to the ground. "Come to think of it, sir, you look burnt to the socket yourself. A war injury?" he added, looking at Charles's arm.

"Portugal," Charles spoke briefly. In spite of Mr. Wills's presence, he held out his arm to Serena. "Sanctuary, princess."

She looked up at him. "Do you really believe that?" she said in a low voice.

His smile faded, and the dark look that already lurked in his eyes deepened. "I don't know."

"You needn't shelter me, you know," she went on, as they entered the Willses' home. It was a comfortable house, dating from Elizabethan times, its plaster walls almost blindingly white, its flower borders colorful and lush. "Not after the last few days."

He placed his hand on her back. "I don't doubt you'll be able to return to London now."

"And I doubt I will," she retorted. "They'll be looking for me, Charles, you know they will."

"They can't watch all the roads to town from here."

She wheeled on him. "You talk as if I'm a ninny! They've done all they can to prevent my escape." She swallowed, hard. "They want me, Charles. God knows why."

"Now, now." Mrs. Wills linked her arm through Serena's. "Things always look worse when you're tired. Are you hungry, lovey?"

"Yes, ma'am, she is," Charles said, after giving Serena a long look. "Shall we discuss this at another time, Lady Serena?"

Serena briefly closed her eyes, and was assailed by a wave of exhaustion so strong it made her dizzy. "Yes."

"You'll be the better for a good meal," Mrs. Wills said, scrutinizing Serena. "A change of clothing, too, I expect."

"Heaven," Serena said fervently, and at last followed the Willses inside.

A little while later, she and Charles sat at the shiny oak table in the Willses' sunny breakfast parlor, overflowing plates set before them. In addition to baked eggs, there were bacon and mushrooms fried together, kippers, thick slices of toast slathered with jam, and strong, hot tea. Replete at last with food, Serena sat back, gazing out the diamond-paned window at the garden, and feeling, for the first time, a spark of hope. Perhaps they'd brush through this, after all.

Mr. Wills, cradling a tankard of ale, sat across from her, frowning. "You have no idea what they want?" he said abruptly.

"None." Serena took a long, deep draught of her tea, and then held out her cup to be refilled. "They never so much as gave me a hint. They've been remarkably persistent, however."

"Hardly surprising, now I know Garnett's involved," Charles put in.

Serena looked at him. "What do you know of him?"

He looked grim. "Nothing good. I didn't know he was in England." Like Mr. Wills, he drank deeply of the ale. "I imagine he was cashiered out of the army."

"Good heavens, why?"

He shook his head. "It hardly signifies. He's not one I'd care to cross again," he went on. "Still." His frown deepened. "I can't see him planning this. He doesn't have the intelligence. Or, I should say, the right kind of intelligence."

"He seemed to know I'd be here."

"True," he admitted, "and he knew enough to turn people against you. He's a manipulative bas— one. Still." He frowned. "I would like to know how he came to choose Oakhurst."

"You don't believe any more than I that he'll give up, do you?"

"No."

She sighed. "Charles." She touched his hand, and then, seeing Mr. Wills's raised eyebrows, pulled back. "Mr. Kirk, this has never really been your problem."

"Don't be more foolish than you can help," he snapped. "We've discussed this already."

"Yes, but 'tis me they're after."

"And I promised I'd see you home safely." He pursed his lips, a look she immediately distrusted. "I've a plan."

"Oh, no," she groaned. "Please tell me it has nothing to do with trees."

"No." He flashed her a smile. "At least, not yet. But I think I know where we might go."

"Now, Mr. Kirk," Mrs. Wills scolded. "You can see how tired Lady Serena is. You'll stay right here for now, until you've both had a chance to rest up."

"Yes, ma'am," Charles said, and suddenly Serena wanted to laugh.

"Where else would you go, until your father can come for you?" Mrs. Wills went on.

Serena's eyes met Charles's. "'Tis not quite that easy," she said. "You don't know these men. They truly won't give up, and I'd rather you weren't involved."

"What you'd like isn't to the point." Mr. Wills sat back, hands clasped across his ample girth. "We're already involved."

Serena flashed him a smile. "I know, and I am grateful. I'd just not see you hurt."

"We may be able to post back to London," Charles said.

"They've likely put our descriptions about at the posting houses."

"True." Charles sat back in his chair. "However, if your father sends his coach for you, or if my brother does, for that matter, you should be safe enough."

"Perhaps." Serena held back a yawn. Privately, she doubted that her captors would ever let her go. There was something preternatural about them. They seemed to know where she would be, before she even did. In London her movements had been predictable, but certainly not since. Certainly not in Mayfield, or here in Ardingly. Now they didn't even have to predict them. They were certain to be close by.

She glanced over at Charles. His face was drawn and his eyes shadowed; occasionally he reached up to rub his shoulder, though he seemed unaware of it. What disruption she'd caused in this man's life. What further disruptions she would cause, should it be known how much time she had spent alone in his company. Certainly by now everyone in Ardingly knew of it, and though most of them were likely sympathetic, there were those who would be scandalized. They were the ones who would write to friends and acquaintances, eager to share this juicy tit-bit of gossip. Certainly the vicar, who was openly shocked and disapproving, would speak out, if only in a letter to her father. Oh, but she didn't want to marry Charles. At least, not this way.

The thought caught her so much by surprise that she didn't hear Charles speak to her at first. "Serena."

"Hm?" She raised her head and blinked at him. "Excuse me, I was woolgathering."

He was smiling at her, an amused, tender smile that did odd things to her stomach. "You fell asleep."

"Oh, dear," she said, and to her surprise and horror, yawned. "Do pray excuse me. I usually don't do such things."

"Tch, you're exhausted, dear. You need to rest," Mrs. Wills said. "You, too, Major. Now, I've had chambers prepared for you—no, I won't listen to any protests. You're safe here, and we'll see to your clothes while you sleep."

Charles smiled up at her, and Serena's stomach did that odd little flip again. She liked his smile. His teeth weren't perfect, but the smile made his eyes crinkle at the corners and softened the severe lines of his face. She wondered what he had been like before he went to war. But then, she mused, had he not gone to fight, he wouldn't be the man he was now.

"Look at her," Charles said, sounding amused, and she started again. "You're becoming an old campaigner, Lady Serena, falling asleep whenever you have the chance."

"Oh, dear." She shook her head to clear it. "I've never done such a thing before."

"Not even when you dance till dawn?" he teased.

She smiled back at him, suddenly more at ease than she had been since her abduction. "I usually sleep the day away, of course. Unless I have fittings with my modiste."

"Or a drive through the park in the afternoon."

"Yes, so terribly fatiguing."

"Now, enough of that." Mrs. Wills took Serena's arm and helped her rise. "It's bed for you. You, too, Major."

"Yes, ma'am," he said with deceptive meekness.

"Oh, go on with you. Get your rest while you can."

"Yes, ma'am. I'll write my letters, and then I promise you I'll sleep."

The mention of letters made Serena's stomach tighten. Charles planned to write to his brother, but she had her own letters to write, to her father. She could not imagine what he must be feeling, or how he would react to her story. The flutter of excitement, so new, that she'd felt earlier was gone. In its place was a cold lump of dread.

"Don't worry so, princess," Charles said softly. "We'll brush through this somehow. Worst comes to worst, I've—"

"A plan." She smiled. "Heaven help me."

Charles trotted down the stairs late that afternoon, feeling refreshed and energetic. He was clean and well fed, and his coat had been sponged and pressed while he slept. Though his arm and shoulder still ached, the discomfort had subsided to a tolerable level. At the moment, he thought he could take on any number of opponents, and win.

Mr. Wills's face turned grim as Charles entered the parlor, and his good humor evaporated. "The plan didn't work," he said flatly.

"No, the plan was sound." Wills handed a tumbler of whiskey to him, and the two men settled into tapestry wing chairs near the windows, overlooking the back garden. "No one paid any mind to my gardener. Who'd think anything of him, leaving the yard with a barrow of grass cuttings and branches?"

"Country dwellers, perhaps, but not someone from town." Charles watched him carefully. "So he delivered the letters to your neighbor with no problem."

"Yes. And his footmen brought them to the posting inns." He took a deep breath. "Which is where there's some difficulty."

Charles went very still. There were three major posting routes in the vicinity. To make sure at least one letter got through to London, he and Serena had each written three copies of their letters, one for each route. "They were there."

"Those two ugly customers? No, they're still about."

Charles sat bolt upright. "They're here?"

"I'm afraid so. Mrs. Taylor, who lives just down the road, saw them."

"When?"

"Not above two hours ago."

"Bloody hell." He frowned and then relaxed, just a little. "We did expect it. Garnett doesn't give up easily."

Mr. Wills shot Charles a look from under his brows. So far he hadn't asked about Charles's connection with Garnett, but likely he would. "Your other guess about him was correct, too."

"He described Lady Serena to all the innkeepers," he said.

"Yes. He asked at Staplefield last night, and the other two this morning. One of the innkeepers," he said reluctantly, "recognized the earl's name and connected it with Lady Serena."

"Bloody hell," Charles said again, though that, too,

was something he had expected when he had outlined his plan. "So there's no going on those roads. Does Lady Serena know, or is she still asleep?"

"No, she's awake and in Mrs. Wills's sitting room. I'll show you there."

"Thank you." Charles rose and followed Mr. Wills back upstairs, to a west-facing room furnished with plump armchairs and a well-padded, faded sofa. A hound was stretched out in front of the hearth, though it held only an arrangement of flowers in a brass urn, and a tabby cat, supremely indifferent to human affairs, sat on the windowsill and stared fixedly outside.

At another time Charles might have appreciated the room's comfort. For now, though, his attention was all for Serena. She looked up at him from the couch, and though she smiled, her face was white and strained. "Well, princess." He smiled down at her. "I do still have a plan."

The words had the desired effect. A sparkle of life returned to Serena's eyes. "Good afternoon, Mr. Kirk. Yes, I suppose I shall just have to trust in it."

"My plans have got us out of a few messes before this."

"And into a few more," she retorted. "Mrs. Wills's maid kept finding bits of leaves in my hair. I can't imagine what she thought."

"Betty is a good soul," Mrs. Wills said as she pulled her needle through the embroidery in a tambour frame set before her.

"Oh, yes, ma'am, I never meant to imply else," Serena said. "You've all been remarkably good to us."

Charles sat with his legs crossed in an armchair. He didn't like the bright sheen in Serena's eyes. In spite of the respite, it was obvious that her nerves were still stretched too thin. "Waxing sentimental, princess?"

She glowered at him. "Not a bit of it."

That was his Serena, Charles thought, grinning at her. "Good. The last thing I need on my hands is a vaporish female."

"Vaporish!" she sputtered.

"Or mawkish."

"I am never vaporish or mawkish, sir."

"You're well liked in this village, Lady Serena," Mrs. Wills said, placidly setting another stitch. "Of course, there are always those few who will be unpleasant, but I never did like that Mrs. Howard above half." She paused, frowning. "Pity her house is so close to ours."

"And the vicar across the road." Serena gave Charles a wry smile. His own grin was unrepentant. He and Mrs. Wills, bless her, had between them managed to break her out of her megrims, at least for now.

"Poor man, he tries so hard, but he simply doesn't understand people. You'll stay the night, of course."

"Thank you," Charles said. "And then, sir?" He turned to Mr. Wills, who sat across from him. "Is there someone willing to take us up in a wagon tomorrow?"

Mr. Wills nodded. "Yes, Mr. Cooper, just three houses away. You won't care for this, Lady Serena," he added as he turned toward her.

Serena eyed him with suspicion. "What?"

"It's a hay wain."

"Hay!" she exclaimed in dismay, and then glared at Charles. "Did you hear that?"

Charles held up his hands in self-defense. "It wasn't my idea, though it's a good one. We'll be covered enough."

"Which is what I fear."

"If it's any comfort, I care less about it than you do." He grinned at her, though, and then turned back to Mr. Wills. "As it's haying season, that should do admirably, sir. What of the horses?"

"I've already sent ahead about that. There'll be two waiting for you."

"We'll fill your saddlebags, too," Mrs. Wills added.

"Someone will bring your horse to London in a few days. A good mount. Arabian?"

"Yes. I got him in Spain." Charles stared down at the floor. It would be cursed difficult to part with Samson, yet that was part of the plan, too. So long as Samson stayed in the Willses' stable, Garnett and Alf would likely believe that he and Serena were still in Ardingly. "He'll give you no trouble."

"Are you certain your friend will be in Brighton?" Serena said abruptly.

He shrugged. "No, but I heard a few days ago that the 10th is stationed there awaiting orders. There are likely to be any number of people I know who will help."

He wouldn't have suggested Brighton as a destination else, should it prove that their way to London were blocked. If that didn't work, he'd think of something else.

He glanced over at Serena and reached for her hand, not caring about what the Willses might think. "It will work, princess," he said softly. "I promise you that."

Geoffrey flipped absently through the post the following morning in the breakfast parlor of his Grosvenor Square mansion, and gave a grunt of surprise. "Good God."

Ariel, sitting across from him and crumbling a piece of toast in her fingers, looked up. "What is it?"

The knife he was using to slit the wax on one of the thick letters stilled as he gazed at his wife. She was pale these mornings, unable to eat much, and her eyes were shadowed. She was carrying his child, and the thought brought with it utter elation and utter terror. "Three letters from Charles."

"Letters? Oh, good." She leaned forward. "I've been so dreadfully worried."

"Mm." So had he, when they'd heard that Charles had never arrived at Oakhurst, though he knew quite well that his brother could handle himself. "I wonder where—good God."

"Geoffrey?"

Without answering, he slit the wax on the second letter, scanned it quickly, and handed it across to her. She gave him an enquiring look as she unfolded it and then gasped. "Heavens!"

He nodded. "Precisely."

"Three copies of the same letter?"

"Read on," he said, already absorbed in the letter. It made for grim reading, the tale of the abducted heiress and Charles's part in her escape. *Good God,* he thought.

"Oh, that poor girl," Ariel said, her fingers trembling as she folded the sheets of paper together. "What a thing to happen to her. If Charles encountered her two days ago—"

"She was held captive for four days," he said. It was an ordeal he'd not wish on anyone, let alone a gently bred young lady.

"At least she's unhurt." Ariel took a shaky breath. "But."

His eyes met hers. "But," he agreed. Her reputation was irretrievably ruined. Worse, she was still in danger. Charles, honorable as he was, likely intended to marry her, but the damage was done. "There's no salvaging her good name."

"No, I fear not. And you know what Harlow is like."

He nodded. He did, indeed, know what type of man Lady Serena's father was. "He'll likely blame Charles for this."

"But he rescued her!"

"It won't matter worth a damn."

Ariel looked mutinous for a moment, her chin out-thrust and her eyes dark. "Then we shall just have to do what we can for the girl. It needed only this, after all he's been through."

"I don't know," Geoffrey said slowly. "It might be the making of him."

She gave him another questioning look, but she must have moved too quickly. Her pallor changed to a sickly green. Clapping her hand over her mouth, she rose so fast that her chair fell back, and ran from the room toward the butler's pantry.

Geoffrey jumped up with equal alacrity, took an involuntary step toward the pantry, and then stopped. There was naught he could do for Ariel, no matter how much he might wish to. His mother assured him sympathetically that his wife's current discomfort would pass; his grandmother scolded him for what she saw as foolish worry. "The gel has months to go yet," she'd said tartly. "You'll see worse than this before she's through."

Good God. Passing a hand across his face, as damp with sweat as Ariel's no doubt was, he sat down and picked up the letter. *Good God,* he thought again.

Promptly at two o'clock that afternoon, Geoffrey was shown into Harlow House. All about him was opulence. Set on Berkeley Square, the mansion was imposing, even by *ton* standards. His gaze encompassed the marble-tiled floor that reputedly had been quarried in Italy, the graceful curve of the U-shaped double staircase, the domed ceiling high above, painted to look like the sky, with cherubs cavorting upon it, and with an enormous chandelier depending from it. Water splashed from a gilded fountain set between the double stairs, and a huge porcelain vase, from China by its appearance, stood against one wall. Even the anteroom, where he was shown after the butler took his hat and walking stick, was opulent, done as it was in the style of Louis Quatorze. Geoffrey had never been in this house. He wasn't certain he ever wished to be again.

Harlow was an odd duck, he thought, as he inspected a delicate Dresden figurine with his quizzing glass. Both austere and sybaritic. Choleric and good-natured. At times he could be the best of good fellows, a fine raconteur with a witty, if caustic, tongue. At others, when his eyes were stormy and his face set, people avoided him. Charles had crossed swords with him more than once in the House of Lords; their political views couldn't be more opposite. He had also jested with him at White's. One never quite knew where one stood with him. One never quite liked him.

It was difficult to predict Harlow's reaction to the news he had doubtless received from his daughter in that morning's post. He was not known as an overfond or indulgent parent, but he certainly was allowing Lady Serena her season. He certainly had allowed her to refuse four eligible suitors. He must be worried about her welfare, Geoffrey thought, though doubt niggled inside him. There was simply no way to predict how the man would react.

At that moment, the butler reappeared and showed Geoffrey to Harlow's study, across the hall and down a corridor. The room revealed the other side of the man. Unlike the public parts of the house, it was furnished plainly, almost ascetically. What furniture there was, however, was of the very best quality. The Turkey carpet, although woven in muted colors, was plush; the club chairs were upholstered in fine Moroccan leather; that same leather padded the top of the massive desk, which itself was made of mahogany that had reputedly been brought from Brazil, to Harlow's exact specifications, by a master craftsman. Yet Harlow himself wore a brocaded waistcoat, and his neckcloth was tied in the complicated *trône d'amour*. A difficult man to know, Geoffrey thought. An even more difficult man, from the man's dark, fathomless eyes and black glower, to face at this moment.

The earl neither rose from behind his desk nor held out his hand, though he did wave Geoffrey toward a chair. He knew quite well why Sherbourne was here, and it had to do with the letter that rested in his desk drawer. The letters that he'd read compulsively, again and again.

"Well, Sherbourne?" he said after a long moment, during which they eyed each other coolly.

"I assume you know why I'm here, sir," Geoffrey said. "You received letters from Lady Serena, did you not?"

Harlow's face hardened as he rose, at last, to cross the room. At a table where several decanters stood, he poured himself a tumbler of Scotch whiskey, drinking deeply before handing a tumbler to Geoffrey and then returning to his desk. He knew how he appeared to the other man, with grizzled hair that had once been red and a face broadened and coarsened through life's hard experience. He knew Geoffrey viewed him as conservative and reactionary, and perhaps he was. They heartily detested each other's politics and felt contempt for the other's way of life. He also held Sherbourne in more respect than the other man likely suspected.

"I did," he said finally. "And so, where is my daughter, sir?" He leaned forward, stabbing at the air with his finger, his anger sweeping over him again. "I'll tell you, shall I? Haring about the countryside with your brother, by God!" he roared, and slammed his hand down upon the desk.

To his credit, Geoffrey did not so much as flinch.

"That is not how I understand the situation, sir," he said coolly.

"True enough." He tapped the edge of the tumbler against the leather blotter. "Your brother has compromised my daughter. What, sir, do you propose to do about it?"

Geoffrey blinked. "What *can* I do? I don't even know where they are at the moment."

"Precisely. As I said. Haring about the countryside."

"May I remind you, sir," Geoffrey said through clenched teeth, "that your daughter was abducted?"

"How very convenient that she just happened to be held in a building at an estate your brother was to manage."

"What are you implying, sir?"

"Your brother is a half-pay officer."

That made Geoffrey come out of his chair. "Are you accusing him of being a fortune hunter?"

Harlow leaned back, fingers drumming on the desktop. "He would not be the first ineligible suitor I've turned away."

"My God." Geoffrey sank back into the chair. "Lady Serena is in danger, and you care only about her reputation?"

"Her reputation is in shreds."

"Which hardly seems important just now."

"She has brought shame to this house, sir. I'll see her banished to the country before I'd ever let her come back to town."

"She is your child."

"She should have been a boy!" he roared again. "By God, she should have been a boy."

"If she were, she wouldn't be in such case," Geoffrey snapped, goaded at last. "She is your daughter, sir, whether you like it or not, and she needs your help."

Harlow gazed at him for a long, long moment. "My

daughter is dead to me," he said flatly. "If you'll excuse me, I've work to see to. Fletcher will see you out."

For a moment, Geoffrey seemed as if he might not accept the dismissal, but then he rose. Without a word, he turned and stalked from the room, closing the door behind him with a definite thud. Harlow gave it a measuring look, and then returned his attention to his desk.

Once again he took Serena's letter from the drawer and read it over. The words hadn't changed. The meaning hadn't changed. His face impassive, he folded it and set it aside. For a long, long moment, he stared into space. Then, his eyes holding a suspicious gleam, he crossed his arms on the desk, sank his head onto them, and stayed that way for a very long time.

SEVEN

The following noon found Charles and Serena snugly ensconced in a small glade, protected from view from the road. They had finished a substantial luncheon of ham, cheese, and buttered bread, with lemonade to drink and small blueberry pastries for a sweet. Ravenous after another nerve-wracking, if uneventful, morning, both had set into the simple meal with a will, until only crumbs remained. "Mrs. Wills's cook is superb," he said.

"'It hath been usual with the honest and well-meaning host to provide a bill of fare,'" Serena quoted absently.

Charles shot up from his lounging position. "When did you read *Tom Jones*?"

"I have had an eclectic education," she said, wiping the crumbs from her hand and wrapping her arms about her knees. He was, she knew, giving her a mistrustful look as he lounged back again, but she ignored it. Instead she looked up at the sun, riding high in a sky so blue that it almost hurt to see it. Time, however, was not their ally, not if they were to reach Brighton by that evening. The back roads they traveled led them on a circuitous route south, through villages and past farms unfamiliar to each. But they were safe. It was extremely unlikely that Garnett would guess either where they were, or what their destination was.

"I am beginning to distrust you when you say you

have a plan," Serena said, picking yet another wisp of hay from the riding habit Mrs. Wills had been good enough to lend her.

Charles, stretched out on his side next to her, took one last bite of his pastry and then rubbed his hands together to free them of crumbs. "They've worked," he said mildly, propping himself on his elbow.

"I should hope so." She huffed out a breath as her fingers found yet more hay in her hair. "But I always end by being so untidy and dirty."

"Going out in a hay wagon was a good idea." He still spoke in that mild tone. "No one knew we were there."

"It was a wonder we could breathe, with all that atop us."

He was quiet for so long that she looked over, to see that his hands were clenched. "The Willses went through a great deal of trouble for us," he finally said.

Frowning, Serena glanced away. In the pre-dawn coolness, she and Charles, both muffled in dark cloaks, had been smuggled through the back gardens to a neighbor's home. There they had clambered into the hay wain, and had been covered with a load of hay. Their hiding place had proved effective. Not until they were past the danger point, well out of the village, did the driver tell them that Garnett had been about, and that he had been supremely indifferent to the comings and goings of farm vehicles. *Thank God,* Serena thought fervently. *Thank God.*

"And we've good enough mounts," Charles went on.

Serena turned and gazed toward the two horses cropping the grass behind them, near the brook, which splashed over stones. They were raw-boned beasts, with nothing of fine lineage about them. Instead they were sturdy and patient. If their gait was slow, at least it was steady and fairly smooth. Serena blessed the neighbor who had agreed to the use of his horses, simply because

Mr. Wills had asked. The Willses had been good to them.

Serena turned back, to admit to Charles the soundness of his plan, only to see him stretched out, his head pillowed on his arm. In the few moments when she had looked away, he had fallen asleep. A soldier's trick, she remembered him saying, to snatch rest where possible. She sighed. Soldier's trick or not, it left her feeling lonely, and very alone in the world.

He was tired, of course. For the past few days they had constantly run from place to place, all in an effort to outpace their pursuers. If it had exhausted her, she didn't have the pain of a wounded shoulder to deal with. She'd seen him favoring his arm on more than one occasion; more than once she'd almost asked him about it. Always, though, she held back, constrained by courtesy and by a certain look in his eyes. He wouldn't welcome what he would probably consider to be pity. More than likely, he'd had enough of that since coming home.

It was odd, she thought, wrapping her arms around her knees and gazing over at the stream. One tended not to think of the war, unless something spectacular happened, such as the defeat at Douro, or Sir John Moore's death at Corunna. One thought only of the gallant, charming officers, so handsome and striking in their scarlet uniforms, making every other man at any *ton* function pale in comparison. She certainly never had thought of what happened to those young officers once they were posted. She was the much-pampered daughter of a wealthy earl, the Incomparable, until terror had come crashing into her life. Until she had been caught up by a former soldier who knew too well how to evade an enemy, she had rarely spared a thought for the grimmer realities of life. It shamed her now, that she could have been so shallow, when she had always considered herself to be a caring person.

A strange, forced clacking sound rescued Serena from her self-recriminations. Glancing down, she saw that Charles's jaw was working back and forth. He was grinding his teeth, she thought. Only great willpower prevented her from reaching out to smooth the furrows from his brow. The horrors he had seen during his time in the army were too far beyond her imagination to conjure up. Certainly he knew how to live off the land. He must have done so before, and that spoke volumes about what his life had been like. A difficult life, and all the time she had been safe and unaware in London's ballrooms.

Charles's face smoothed out, but still Serena gazed at him. Still she wished to touch him, for a different reason this time, a reason she didn't quite understand. She wished to stroke those lean, chiseled cheeks, that tarnished gold hair. In repose his features were softened, his face less gaunt, his eyes less shadowed. He looked so much younger that for the first time she wondered how old he was. He was so very competent, so self-assured, that she had thought him to be older than she. What she could guess was that he was, in many ways, too old to take part in the pursuits of the *ton*. War had done that to him, she thought. It had brought that certain bleak look to his eyes.

Uncomfortable with that thought, she looked at the stream again, finding no surcease there. If Charles faced his own private hell, so did she. So did she have nightmares, of all that had happened to her, of all that might have happened. Again she shuddered. If Charles hadn't come along when he had . . .

Beside her, she heard an odd, strangled sound. Charles's face was contorted, and he was groaning deeply, painfully. Another nightmare, or perhaps the same? Whichever it was, he was clearly in distress. Serena couldn't bear it. She reached out to touch his shoulder.

Charles threw back her hand and jerked upright violently. "Luz!" His cry was hoarse and agonized. "Oh, God, Luz, *men querido,* Luz."

"Charles." Serena grabbed his shoulder to shake him, and again he threw her off. Caught off guard, she toppled to the ground, and sharp pain shot up her arm from the unintended hurt he had inflicted on her elbow. "Ow!" she exclaimed, unable to help herself. "I'm not Luz!"

That seemed to do it. He swiveled his head toward her, and the blank, blind look in his eyes turned gradually to awareness. He stared at her for a moment more and then sat up, sinking his head into his hands. "God," he said shakily. "Oh, God."

Serena rose more slowly, wincing a little and rubbing at her elbow. It was her right arm, and she suspected it would pain her for some time. "What happened?" she asked, though she knew.

"A dream. A damned dream."

She gazed at him with disfavor, not wanting to speak, yet knowing she had to make some effort. She owed him so much. "Do you want to tell me about it?"

"No," he said in a clipped voice.

Well. That was that. She had asked and had been rebuffed, leaving her with no further obligation. And yet . . . "Who is Luz?" she asked.

He turned sharply toward her. "How do you know that name?"

"You called it out in your sleep. Who was she?"

Charles took a long time to answer. "A girl I once knew."

"A señorita?"

"You ask too many questions," he snapped. "Have I asked you exactly what happened to you?"

Serena lurched clumsily to her feet and began running blindly toward the stream and the grazing horses. For a time she had held them back, the ghosts of horror that haunted her dreams, but his words brought them back all too clearly. She had to escape. Somehow she had to outrun them.

Behind her she heard someone call her name, and she redoubled her efforts. They were after her. Panting, with fingers that felt too large for the task, she fumbled at the reins of her mount, fastened loosely to the branch of a tree. A hand caught her arm, and she cried out with pain and terror, striking out blindly. "No! Leave me alone—"

"Serena!" Charles said in a voice she'd never heard before, and swung her around. Her other arm reflexively came up to shield her face. Now it would begin again; now it would start. "Serena," Charles said again.

This time she heard him. "Ch-Charles?" she whimpered.

"Yes, princess."

"Oh." She was safe, she realized, safe, and yet the horror still gripped her. "Oh, God," she said, her voice a high, thin wail. "Oh, God."

"Princess, it's all right." Charles drew her into his arms, and she went, docile, unresisting, and shaking uncontrollably. "Oh, my dear," he said into her hair, holding her tight against him. "I'm sorry. I didn't mean to scare you."

"Ch-Charles." She clutched at him. "I was so frightened. I didn't know what they wanted. I didn't know what they'd do, and the way they looked at me—oh, if they catch me—"

"They won't." He sounded grim. "I promise you that, princess. I won't allow anyone to lay a hand on you."

"But what do they want?" she cried. "What do they want from me?"

"Shh." He cradled her against him. "You're safe, Serena. I'm not going to let them hurt you."

Serena pulled back and studied his face. She knew tears were coursing down her cheeks. She knew that when she cried she was not particularly pretty, not with her eyes and nose red and her ordinarily fair skin blotchy. Yet the way he was looking at her, his eyes intent, heavy-lidded—oh, it took her breath away. It made the darkness fade. Unable to look away, feeling the strength of his arms around her and the tenderness of his hand cupping her head, she lifted her face, just as his lowered.

She had been kissed before and considered herself to be quite experienced and knowledgeable on the subject. Led out onto terraces or into gardens or shady paths by various young men, she had always felt a little daring, a little excited. Some had bestowed upon her shy little flutters; some had seemed determined to mash her lips with theirs, all the time squeezing her much too close; some had been slobbery and wet. All had been disappointing, leaving her vaguely depressed and very uncertain. If those kisses were an indication of what life with a man was like, she thought she'd rather be a spinster.

Charles, though, was different. Somehow she had known he would be. His lips were warm, and they neither mashed nor fluttered. Instead they slanted softly across hers. And they moved. That was her first surprise. They parted slightly to draw in her upper lip, just for a moment, and then her lower lip. They sucked lightly at the corner of her mouth; they slid, still parted, across her lower lip to nibble at the other corner. By the time they settled on hers again, firmer now, more demanding, she was more than willing to meet him. When his tongue slid across the closed seam of her mouth, she opened hers slightly to it. And when he instantly took advantage of that little surrender, stroking along the soft flesh, probing insistently at her teeth, she gave in. She had no choice.

Immediately his tongue plunged into her mouth. No softness now, no gentleness. All was need and longing and desire. At some point her hands had come up to encircle his back. Now they clutched at his shoulder blades in rhythm with what he was doing to her. He was stroking in and out, and within seconds she felt compelled to do the same. At first, it seemed awkward. At first, she didn't know if she were doing it quite right. But then he drew her tongue into his mouth and sucked on it lightly, and all reason fled, leaving behind only feeling. Oh, this was nice, this felt very good indeed. She rose up on her toes and pressed herself against him. If he were to tumble her upon the ground right now she would gladly go with him. . . .

Serena wrenched her lips away, gasping in sharply. His eyes were puzzled; his lips were fuller and darker than they had been moments ago. She wondered if hers looked the same. They certainly felt different, swollen and tight.

"I scared you, didn't I?" Charles said softly. "I'm sorry, princess."

Serena looked down, her eyes roughly at a level with his chest. "I know."

He stroked her cheek with the back of his fingers. "I never meant to."

She swallowed. Even that light, gentle touch was enough to set up a thrumming in her blood. Pressed against him as she was, she couldn't help but be aware of how much he wanted her. What surprised her, what frightened her, was how much she wanted him. "I know that, too," she said, and felt the truth of it. Being abducted and then held captive had, she realized, destroyed something within her. Never again would she be so blithely unconcerned about other people, and what their intentions toward her might be. Yet she trusted Charles. That she knew in her heart, in her soul. And she was, she knew in the same way, well on her way to falling in love with him.

"Why do you look at me like that?" Charles asked, his gaze puzzled and wary.

"Like what?"

"I don't know. I'm not sure I like what you're thinking, whatever it is."

"I was thinking how brave of you that was."

His brow furrowed. "Why?"

"Kissing me when I look a perfect fright from crying."

"You look beautiful, princess," he said, with such sincerity that it both alarmed her and made her feel warm.

"Certainly no one in London would think so."

"They're superficial in London."

"Yes," she said slowly, admitting it for the first time. Until a few days ago, she had been part of that glittering, artificial world, accepting as her just due that she was the Season's reigning belle. How foolish that was. "They are, aren't they?"

"Yes." They looked at each other in perfect understanding, two veterans of hell, until it became too much. "What will your father do, do you think?" Charles asked, as he had once before.

"I've no idea," she said. They had crossed to the horses, and now he threw her up into the saddle. "In some ways appearances mean a great deal to him, and in others, they don't."

Charles handed her her reins and swung onto his own mount. "He won't want you marrying a second son who also happens to be a half-pay officer, will he."

It was not a question, and it made her look at him curiously. "Do you wish you had the title?"

"No, Geoffrey's welcome to that. But as to money, I'm not precisely poor."

"I don't see how that's to the point."

"Your father can be assured that I can take care of you."

"Take care of—we aren't marrying, Charles. I told you that before."

"And I've told you that you've been compromised."

"Not by you."

"Yes, by me. We've spent days in each other's company. Society will believe we've been together all along."

She dismissed that with a wave of her hand. "I believe we just agreed that society is superficial?"

"What of your father, then? What is he thinking, since I've not brought you home?"

"He'll not force me to marry where I don't wish to."

"I suppose he wanted you to make a good match. Another earl at the least, or a marquess. Or a duke."

"Not if I didn't at least like the man," she shot back.

"You yourself told me that you don't believe in love."

She pondered that for a moment before she answered. "I don't," she said carefully, in spite of her growing feelings for him. "I believe in affection, though, and respect."

"And if those happen to come with a title and a fortune, so much the better."

"Now who's being superficial?"

He shifted in the saddle, and the horse tossed up his head. "It matters not. I'm marrying you."

"No, you're not."

"Yes, I am."

"I'm not going to marry," she said firmly. "Not now."

"We'll see."

"We won't," she said, and, setting her horse into a canter, rode away from him.

Charles caught up with her at last, and for a long time neither one of them talked. "Seriously," he said finally, "how will your father take this? Will he banish you to the country?"

She glanced at him. "He may. My sister will be appalled, of course," she added.

"Will she? Why—oh. She was the Season's Incomparable some years back, was she not?"

"Yes." And now conventionally married to a prosy old bore of a man who kept mistresses and gambled away his nights. Lady Anne resented it that now her younger sister was acclaimed as she once had been. She might be just a little pleased at Serena's downfall. "It's not worth looking ahead, is it? It will be unpleasant for a time, but then 'twill all die down."

"Your name will forever be ruined."

"Better that than being held captive," she shot back, and again cantered away.

Charles caught her up within a few minutes, riding in silence beside her, while she fumed with a mixture of anger and helplessness and fear. Fear? Of what? Except for the fact that she had not yet reached home, she was safe. To feel as she did was irrational, and yet she couldn't shake it. She was afraid.

"I wondered when that would happen," Charles said quietly.

She glanced at him. "What?"

"When you were going to break, as you did back there."

"What!"

"I saw it often on the Peninsula. Men who went through the worst battles, who fought as bravely as anyone else, perhaps more so, were the worst when the battle was done."

Her grip on the reins was tight. Was he saying that she

was brave, that what she'd gone through was terrible, or both? "What is your meaning, sir?"

"They were the ones who took it the hardest. Always. The ones with nightmares, the ones who shook or screamed when it thundered. Some went along normally," he went on, "but it always came out." He took a deep breath. "Most of them recovered, at least enough to function," he went on, as if she hadn't spoken, "but some didn't. They had to be sent home."

"You're saying that's what's happened to me."

"Yes, princess." His voice was gentle. "It did happen."

She blinked back tears. She didn't like this man seeing so deeply into her soul. "And you're afraid I'm one of the ones who won't recover."

"No, princess," he protested. "The opposite. But don't think you must be strong all the time."

"I don't," she began, and then stopped. But she did. She always had. "Never mind." She was so tired, tired of living with what had happened to her, tired of always having to run. What would she have done without Charles? "Heaven help me, but do you have a plan?"

He grinned at her. "Of course."

Serena noticed, not for the first time, that one tooth, though white and obviously strong, overlapped the other. It was an endearing feature, and it kept his face from being too austerely handsome. "I thought as much." She pretended to grimace as they ambled toward the road. "What does it involve this time? Not leaves or hay, we've already tried those. Twigs? Cornstalks? No, no, don't tell me. Mud."

His smile this time was a little strained. "Hardly. I had enough of that on the Peninsula."

There it was again, the reminder that his past had molded him into a person far different from most she had encountered in her life. He was lean, capable, hardened by his experiences. Yet he had not failed to come to her aid. Reluctant hero though he was, he had still found ways to keep her safe. And yet, there was the nightmare. Very well, she thought suddenly. If he could probe into her feelings, then she could do the same. "Who is Luz?" she asked again.

Charles's face went tight. "Why do you keep asking?"

"Because of your nightmare."

"I knew her in Portugal," he said, his tone indicating that, so far as he was concerned, the subject was closed.

"Where is she now?"

"Still in Portugal."

"Oh." Her mind teemed with questions. She wondered if he had loved her. Probably he had, she thought gloomily. Mayhap he always would.

Not that it mattered, she reminded herself quickly. Mayhap that kiss had meant something only to her. Mayhap she *was* close to falling in love with him. More fool she. She was levelheaded enough to know that much of what she felt came from the remarkable experiences they had shared. Gratitude was likely the base of her feelings. For she was not going to let herself be forced into marrying Charles. It was a terrible reward for having rescued her, when he had not been the one to ruin her reputation. Foolish rule, she thought. Being abducted and then held captive by two men certainly had not been by her choice. Neither was the situation she found herself in with Charles. Most of all, it was not her choice that he still loved another woman.

She sighed. Well. That was quite enough self-pity. She lifted her head in defiance of the difficulties that still faced her. "What is your plan?" she asked, breaking the mood.

"Hm?" Charles looked up, and his gaze was so distant it was apparent he had been lost in thought. "Yes. The plan." Again he grinned. "We'll go to my friend,

Lieutenant Cathcart. He'll find a way to get us away, even if we have to go in disguise."

"Disguise!" Startled, she turned toward him. "Such as?"

"I don't know yet. But I have—"

"Yet another plan," she finished. "I don't trust you."

"Actually," he said, and stopped. His look was arrested. "If I had planned better, we'd have made for Canterbury."

"Canterbury? Why?"

"Going east 'twould be the last thing Garnett and Alf would expect, for one thing."

"How did they know where I'd go? That bothers me."

"I don't know, princess." His face was grave. "They obviously know a great deal about you."

"They planned well, didn't they?" she said in a small voice. "They must have learned all they could about me."

"I'm afraid so, princess," he said, his voice gentle.

"But why? We still don't know that. If it were for ransom, surely I would have been released within a day or two. Why four days? Why," she gulped, "perhaps longer?"

"They didn't touch you?" he asked, as he had once before.

"No." She gulped again, and closed her eyes. "But if it had gone on much longer, I think they would have."

"Easy, princess." He laid his hand on hers, and she realized in dim surprise that they had stopped. "It didn't happen."

"I—I know."

"Come." He released her hand and took up his reins. "Time is passing, if we're to be in Brighton before evening."

Serena blinked several times and then, breathing deeply, began to ride as well. "Why Canterbury?" she asked again, more to distract herself than anything.

"Hm?"

"You implied there was more than one reason."

"So there is." He smiled at her. "It so happens that my father was well acquainted with the Bishop of Canterbury."

She frowned. "So?"

"Think, Serena," he said patiently. "Where better to get a special license?"

"No!" Again she rode ahead; again he caught up with her easily. "You really can't be serious about this," she said.

"I've never been more so."

"No. And I'm serious."

"Serena." His voice was patient. "Why are you so set against marriage?"

"Because you still love someone else."

Charles's face suddenly went fierce. "We will not speak of her again."

"It's true," she insisted. "Tell me it's not."

"She's in the past."

"I don't think so."

"Dammit, Serena! She has nothing to do with us."

But she does, Serena thought, and in that moment knew that she was not on her way to falling in love with Charles. She was already there. "Charles, I'm not marrying you," she said as gently as she could. "Accept it this time. You may have made your decision, but so have I, years ago." She took a deep breath. "Unless you can tell me you love me—maybe not even then—I will not marry you."

"Am I not acceptable, then?"

His tone was so aggrieved that she stifled a laugh. Apparently he had his share of male vanity. "Of course you are." Too much so. She would not willingly go into a marriage where she loved a man who didn't love her. And there it was again. Love. Long ago, watching her parents, she had decided it brought only trouble and pain. "Brighton is a better idea, Charles."

He looked at her for a moment longer, his eyes still hard, and then turned away, nodding. "Brighton it is, then."

Brighton was surprisingly filled with people, exposing both of them to danger. Charles swore under his breath. "I should have realized," he muttered. "Brighton is fashionable now."

"I should have remembered this is the season for it. I've had a different sense of time lately."

Charles sent her a swift glance. Her face was smooth, serene. She was bearing up surprisingly well, he thought, considering how she had broken down just a few hours earlier. "We need to find a place for you to stay."

"That won't look very good, Charles, a woman alone."

He frowned. Once again he'd forgotten the etiquette of polite society, because of the urgency and danger of what they faced. "For both of us, then," he said reluctantly. "We'll say we're brother and sister."

"We won't be believed."

"Nevertheless, it's what we must do. I need to see Lieutenant Cathcart. It's not proper for you to go to his lodgings."

Serena burst out laughing. "Oh, Charles! As if propriety has even been considered these days past."

"You thought of it just now," he pointed out, grinning. It was the first time Serena had laughed since she had broken down.

"That's different." Together they turned their mounts and rode away from the center of town. "That has more to do with my safety than what is proper. Proper." She chuckled again. "I do believe I'll not give two snaps for that again."

He gazed at her riding by his side, unaware of his scrutiny. When they returned to London, propriety would be important indeed, with her reputation as damaged as it was. No matter what she said, he had every intention of marrying her. "Perhaps, princess. Perhaps not."

Wisely, Charles ignored the better inns they passed, those that served as posting inns or catered to the Quality, and even those a notch below. When they did stop at last, the inn they picked was inferior, judging by its untended look. All the better for their purposes.

"Here?" Serena looked in dismay at the ramshackle building.

"How likely is it we'll meet someone we know?" he said, and swung off his horse before turning to help Serena down. "Come." He held out his arm to her and led her into the inn.

The innkeeper was inclined to sneer when told of their claim that they were brother and sister. Charles, however, had not been an officer on the Peninsula for nothing. He drew himself up to his full height, spreading his feet apart, "We require two rooms, for my sister and me," he repeated, in the voice that had commanded so many men, and the innkeeper blinked.

Serena, ignoring completely the innkeeper's stammered apology, turned to Charles. "Must we put up with this maworm?" she said with such bored, aristocratic hauteur that Charles bit back a smile. "Surely we are not reduced to this."

"I fear so," he said gravely, looking at her as if she were his sister, and finding that surprisingly hard. She was indeed a beauty, his Serena, and yet she was something far more. It was as if he could see past her surface loveliness, to the beauty within. The feeling was unsettling.

The moment must have stretched on longer than he

had realized. Serena was again staring at him with her chin raised. Her eyes were puzzled, though. "We have come far down in the world, my dear," Charles said.

"But to be in Brighton and not to partake of any of its pleasures." She actually pouted. "Really, it's too bad."

"Yes, it is. Come." He turned from the counter. "Our custom is not wanted here."

"Wait," the innkeeper called, and Charles had to resist shooting a glance of amusement at Serena. "Might be I just have something for you."

"Indeed?" Charles turned back. "Two rooms?"

"Yes, yes, Major."

That hit too close to home for comfort. "A private parlor, too, of course," he said, voice crisp again.

"Yes, yes, of course. If you'd just sign, sir?" His eyes glittered suddenly. "You can pay the shot, of course."

Charles looked up. "Of course," he said, and proceeded without hesitation to sign the name of a comrade who had died on the retreat to Corunna. "Our bags are with our horses. See to them. And send up water," he threw back over his shoulder as he escorted Serena to the stairs.

"Yes, yes." The innkeeper's voice was nervous as he came around the counter. "As quick as can be, Major."

"Captain," Charles said, in that crisp voice. "As you would know if you'd bother to read the register."

"Yes, yes," the innkeeper said, and at last led them to their private parlor. Charles looked about the small, dingy room, furnished with a scarred table and several tired-looking chairs, and raised his eyebrows inquiringly at Serena. She was looking down her nose again, this time with her nostrils pinched, as if she smelled something bad.

"I suppose it will do," she sighed at last.

"It has to. You are dismissed," he said curtly to the innkeeper, who bowed himself out of the room.

Charles looked over at Serena as the door closed, leaving them at last alone. Her hand was clamped over her mouth, but above it her eyes danced with merriment. "Well?" he said, still in the manner he had assumed for the innkeeper's benefit, and she collapsed into a chair.

"Oh, did you see his face?" she gasped, when her first gust of amusement had passed. "I could almost pity him."

Charles grinned. He did enjoy her laughter, so free and unfettered. "But not quite." He leaned back in the rickety chair, hands clasped behind his head. "'I suppose it will do,'" he mimicked, and that set her off again.

"And yet." Her face was suddenly serious. "Anyone checking here would certainly know who we are."

He shot her a look, his own amusement gone. "Why should anyone do that?"

"I don't know." Her eyes were troubled. "A feeling, perhaps. I can't think they'll give up yet."

She was right, curse it. He sat forward, and the front legs of the chair banged onto the floor. "I did sign a false name, if anyone should come." *If.* Garnett would know immediately. "'Tis a remote chance."

"I suppose it is," she said after a moment, her gaze on her fingers, which were pleating her skirt. "But what if the innkeeper should describe us?"

"We'll be gone by then. He won't know where."

Her eyes were as haunted as he had ever seen them. "Have you a plan where?"

"A few ideas."

"Merely to find your friend."

"Yes. He knows this town better than we do. He'll find us better lodgings than this. Come," he called out. This, as there was a soft knock at the door. It opened to admit a tired-looking maid, carrying a tray. She set it down on the table, bobbed a curtsy, and then was gone.

"And then home," Serena said, when the maid was gone and they no longer needed to keep silent.

"And then home." Their adventure was nearly over, which was, in so many ways, a relief. Which was, in other, more subtle ways, a disappointment. It was for the best that they returned to their normal lives, though that prospect appeared flat and dull to him. Now that he had been in action again, so to speak, now that he had found some purpose in his life, at least for a brief time, he could not imagine living as he had planned. He wondered if she felt the same, since they faced one enormous problem. They still didn't know why she had been abducted.

EIGHT

Lieutenant Sir Edward Cathcart, of the 10th, Prince of Wales's Own Royal Regiment of Hussars, and a friend of Charles since their days at Cambridge, looked surprised when Charles was shown into his quarters in a house just off the Steyne, Brighton's main street, the following morning. "Charles?" he said, coming forward with hand outstretched. "What the devil do you do here? And," he wrinkled his nose, "dressed like that?"

Charles looked down at his clothing, vaguely surprised at his friend's reaction. In the last days he had become accustomed to looking less than his precise self. Such things simply had not seemed important. "Not my best," he admitted, and strolled to the window to look out on the street. For all the bustle and busyness of the rest of the town, it was relatively peaceful here. "How do you find Brighton?"

"Dashed boring," he said promptly. "I feel like a paper soldier, waiting on Prinny's whims. I'd rather see action."

"Believe me, you hadn't," Charles said gently. "Trust me."

An awkward silence fell between them. "I didn't buy my commission merely to sit out the war." Cathcart's voice was low. "Boney has to be defeated, and yet I sit here while my friends lie wounded or dead."

It was far worse than that, Charles thought. "Do you know the town well enough to secure lodgings?"

"Lodgings?" Cathcart stared at him in blank surprise. "For you? Why?"

"Someplace quiet," Charles went on, "but in a decent neighborhood."

"For you?" Cathcart repeated, grinning. "Do you intend to take up residence here then, Kirk? Become part of Prinny's set? Oh-ho. I know what it is. You have found a, er, lady who wishes to be fashionable."

Charles swung around with a violence he had never thought himself capable of feeling, not even in Portugal. "If you breathe one word of this I shall thrash you," he said through gritted teeth.

"I say!" Cathcart stared at him, his smile fading. "I've hit on it, haven't I? Who is she?"

"A lady. A true lady." Too agitated to sit down, certain he would plant Cathcart a facer should he look at him, Charles paced the floor and told him of all that had happened since he'd met Serena. When he finished, Cathcart was staring at him in blank astonishment.

"Lady Serena Fairchild," he said, and grinned again. "Trust you to find a beauty. No, hold your fire!" He held up his hands as Charles swung around. "I mean no disrespect to the lady. You do realize you've compromised her."

"I'm aware of that," Charles said, irritated. "If I could get a special license I'd marry her right now, except for a slight problem. She's refused me."

"Serves you right," Cathcart said without sympathy. "After the wide swath you cut through Cambridge."

Charles ignored that. "Doubtless she'll see sense before long. In the meantime, we need a place to stay."

" 'We?' "

"I'm not about to leave her there alone. And do not dare say what you are thinking."

"I believe the lady is safe at last, Kirk."

Charles frowned. He had this niggling, nebulous feeling that all was not as it should be. They should have shaken off pursuit by now. No one could know they were here, yet he couldn't shake it. Mayhap 'twas nothing more than that he'd lost his own sense of security. His instincts had served him more than once on the Peninsula, however. He'd be foolish to ignore them now. "I said I'd see her home safely, and I will."

Cathcart studied him for a moment and then nodded, as if he'd expected such an answer. "I'll help any way I can, Charles," he said quietly.

For the next hour the two proceeded to talk and to make plans, until finally they had one which seemed workable. Some details remained vague, but all in all, events seemed at last to be working for them, rather than against. He could return Serena safely home to London, and he would, despite her current protests, marry her. 'Twas the honorable thing to do. It was also far more enticing than he would ever have expected, he thought, pausing at the top of the stoop to Cathcart's lodgings to put on his hat. Who would have believed that? Feeling well pleased with himself, he stepped briskly down the stairs and onto the pavement, striding in the direction of the inn.

And, across the street, a silent figure slinked from the shadows near a house, and fell into a loose pursuit behind him.

The rooms Cathcart found for Charles and Serena were in a genteel section of narrow, twisting streets not far from the waterfront, dating from the time when Brighton had been known as Brightelmstone and had merely been a fishing village. Serena, dressed properly in a muslin afternoon dress, with a spencer over it and wearing a bonnet, looked about and sighed. The rooms, consisting of two bedrooms, a dining room, and a sitting room, were clean, and there were a manservant and his wife to see to their needs. That the furnishings were drab was beside the point. For the moment, she was safe. She was also, she admitted to herself with a sigh, badly compromised. Were the *ton* to hear of this, her reputation would indeed be damaged beyond repair.

She turned to see Charles looking at her, his gaze level and direct, his bearing as erect as any officer's should be. "It will have to do, won't it?" she said.

He inclined his head and strolled over to the mantel, laying his arm across it. A moment later he lifted it, frowning. "My apologies, princess, if your sensibilities are offended. I do wonder, though," he went on, looking at his arm, "when this place was last dusted."

"Oh, Charles." She walked toward him, though his cool gray eyes were uninviting. "I do not mean to criticize what you've done for me. It's just that I'm so tired." And she wanted to go home. She wanted to be safe, though with Charles she knew she was. He had made her feel that way from the beginning. She was simply weary of running from place to place, without knowing why.

His face had softened. "I know, princess. We're nearly there, though." He paused. "If I could get a special license, I could protect you better."

She closed her eyes. Protection. That was what this was about. Not affection, not, heaven help her, the same desire that she felt, and certainly not love. "Oh, Charles, not that again."

"Yes, princess. I'll keep saying it, until you give in."

" 'Tis odd." She continued to stare out. "I always imagined that when—if—I married it would be at St. George's. A splendid wedding, of course. My father would insist on it. I always preferred the chapel at

Harford, our estate, and a quiet ceremony. If I ever say yes to you, 'tis probably the most my father will approve." She turned at last. Charles really was standing far too close, and his gaze was too steady on her. Unsettling, she thought again. "What does Lieutenant Cathcart think we should do?"

Charles at last moved away, and she took her first breath in what seemed like ages. "We both agree that we shouldn't go along the direct route from Brighton."

"You believe 'tis still watched?"

His eyebrows rose. "Don't you?"

"Yes, it likely is." She sighed. "Well, then?"

"I thought of hiring a post chaise, but I suspect that would make us more conspicuous now. We would still have to change horses, too. That problem hasn't changed since Ardingly."

Alarmed, she clenched her hands into fists. "You surely don't believe they're here, do you?"

"I don't know. They could have an idea which direction we traveled. Why leave our names at the inns, else? No, I believe our best chance is to take a road going west of here. Of course, if we went east and stopped at Canterbury . . ."

"No," she said firmly. It would be such a bad marriage. She had long ago resolved never to enter into one willingly.

"I'll change your mind yet, Serena."

"I doubt it." She turned away again, biting her lip. It hadn't taken her long to fall in love with him. Looking back, she could pinpoint the exact moment. It was in Ardingly, when he'd put himself between her and danger. From the very beginning she'd been aware of his lean strength; from the very beginning she had been aware of him as a man, far more than she'd ever been of her town beaux. He was all male, using not only the strength of his body, but of his

We'd Like to Invite You to Subscribe to Zebra's Regency Romance Book Club and Send You 4 Free Books as Your Introduction! (Worth $19.96!)

If you're a Regency lover, imagine the joy of getting 4 FREE Zebra Regency Romances and then the chance to have these lovely stories delivered to your home each month at the lowest price available! Well, that's our offer to you and here's how you benefit by becoming a Regency Romance subscriber:

- 4 FREE *Introductory Regency Romances are delivered to your doorstep (you only pay for shipping & handling)*
- *4 BRAND NEW Regencies are then delivered each month (usually before they're available in bookstores)*
- *Subscribers save almost $4.00 off the cover price every month*
- *You also receive a FREE monthly newsletter, which features author profiles, discounts, subscriber benefits, book previews and more*
- *There's no risks or obligations…in other words, you can cancel whenever you wish with no questions asked*

Join the thousands of readers who enjoy the savings and convenience offered to Regency Romance subscribers. After your initial introductory shipment, you'll receive 4 brand-new Zebra Regency Romances each month to examine for 10 days. Then, if you decide to keep the books, you pay the preferred subscriber's price, plus shipping and handling.

It's a no-lose proposition, so return the FREE BOOK CERTIFICATE today!

A $19.96 value – **FREE** No obligation to buy anything – ever.
4 FREE BOOKS are waiting for you! Just mail in the certificate below!

FREE BOOK CERTIFICATE

YES! Please rush me 4 FREE Zebra Regency Romances (I only pay $1.99 for shipping and handling).I understand that each month thereafter I will be able to preview 4 brand-new Regency Romances FREE for 10 days. Then, if I should decide to keep them, I will pay the money-saving preferred subscriber's price for all 4... (that's a savings of 20% off the retail price), plus shipping and handling. I may return any shipment within 10 days and owe nothing, and I may cancel this subscription at any time.

Name_____

Address_____Apt._____

City_____State_____Zip_____

Telephone (___)_____

Signature_____

(If under 18, parent or guardian must sign)

Offer limited to one per household and not to current subscribers. Terms, offer and prices subject to change. Orders subject to acceptance by Regency Romance Book Club. Offer Valid in the U.S. only.

RN063A

Treat yourself to 4 FREE Regency Romances!
A \$19.96 VALUE... FREE!
No obligation to buy anything ever!

REGENCY ROMANCE BOOK CLUB
Zebra Home Subscription Service, Inc.
P.O. Box 5214
Clifton NJ 07015-5214

mind as well, to pull her from dangerous situations. If he refused to express his own emotions, he was certainly aware of hers, comforting her when she needed it. Of course she'd fallen in love with him. After what she'd faced, how could she not?

Had she felt only the giddy excitement of being in love, though, her breathlessness when he was near, her low spirits when he wasn't, she would eventually have realized that she was merely infatuated, as her parents once had been. But he, drat the man, had made her love him. Drat him, he'd had to go to sleep on the road, making her long to stroke his face, to ease away all the lines of care and worry that creased it even in repose. He'd had to make her ache to hold him when he'd jolted awake from a nightmare about another woman. Most of all, he'd had to make her feel warm and surrounded by safety as he'd held her when she broke down. For that alone, she would never forget him.

And then, he had kissed her. Then he had aroused in her an uprush of feelings she knew had to be desire. Oh, yes, she loved him, more than she'd ever known possible, and, when the time came to part, it would break her heart.

"Charles," she said in a low voice, as if she hadn't just had a momentous revelation, "do you truly want this marriage?"

"Of course," he said, but he hesitated just a bit too long. "I believe we'd deal quite well together, after the days past."

Deal well together. Dear God, and she was so in love with him. Serena turned away from the window, her stomach churning. Oh, she didn't want to marry him if that was all he felt. "Charles—why do you keep looking out the window?" she asked, frowning. "Is there something out there?"

"Naught that I can see." His tone was easy, relaxed,

as he turned back, but there was a certain wariness in his eyes that put her instantly on guard.

"You sense something."

"No. It's good soldiering to be prepared."

"Why?" she asked bluntly.

"They've turned up wherever we have. How do they know—"

Whatever he had been about to say was interrupted by a loud knock on the door. For a brief moment they looked at each other, tension and fear crackling between them. "In there," he mouthed, and motioned sharply toward the dining room. Serena scurried across the room without even thinking of disobeying his command, leaving the door only a tiny bit ajar. From her position at the doorjamb she could see Charles gesturing to someone else, most likely Haley, the manservant. He must have been a fine officer, she thought, quick to react, equally quick to take action. Why was it, then, that he seemed so hard on himself?

"May I ask who's calling?" Haley called, apparently not opening the door. Serena let out her breath in relief. In London such a thing would be a horrendous breach of etiquette. Here it was only a precaution.

"Lieutenant Cathcart," a cheerful voice came back. "Now open the dashed door, Haley. I have rather a large package."

Serena slipped back into the sitting room just as Cathcart came in. "Lady Serena." He bowed to her. "And Charles."

Charles nodded. "I assume this isn't just a social call."

"As it happens, no. I've a plan," he said, making Serena want to groan, and placed the large, paper-wrapped parcel on the sitting room table. "And this is it."

* * *

The following morning Charles strolled along the Steyne, thoroughly disgruntled, thoroughly annoyed. He looked far more presentable, if not *au courant*. His buff pantaloons were of inferior quality, his boots were obviously not new, and his coat of brown merino, far too warm for a day like today, had been made for a man smaller across the shoulders than he was. Still, this outfit was preferable to the clothes he'd so recently worn, ragged as they were from several days of rough living, and he had Cathcart to thank for it. It was the other clothes Cathcart had brought that disgusted him.

Cathcart had earlier brought Serena clothes as well, damn his eyes. Certainly she'd needed them, and certainly she delighted in them. Certainly it was a pleasure to see her garbed in light muslins and to realize, again, how truly lovely she was. Not just pretty, but lovely, bone deep, soul deep.

What he wondered, though, was how Cathcart had known exactly what would fit her. When had he looked at her figure and known the exact size to buy? He had taken her measure too closely for Charles's comfort. Charles had a mind to call the man out.

But why? he wondered as he stepped aside to let a lady and her maid pass, tipping his hat as he did so, though they ignored him. Fool that he was, he felt almost jealous, and for no reason. Serena was the Incomparable, the toast of London. This time last week he'd barely known she existed. This week, today, she was near to being his fiancée, if ever he convinced her to marry him. Why would she not agree? Compromised or not, Serena was his. He would never love her as much as he had Luz, but a bond had grown between them during their days on the road. If it had been born of need and danger, still it was too strong to break.

They were comrades in arms, and something more. What that more was, however, he couldn't begin to fathom.

"Kirk, is that you? I say, Kirk! Hello!"

Charles stiffened. Who knew him here in Brighton? Instantly on guard, he turned, and relaxed. "Oh, Hyatt," he said, watching the man he had always considered a fop and something of a bounder mince his way across to him. "You here?"

"As you see." Osbert Hyatt gave him a short bow, and then made a *moue* of distaste. "A most abominable coat, Kirk. Never say a London tailor made it."

Charles grinned, diverted for the first time in days. "As a matter of fact, no."

"I'd not be caught dead in it."

"That I can well believe," he said, amused. Hyatt's ensemble was startling to see, especially since he was already running to fat, though he was about Charles's age. He was attired in pantaloons of the palest yellow, worn with a waistcoat striped startlingly in violet and scarlet. His coat, of a lighter orchid, was nipped in tightly at the waist and broadened considerably in the shoulders with buckram; it had extremely wide lapels and extremely big buttons, and his neckcloth was a masterpiece of the valet's art. He was, in short, the kind of dandy Charles had come to hold in contempt, though in the past he'd found the man to be pleasant enough. "What do you here?"

"All the world's here now, don't you know, since Prinny made the place popular," he said in his plummy voice. "Strange place to be, if you ask me, but one never knows what Prinny will do."

"No, one never does. I won't be staying here above a day. If you'll excuse me—"

"Oh? Where do you go from here?"

"London, most likely. I've had a letter from my brother," he added vaguely.

"Do you have business to attend to, Kirk?"

Charles was instantly on guard. It was an impertinent question at best. "A trifle, nothing more."

"P'raps I'll walk along with you, then."

He forced himself to grin. "The lady wouldn't like it above half."

"The lady—oho, I see. So there's a woman here, is there?"

"Yes. So if you'll excuse me, I'll be off." He looked down. "It's a long walk, at any rate. I don't believe your boots will withstand it."

For a moment anger flashed in Hyatt's eyes. It was doubtful he cared to be reminded of his stoutness, or of his labored breathing. He must wear a corset, Charles thought suddenly, and held back a smile.

"I see," Hyatt said after a moment, leaning upon the silver knob of his ebony walking stick. "I won't keep you. Been invited to the Marine Pavilion this evening, d-don't you know. I'm on my way to my tailor."

Charles bowed to him gravely. "Good day to you, Hyatt," he said, and turned away. Hyatt was harmless enough, though one had to watch him closely at cards, and though he had pockets to let. He had been hanging out for a rich wife anytime these years past. Thank God he'd managed to shake the man off. Charles didn't want anyone to know of his errand, not when he was on his way to a posting inn to buy tickets for a coach headed west.

The eastern route was not a good one, he had decided reluctantly after discussing the matter with Cathcart. It was too close to the Brighton road, and so the inns along it might have been alerted as well. The western route, toward Chichester and then inland to Guildford, was more roundabout. Thus it would be more unexpected. They had not seen Garnett or Alf since leaving Ardingly; it was likely they had no idea where he and Serena were. It was best to be prepared, though. With luck they would, according to Cathcart's ridiculous plot, board the coach with no one being the wiser as to their identities. There was the problem, though, Charles thought, even if they would likely be safe back in London in two days. He now understood why Serena groaned whenever he said he had a plan.

Some distance away, Hyatt, leaning on his walking stick, watched Charles go. It still gave him immense satisfaction that he had guessed Kirk's destination. Oh, he knew people better than they thought. They tended to underestimate him. In fact, one of the reasons he dressed as he did was to keep them off guard. He knew, as well, that his reputation was slightly unsavory. So much the better. He could get away with more than any upright citizen could.

He couldn't trust Garnett or Connor, of course. He'd known that from the beginning. Thus he hadn't been surprised when he never heard from them after they left London. It was from the spy he'd set upon them that he'd learned that Kirk had last been seen in Ardingly, though the two had disappeared after that. It was doubtful that Kirk would stay in that godforsaken village, tiny as it was, nor was Oakhurst safe for him. Brighton, then, Hyatt had thought with a flash of inspiration that he still considered brilliant. Brighton, not fifteen miles from Ardingly by back roads, and where the 10th regiment was based. Kirk was likely to have an acquaintance there who would help him.

So it had proved to be. By asking some questions in an oh, so casual manner, he'd learned the friend's name. After that it had been a boring, if simple, effort to watch the lodgings of this Lieutenant Cathcart. He had been amply rewarded when Kirk indeed appeared there. He'd been more than rewarded later, when he saw Kirk and Lady Serena together. His Lady Serena, he thought with a wave of possessiveness. All that beauty. All that lovely money. His.

Now it behooved him—Hyatt liked using words like that, though simpler ones would do—now it behooved him to find out exactly where Kirk was going, should it have any bearing on his next destination. He looked down at his boots with distaste. Kirk had been right about one thing. They had indeed been made more for appearance than for walking. Yet he had to try, lest he lose Kirk's trail again. Of course, in that case he could return to the lodgings where Kirk was staying, but following him promised to be far more rewarding.

Taking a deep breath, holding tight to his walking stick, Hyatt stepped off after Charles. And behind him, a figure slipped out from the shadow of a building, and followed him.

Sometime later Quigley Garnett walked along the narrow street where Charles and Serena lodged, being careful to keep close to the houses on that side. That way, no one looking down would see him. Crossing the street a moment later was a risk, but a necessary one. How else could he reach Alf?

"Anything?" he said in a low voice.

"Naw." Deep in the shadows of a service alley directly between two houses, Alf stared at the lodgings. "Don't think she goes out, Guv."

"Dear, dear, and not deliver herself into our hands? How inconvenient."

Alf didn't appear to catch the mockery. "I did thinks I saw something at the window, but might be it was only the sun."

Garnett was suddenly alert. "Did she see you?"

"Naw. I was back 'ere." He gestured toward the house with his chin. "What about 'im?"

"Kirk? I followed Hyatt," he grinned, "who was following Kirk. Dear, dear, we must have looked like a parade."

"And?" Alf demanded.

"Kirk went to a posting house."

"They're scarpering."

"So it would appear."

"You find out where?"

"With Hyatt there? Hardly. We don't want him to know yet he's been cut out."

"Wonder how 'e know how to come 'ere."

Garnett shrugged. "No matter. Following him here was an inspired idea, if I do say so myself."

"You know 'e's playing 'is own game, Guv."

"Oh, I'm well aware of that. Still and all, it's made it convenient for us."

"So now we grab 'er," Alf said with considerable relish.

"Not here, you fool," Garnett hissed. "There are too many people about. Not to mention Hyatt, and Mr. Bloody Kirk."

Alf looked at him curiously. "What you got against 'im, Guv?"

"Nothing," Garnett said in a clipped voice, and for a while there was silence between them. "We'll take them when they're outside of town. At an inn, when they're off guard. We'll have to think of some way of getting Hyatt out of the way, though."

"You take one, I'll take the other," Alf suggested.

Garnett shook his head. "It won't work. Kirk is the very demon to fight, and even if he wasn't, the girl could get away for help. No, we have to take Hyatt apart from the others."

"And do 'im, Guv."

Garnett gave him the loathing gaze one gives to a

worm, at the relish in his voice. "Certainly not. Killing a member of the *ton*, even so repellent an individual as—"

"Huh?"

"As ugly a character as Hyatt is," he explained patiently. "It would raise a dust-up. It would be worse with Kirk. No, we'll have to think of something else for them. Tie them up for a few days, mayhap, and then it will be too late."

"I'd loikes to tie the girl up again. Or down."

Garnett's stomach lurched with revulsion again, this time directed as much at himself as at Alf. The bitch deserved it, after all she'd put them through. The problem would be, he thought uneasily, keeping Alf in check. "Simple ransom this time," he said, as if they hadn't reached this decision already. "With the assurance the girl won't be hurt."

"Auw, Guv." Alf was frowning. "She's seen our faces, she has."

"With what we'll be getting we can go far away. Besides," he grinned again, "who says she'll remain unharmed?"

Alf chuckled. "Toss you for first go at 'er."

"Quite." Quigley nodded, but inside his uneasiness grew. Alf was fast becoming a nuisance. A necessary one, of course, but he was too wild, too unpredictable. Who was to say that Alf wouldn't attack him one night, if only for the money? No, Alf would have to go, he thought without remorse. And then it would all be his, the girl and the money.

Footsore, weary, and more than a little apprehensive, Charles trudged along the street toward their lodgings. Under other circumstances the walk to the coaching inn and back would have been little more than a brisk stroll, but today it had been an ordeal. Poetic justice, he supposed. For if Hyatt's boots had been made for show, as he had jibed, Charles's own had been made for another man. They pinched in the toes and slipped off his heels, which felt rubbed raw. He was not one to complain about pain. He had fought the surgeon in Portugal who'd wanted to take off his arm, and lived with that pain as quietly as he could. He knew, however, how important to morale it was for a soldier's feet to be comfortable. Such a little thing, and yet on such things battles could be won or lost.

Frowning, Charles turned around suddenly. There it was again, that feeling that he was being watched, that he was being followed. All nonsense, of course, he assured himself, though he was uneasily aware that in such a busy town as Brighton it was nearly impossible to spot a pursuer. On this quiet street there were enough hiding places where some could lurk. Every so often the skin between his shoulder blades tightened, as if he could feel the gaze of unseen eyes. It was a sense of danger that had served him well in the army. It was a feeling he dared not ignore. Yet, when he stopped at the top of the stoop to gaze about the street, he saw no one. Mentally shrugging, he went in and climbed the stairs to the lodgings he and Serena shared.

The room was quiet as Haley let him in. "Where is Miss Devon?" he asked, using the name they had picked at random for their surname.

The servant bowed. "In her bedchamber, sir. I'll send Mrs. Haley to fetch her."

Charles inclined his head. "If you would," he said, and at that moment there was the sound of a door opening and crashing against the wall. Reacting instinctively, he reached for a sword that wasn't there, but he didn't relax even when he realized that Serena was hurtling herself across the room toward him. Her face was parchment pale and her hands were outstretched to him. "Oh, Charles!" She threw herself into his arms. "I think I saw Alf!"

NINE

"Bedamned! Where?" Charles demanded, grasping Serena by the shoulders and holding her at arm's length.

"Over—over there," she said on a little hiccup. Since she had glanced out the window not half an hour ago and seen that horrible, familiar face, she had lain curled in a ball in her bed, shivering and sobbing. They had found her. She didn't know how, but they had found her.

Charles prowled across the room, as if someone outside could see, and looked out. He was not so foolish as to pull back a curtain, but she had no doubt that his sharp, farsighted eyes were taking everything in. "Nothing," he said finally. "But I had the feeling when I was coming home . . ."

"What?" she said when he broke off.

He shook his head. "It's of no moment." Crossing the room, he took her hands in his. To Serena they felt very large, very strong. As usual, his touch soothed her, and, even at this most inappropriate time, sent a shivery shock through her. "I'll get us through this, princess. I promised you that already."

"Ye-es."

"Do you doubt me?" To her surprise he lifted her hands and pressed a soft kiss on each, though she was aware that Haley had remained, an interested bystander to this drama.

"No, but—"

"Trust me." His voice was soft. "I really do have a plan."

Serena gazed uncertainly up into his eyes, and then nodded. He had brought her this far, and though she had suffered discomfort, she had not been hurt. "I do trust you, Charles," she whispered.

He lifted her hands again. The touch of his lips, feather light, sent that shiver through her again. "That's my girl," he said, and released her. "Now." He was suddenly brisk. "We've much to do."

Early the following morning, a man walked down the stairs of the lodging house. He was garbed in ill-fitting pantaloons, a coat that was too small, boots that were desperately in need of polish, and a beaver hat that, though bare in patches, was large enough to hide his face from view. In spite of that, his bearing was military, and he strode along at a brisk pace. He appeared unaware of unseen eyes watching him as he turned the corner onto the Steyne and was gone from sight.

"Is he gone?" Serena asked.

Charles, staring out the window, nodded. "I think he might just fool them." He shook his head. "He should have tried for a career on the stage."

"He's been a good friend to us."

"So he has," Charles agreed bemusedly, making her smile in spite of the situation. Dressed in Charles's shabby suit of clothes, Lieutenant Cathcart somehow had managed to take on Charles's appearance, though in truth they looked nothing alike. She only hoped their pursuers would be fooled.

"Is there anyone following?" she asked now.

"No—yes." Though he could see out the window, he was careful to keep to the shelter of the wall. "Garnett."

Serena stayed where she was, her heart beating loudly in her ears, her hands clammy. "Not Alf?"

"No. Just Garnett and—bedamned!"

"What?"

"There's someone else."

"What?"

"No, stay back." He held his hand out, preventing her from moving to the window. "Damn."

"Who is it?"

"I don't know. He's too far along the street for me to see." This time Charles did lean toward the window. "I think—no, curse it, he's gone."

Serena clutched her hands together tightly in an effort to ward off panic. It had been bad enough before when she had known that Alf and Garnett were there. If this unknown enemy were in league with them . . .

She must have made some noise. Charles turned from the window to look at her. Within a moment, he was crossing the room to her.

"No, no." She held out her hands to ward him off. She was tired of being weak, of needing to depend on him. "I'm all right. Truly."

He looked at her, hard. "Are you sure?"

"Yes." She let out her breath. "I won't deny I'm scared. Oh, but Charles, I'm tired of it," she burst out, surprising herself. "I'm tired of forever being chased, and not knowing why, and of being a victim. Oh, I want to turn it about! I want to be the pursuer for a change."

There was an odd expression on his face. "Serena."

"Well, I do. Don't you? You're a soldier, Charles. What would you do if I weren't involved?"

"Fight them," he said promptly.

"Then why should I feel differently? I'm in danger, and yet I can't even protect myself."

"Princess, how can you protect yourself from them?"

"I don't know, but sometimes I get so angry." She took a deep, calming breath. "I also know we can't stay in hiding forever. Especially since they've discovered we're here." She paused. "Do you think these disguises will work?"

Charles scowled. "God knows."

Serena laughed. "Oh, if you could have seen your face when Lieutenant Cathcart told us his idea."

"I should have known he'd come up with something like this. He ever was a jokester at Eton."

"And at Cambridge?"

This time he smiled. "He and I played some memorable pranks there. It's a wonder we both weren't sent down." He paused. "Of course, he was a brilliant scholar."

Serena suspected that he had done well enough, too. "Well." She crossed to the window, standing as he did, far enough back to avoid detection. "Should we go, do you think?"

"I don't like it that only Garnett went. And that other man." He frowned. "But, yes, if we don't go we'll miss the coach." He picked up a bandbox, a large satchel, and a bonnet from the table. "We'll have to go. Haley." He held out his hand. "Thank you. You and your wife have been of great help."

"Glad I am to help, Major, Lady Serena." Haley took Serena's hand as well, and then released it. He had seen through their story almost immediately, they'd learned later. He also had been privy to their planning. "You can count on me, sir. I won't give you away. Not with a nephew in Spain."

"I'm certain of that." Charles's voice was grave. "Watch out for those ruffians, though. They're not above murder."

Serena looked up sharply at that. Of course she knew Garnett and Alf were capable of violence, but murder? Why would Charles say such a thing? "I must thank you as well. Should you ever need anything, do call on me. I'll help all I can."

"Thank you, my lady. I'll do that."

"Good." She turned to Charles. "Should we go?"

He took a deep breath, and for the first time she realized he was as apprehensive as she was. "Yes," he said, and held out his arm to her.

A little while later, two people walked out of the back door of the lodging house and strode along the service alley that would eventually lead them to the Steyne. They were an ill-assorted couple—a slender, small lad with his hair covered by a large cap, wearing a shabby jacket and loose breeches. Beside him was a very big, very broad woman, her face shaded by a large bonnet. Her gloved hands carried a satchel and a bandbox, and she strode as confidently as she could beside the lad.

"Curse it," the woman said. "How the devil do you walk in skirts?"

"Do please try not to swear before me, or you may corrupt me in my youth."

The woman gave the boy a sour look. "You're pert."

"Aye, that I am." The lad kicked out a leg suddenly. "I do love wearing breeches. There's such freedom!"

"Stubble it," the woman growled, as they neared the end of the alley. "Or I may take a strap to you, son."

Serena gave Charles a glowing smile. "Yes, Mother. It was a brilliant idea the lieutenant had, to bring theatrical makeup. Why, when your beard starts to grow out, no one will know at first."

"Serena—"

"Oh, but Charles, 'tis funny! You must admit that. And it just may work."

"Not with the way you walk." He leered at her, making her laugh. "No one will believe you're a lad."

"That is a problem. You still bear yourself as a soldier."

"What? How?"

"It isn't so bad, really, a woman of your stature would be likely to stride along. Still."

"Still?"

"Do we have time? Yes, I think we do. Walk back into the alley a bit."

"What the devil?"

"Oh, just do it, Charles!" she said impatiently.

He glowered at her, but he did turn to walk a few paces away. "Well?" he demanded, looking back at her.

"'She walks in beauty, as the night,'" she quoted.

"What!"

"It seemed appropriate. Hm." She frowned, her hand resting against her chin and one finger tapping her cheek. "You need to roll your hips a bit more, side to side."

"Serena," he protested again.

"Do it."

"Oh, bedamned," he said, obeying her order with such a look of disgust that Serena stifled a smile. "Are you satisfied now?"

"It's a bit better," she conceded.

"Thank you so much," he bit out. "Your turn now, Serena."

She took a deep breath. "Why didn't I realize you'd do this?"

His smile was devilish. "Turn and turnabout."

Serena gave him a look, but she, too, walked back into the alley. Having watching Charles, she tried to keep her own hips as straight as possible. "Is that all right?"

Charles was grinning. "Those breeches do wonderful things for you, princess."

She whirled. "Charles!"

"You make a fetching boy." He quirked his lips. "Walk back here. Now slouch."

"Slouch?"

"Yes. You're too straight. I imagine you had a governess who drilled you on posture."

"Oh, unmercifully."

"Forget her for the time being. Drop your shoulders. Good. Now shove your hands into your pockets."

"Like this?" she said dubiously.

"Yes." His face was still as she reached him. "It's better, if not enough. But there is one problem, princess."

"What is that?"

He stroked her jaw with a fingertip. "You're too pretty."

Serena drew her breath in as his caress continued, along the other side of her jaw, and then, disconcertingly, across her lips. An ache started within her, down low in the pit of her stomach. "Oh, what are you doing to me?"

"I'd like to kiss you again."

She closed her eyes as his thumbs brushed across her lips, parted now, again and again. "Charles . . ." This as his thumb slid just inside her lips, stroking, stroking. Her mouth was dry, she could tell by the way his thumb dragged, and so of course she had to moisten her lips. Of course, she touched the tip of his thumb with her tongue.

"Ah," Charles said again, his hand still now as Serena took the initiative, her tongue circling and exploring his thumb. All thoughts of behaving like the farm boy she was supposed to appear, with catching their coach, even of needing to escape, fled. She could concentrate only on the here and now.

"Serena," Charles gasped, and set his arm about her waist, drawing her to him.

"Mm," she murmured in return, raising her face for a kiss.

"Serena," he said again, and this time abruptly withdrew his finger, his arm. "If we don't stop now, I'll have you up against that wall kissing you, and God knows what else."

Her eyes were closed; her lips were still parted. "Oh," she breathed. That sounded like so very good an idea.

"And if anyone looked down the alley and saw us, a woman with a boy . . ."

Reality came flooding painfully back. He was right. Anyone seeing them kissing, touching, would wonder very much why such a thing was happening. This was not the time or place. She wondered if it ever would be. He was still in love with another woman, she reminded herself. *Oh, dear God.*

At that thought she straightened her shoulders, remembered the admonition to slouch, and breathed deeply to fortify herself. "You're right, of course. We'd best go."

Sometime after Serena and Charles had departed, Quigley strode back toward the lodging house, his face thunderous. "Did she come out?" he demanded of Alf, who was leaning against the wall of a house that bordered the alley across the street.

The bread he was chewing fell out of his mouth as he gawked at Quigley. "Lady Serena? Naw, Guv, ain't seen hide nor hair of 'er. Ain't she in there?"

"I don't know, damn it." He glared across the street. "They were to have boarded the coach this morning." He stared across the street. "A ruse. A bloody ruse."

"Guv?"

"To make us think they would leave at another time. That man," he spat out.

"Eh, the one you followed?"

"Yes, damn it, him. He headed toward the waterfront."

Now Alf frowned. "So where is 'e, Guv?"

"God knows." Quigley's tone was grim. Somewhere along the waterfront he'd lost Kirk, who'd ducked into a warren of streets and buildings until he was surprisingly caught up in a troop of soldiers. After that, no matter how hard he looked, Quigley couldn't find him. The man was gone. So, possibly, was Lady Serena.

He looked over at Alf, who was staring blankly at the house, and frowned. More and more, Alf was proving to be a liability. He was good enough for the rough stuff, but they'd had no need of that since being at Oakhurst. Even then he'd botched it, letting Lady Serena escape while he dozed. Quigley was beginning to think he could handle the rest himself. After all, he'd managed to take care of Kirk in Spain when the stakes were much higher, hadn't he? This time he'd be more direct, he decided. Kirk was not going to keep him from his goal.

"I think that when Kirk went to the coaching inn yesterday, that was a ruse, too," he said.

"Eh?"

"Another trick, to make us think they were traveling today. Now I wonder." He paused, glad of the way Alf was looking at him, attentive and yet not very intelligent.

"So, Guv?"

"I think their friend helped them to travel by boat."

"But she didn't come out, Guv," Alf protested.

"Oh, they got her out somehow," Quigley said grimly, knowing in his heart it was true. *Damn it.* To have been so close, and to have missed his chance. He would prevail, though. No matter what he had to do, he would have Lady Serena back. It was no longer a matter of money, but of pride, and vengeance. He wanted revenge on Major bloody Kirk more than he'd ever wanted anything.

"Come." He walked out of the alley.

Alf followed, looking perplexed. "Where, Guv?"

"To the waterfront, to find out if they went by boat."

"But, Guv, the house—"

"They're gone," he said in a clipped voice, glaring at Alf. "God knows how."

"I watched, I did," Alf protested.

"Huh." They turned onto the Steyne and walked toward the sea, an ill-assorted pair that drew more than one startled glance. Alf gawked when they passed the Marine Pavilion, the Prince's country mansion by the sea, but Quigley gave him no time to see more. Instead he turned along a street bordering the sea front, going past the Parade Grounds and the beach where people of Quality took the air or bathed in the sea. They came at last to more prosaic areas, where the fishing fleet went out. Passenger boats left elsewhere, but Alf didn't need to know that.

The fishing fleet was out, and so the long pier where Quigley led Alf was deserted. Alf took one sniff and frowned. "Smells too much like fish, it does."

"I know." Quigley frowned. "I thought passenger boats left from here." His face suddenly cleared. "I have it. Of course."

"What, Guv?"

"They didn't wish to chance going by an established route! I wonder if anyone saw them here."

"You mean someone took them on a fishing boat?" Alf said doubtfully.

"Haven't they used other tricks? Yes." He pretended to gaze about. "I wonder if any are tied up at other piers."

Alf shaded his eyes and gazed doubtfully along the seafront toward other deserted piers. "Dunno, Guv. Don't look that way."

"We need to ask. Look, there's a building at the end of this one." Quigley pointed toward a deserted-looking hut at the end of the pier, and confidently strode forward toward it. Heavy footsteps echoed on the gaping boards behind him, making him smile. "I do believe I see someone."

Alf's steps quickened, just as Quigley's did. "Where, Guv?" he asked as they reached the end of the pier.

"Here," Quigley said, and his foot shot out. It caught Alf by the ankle, and made him stumble forward off the pier.

"Guv!" Alf screamed as he fell, far, far into the sea. "I can't swim!"

Quigley didn't answer, but instead watched expressionlessly, just long enough to make sure Alf wouldn't rise again. Then, still impassive, he walked off the pier. Someone dressed in rough clothing, passing along on the road, looked at him curiously, but Quigley paid him no heed. He would be away long before anyone connected him with Alf.

Just now he had more pressing business to attend to. He was certain Alf had let the fugitives escape, but how? Damn, he wished he'd gone to the posting inn, but it was too late for regrets. What he would do instead was inquire at their lodgings, and shake the information out of someone there.

Slowly, as befitted the man of substance he intended to portray, he sauntered to the lodgings and then climbed the stairs within, to where he thought might be the apartment where Alf had seen Lady Serena. "My name is Tyler," he said to the man who opened the door, improvising on the spur of the moment. "I believe you have a young man and woman staying here."

The man gaped at him. "Sir?"

"A young man and woman." Quigley impatiently leaned forward on the balls of his feet, making the servant prudently take a step back. "Are they in?"

"Is it Mr. and Miss Devon you're meaning? Yes, a lovely couple, sir. No, no, they're gone."

"There's a pound in it if you tell me where."

The man licked his lips as he looked at the coin. "A pound?"

"Damn it, make it a guinea, then. Well?"

The man licked his lips again. "I may have heard something about Basingstoke."

"Basingstoke?

"Yes, sir. Basingstoke."

Basingstoke! he thought as he ran down the stairs a few moments later, after trying to learn more from the servant, and failing. What the devil was in Basingstoke?

It was in Arundel that Osbert Hyatt had his first bit of luck.

Unlike Garnett, he had not made the mistake of following the man who appeared to be Kirk. After going a few paces, he'd seen the man's face too clearly for that. He'd known then that his quarry must be escaping by a different way. Thus he'd made his way to the coaching inn, only to hear that not only had it already left, but that no one such as he described had been on it. Still, he went west, on the road he'd learned yesterday that Kirk and Lady Serena planned to take.

He was not a particularly happy man as he stomped out of the inn and called for his curricle, though he truly had not expected to have any luck. "Here." He threw a coin to the man who'd held his horses as he climbed aboard. Without further ceremony he began to drive off. After going only a few yards, though, he stopped. Almost carelessly he backed into the inn yard. "You," he said, snapping his fingers.

The ostler came forward, his face sullen. "Sir?"

"There's a half-crown in it if you answer a few questions." Inwardly he winced at the expense, especially since he'd paid as much to the servant at Kirk's lodgings in Brighton. However, the ostler may have noticed something out of the way, such as people who hadn't gone inside to take a hasty breakfast.

The ostler's eyes flickered briefly. "Help you if I can, sir."

"Good," Hyatt said, and went on to describe Serena and Charles. Before he was even halfway through, the ostler was shaking his head. "No?"

"No, sir. But . . . make it a guinea, and I might make it worth your while."

A guinea! "If the information is helpful," he added, sounding bored more than anything.

"There was two people here, sir, didn't go inside," the man said in answer to Hyatt's question. "A big woman, strapping, like, and a lad."

Hyatt had already heard these people described at the coaching inn in Brighton. "Yes, so?" he said impatiently.

"They sat outside on that bench, there." He indicated a backless bench near the door. "It being a nice day and all, and had something to eat from a satchel."

Hyatt's impatience rose. "I see nothing unusual in that."

"The woman, sir. Awful big, she was. Awful deep voice, too. And," he added thoughtfully, "never seen no woman with an Adam's apple."

Hyatt straightened so quickly that his horses stepped sideways in their traces. "What color was his hair?" he demanded.

"Couldn't tell, sir, with the bonnet and all. I know that everyone else on the stage thought he had a putrid sore throat, so why was she—he—talking?"

"The lad, man, the lad." Quickly he described Serena. "What color was his hair?"

"Couldn't see again, sir," he said regretfully. "A cap this time, sir. But I've never seen no lad shaped like him."

It was them! Hyatt exulted in the knowledge. It had

to be. What other pair would be in such a disguise? "Did they say where they were going? And, no, you'll not get any more than a guinea from me. In fact," he went on at the crestfallen look that came over the ostler's face, "you might not even get that much if you don't answer my questions."

"But I have, sir," the ostler protested.

Hyatt pursed his lips, and then nodded. "I suppose you have, at that. Did they say where they were going?" he repeated.

"No, sir, only the stage goes by Chichester, and I heard them mention changing there."

Chichester! They could still be going to Basingstoke, as the servant at their lodgings had said; that road went through Chichester. Or they could be going elsewhere. On consulting his map, he'd learned that that road was a direct one, with no stops where passengers had to get out and change. That meant that their actual destination—for he had little doubt as to who the woman and lad were—was elsewhere. The question now was, where. "Thank you," he said, and, tossing the man his guinea, drove off.

Chichester, he thought again, and briefly smiled. Kirk and Lady Serena didn't know it yet, but their bid for freedom was nearly over.

TEN

The morning air was fresh, with just a hint of the approaching autumn. Charles, dressed in his hated guise of the mute farmer's wife, tried to moderate his strides as he walked across the inn's back garden toward the necessary. Anyone seeing him would think what he was doing odd, as he was supposed to be a mother with her son. Anyone seeing him could tell a pursuer about his strange actions, thus putting him under suspicion, though he thought they'd shaken off any pursuit. Had he stayed within to take care of matters, it would have been acutely embarrassing to both him and Serena. The last thing they needed was to add to the strain that already stretched between them. If this flight from her captors, with its accompanying deceptions, went on much longer, one of them was likely to snap. He thought he might be the one to do so.

Last evening, as well as their day of traveling, had been an ordeal. Though there was a direct route from Brighton to Guildford, they'd decided against it, again in the hope of doing the unexpected and shaking off any pursuit. The problem was that the road to Chichester kept along the coast, rather than turning inland. Thus he and Serena had to pass the night there before the coach to Guildford, and eventually London, departed the following morning. They had also reluctantly decided, one stop back, that they would have to take one room rather than two. For one thing, their hoard of money was pitifully small, and they would have to pay not only for a room but also for food and fares to London. For another, they were posing as mother and son. As such, it was not only reasonable, it was to be expected that they would share a room. The trouble was, what Charles was beginning to feel for Serena wasn't motherly at all, he thought now as he waited in the inn's garden for his turn. What it was, he didn't quite know yet, but he did know that he felt alive in a way that he hadn't since he'd last seen Luz.

Thus, when the stage had left them at the inn early the previous afternoon, they had engaged their room, left their bags there, and made arrangements for the following day. Then, needing to do something to pass the time, they had gone out to explore the town.

Their first stop was at a tavern that was closer to the town's center and promised considerably better fare than their inn's taproom. They ordered warm, savory pasties filled with chunks of beef and potatoes and bursting with juices, small mince tarts, and two tankards of ale, though Serena had never had the drink before. Thus fortified, they set out to explore the town.

Fortunately it wasn't a market day, or Chichester's narrow streets would have been all but impassable. Their path took them along North Street, leading them inevitably to the market square, where there stood a startling edifice of creamy stone, with Gothic arches, a clock, and a cupola soaring high against the sky. In wonder they wandered through the open arches, while around them the traffic of a busy town ebbed and flowed. At last, however, they went out again, more concerned about avoiding the inn and the room that awaited them than taking in any sights.

Charles had obtained a guidebook, amusing Serena.

He grinned at the joke against himself and his tendency always to wish to know where he was, simply because he was enchanted, again, to hear her laugh. Studying it for a moment, he pointed the way along West Street, one of the four streets branching out from the market square, to the cathedral, whose spire, oddly separate from the main building, soared even more impressively than that of the market cross. Like the cross, it glowed almost blazingly and surprisingly white against the sky. Dutifully they wandered about inside, trying to ignore the guide who droned on about the depredations the building had suffered, most notably at Cromwell's hands. Both noted that there was no stained glass to speak of, nor any impressive monuments. Both agreed that, while it had a majesty and a dignity of its own, it was friendly and open in a way that Canterbury cathedral was not. Discussion of Canterbury, however, made Charles inevitably think of a special license. Serena's protests notwithstanding, it wasn't too late to head toward that city, the aim of so many pilgrimages. Certainly it would confound any pursuers, had they been bold enough, or smart enough, to follow them here. Sometimes Charles felt that prickling between his shoulder blades again.

Saint Mary's Hospital, built during the 1500's, didn't interest them enough to tour it. The remainder of the Roman walls, however, did. Chichester was both Roman and Georgian, and they were amused at the classically beautiful house that bore the unfortunate nickname of "Dodo House," because of the odd birds that topped its entrance pillars. Finally, though, they climbed to the promenade inside the Roman walls and surveyed the city. Here they sat for a while, content as they had not been since the beginning of the pursuit, simply to relax.

At last, though, it was time to return to the inn, and the complications that awaited them. In the taproom they chose a high-backed settle as close to the wall as they could, for their supper, with Charles, as ever, facing the door. To Serena's great discomfort and to Charles's great amusement, the barmaid, whose blouse was pulled down as far as it could possibly go, delivered their meals of chicken stew and managed more than once to bump her hips against Serena's shoulder. It didn't help that the patrons of the taproom, all men, were obviously amused at what appeared to be the seduction of a downy-faced lad.

"This stew is quite good," Serena said, her voice coming out as a squeak. "I mean, surprisingly good."

Charles grinned at the change in her voice. Though anyone listening to her could tell she was educated, as least she had lowered its tone. "Quite good," he agreed, his own voice higher pitched than usual. That made Serena cast him a startled look, and he strove to look as innocent as possible. It was good to be talking again, after a morning spent pretending he suffered from a sore throat. If he had to disguise his voice, it was a small price to pay.

Face determined, though she was as flustered as ever he had seen her, she pressed on. "I doubt they serve the ordinary traveler such fare, don't you?"

His nod was grave. "I misdoubt, as well."

"Are you making mock of me?"

"I would hardly dare, prin—Peter."

This time she bit her lips, and her eyes danced with merriment. "This is absurd, is it not?"

Something within him relaxed. "Rather."

"And," she leaned back, "there is still tonight to consider."

His amusement faded. "Yes."

"Do you think," she said, her voice falsely bright, "that we should obtain lunches for tomorrow's journey, as we did today? Then we need pay only for coffee along the way."

"Or ale."

She made a face. "Vile stuff. I don't know why you drink it."

"Are you feeling a trifle well to go, son?"

She bit her lips again. "Do we have money enough?"

"We've the fare to London paid, so there is some remaining. Yes, if we're not extravagant, we should have enough."

"Then one room tonight—"

"'Tis for the best, as you well know."

She sighed and glanced away, obviously ill at ease with what the night might hold. Somehow, sleeping close together under the stars was one thing; sharing a bedroom indoors, with all its implications, was another. "I suppose so."

Charles watched her with sympathy and speculation. She ate her stew with far less gusto than she had. She hadn't yet admitted they had to marry, let alone agreed to it, but tonight would settle matters. They would both be social pariahs after this strange journey. He was rather surprised that he minded the idea of that less for himself than for Serena.

"There's something we need to discuss," he said in a low voice, leaning toward her.

She laid down her spoon, her eyes wary. "What?"

"What happens when we get to London."

"I've already told you. I won't mar—"

"So you have." He gave her a warning look. "Still, it needs to be discussed again, if not now, then tonight."

"To clear the air?"

He nodded. "As it were."

"Yes," she said after a moment. "I suppose we do."

"I'd like to know," he said, picking up his spoon again, "why a certain action is so repugnant to you."

"I never said it was repugnant." Her words were hasty at the frown he gave her. "At least, not for others. 'Tis simply that I don't wish to be coerced into anything. Or you, either," she added. "I've told you that."

He glanced about, but none of the patrons of the taproom seemed to pay them the least heed, in spite of his bonnet and her disreputable cap. For the first time he wondered what her true reasons were, since her aversion seemed to go so deep. "As for coercion, none of this journey was my idea."

"Yet you went along with it," she retorted. "It seems even as if you've enjoyed it at times."

"Don't make me to be something I'm not. I have no desire to play the hero."

"Heroine."

"What?"

"Heroine," she repeated, a little smile on her lips.

"Very well, but the words don't matter. The matter stands."

"Reluctant or not, you're here, and there's a certain action that you insist on discussing."

"I'd think you'd want to, as well."

She lowered her head. "No."

"Why not?"

"Would you, else?"

He glanced about the room again. "You're a bit above my touch, but—"

"Why?" she challenged. "Being who you are."

"The second son."

"What of it? You're not really half-pay."

"Marriage is not something I aspire to," he said quietly.

"Do you mean just now?"

Dear God, dear God. The pain that coursed through him was staggering. And yet . . . "Not ever, I think."

"Because of Luz."

He could feel his face harden. "We'll leave that person out of this," he snapped, and noticed for the first time someone turn toward him. *Damn.*

"I don't think we can."

"Keep your voice down. I believe—yes?" he broke off, as a giant of a man loomed up beside their table.

"Couldn't help overhearin' ye." His voice was unexpectedly apologetic, but his eyes were lively and aware. "You talking about Luz, and all. Don't hear that name much, pronounced just that way. You on the Peninsula, Captain?"

Major, Charles almost said, almost falling into the trap. "Dear me, no." He turned away, fumbling in his pocket for the handkerchief that refused his every effort to come out, and hoping his voice was high enough. God help him, but Serena seemed to be choking back laughter. "My dear husband—a private with the 50th foot, you see—died in Portugal. My poor boy"—he indicated Serena with a mournful look—"is left an orphan."

"Aye. I see," the giant said, and just what he understood was worrisome. "I'm sorry for it, ma'am. Who is Luz, ma'am?"

"Oh, well, I," Charles began, and sputtered into silence.

"I ask only because o' my son. He died at Torres Vedres."

Any laughter in Serena's face died. "I'm sorry, Mr.—"

"Lamb. Aye, been hard on my wife and me. We had just the one son, you see."

"I'm that sorry, too," Charles echoed. "Lot o' fine men died there."

"More will, 'fore we're done. Well, sir. Miss." He pulled at his forelock. "I'll leave ye to your supper now."

Charles took up his spoon after Mr. Lamb had left

and had just taken a bite when he choked, making Serena look up in alarm. "Are you well? Is it a bone?"

"No." Charles waved her back to her seat. "But we've trouble."

Alarmed, Serena looked covertly around the taproom, at least the part that she could see around the back of the settle. "Not Garnett and Alf!"

"No. Lamb. He called me 'sir' and you 'miss.'"

It took a moment for that to penetrate, as it had with him, but when it did, Serena's eyes grew wide. "He knows!"

"Keep your voice down," he said in a furious whisper, leaning forward. " 'Twas bad enough before, your voice going up and down like a boy's, but too much of it . . . No, he only suspected, and we simply confirmed it."

"Oh, no." Serena's eyes were distressed. "What will he do, do you think?"

Charles glanced quickly over at Lamb, who looked to be in a genial conversation with another man. "Nothing for now. No one's looking at us. I don't believe he's said a word."

"But he might." Her gaze was apprehensive. "And then?"

Charles looked at her, filled somehow with more worry than he had been even when it seemed she might be the victim of ruffians. If the mob here—for that was how the group of genial, rough-garbed men suddenly appeared to him—were to get wind of her true sex, he had no doubt what would happen to her. So, by the way her shoulders were hunched, did she. Poor girl, she'd had enough of that particular fear to deal with lately. She looked so small, so fragile, that he longed to take her into his arms and comfort her. Unfortunately, he couldn't.

Abruptly he threw down his spoon. "Early rising tomorrow, son," he said, careful to keep his voice pitched both high and rough. "Time and more we were abed."

Serena rose a bit more slowly. "Yes, Ma," she said, forcing him to hold back a smile. Certainly he was no hero, but he suspected he would remember this adventure for a very long time. He would remember her indomitable spirit, in spite of her natural moments of fear; he would remember her humor in the face of danger. Above all, he would remember that he loved her, though he knew well she would never return his feelings.

The thought almost made him stop still, except that he was well aware that they were still visible from the taproom. He was too old a campaigner to allow the enemy any advantage. Good God, when had this happened? he thought with real dismay. Love brought with it too much pain, too much responsibility. She was in his care, poor, brave girl, and the last thing she needed was to have him pressing attentions on her that were sure to be unwelcome. From the very beginning she had told him she didn't wish to marry, and even if he didn't understand why, he had to respect that she had her reasons. But there was this damnable matter of her reputation being completely ruined. He could not allow her to go through life with that burden.

Abruptly he passed a hand over his face. He couldn't be in love. Always and forever, he would love Luz. Yet the name didn't resonate within him quite as much as it had. Luz was in the past, he realized with a shock, and so was the life he'd lived since he'd lost her. Somehow, and very recently, he'd come alive again, and he owed it to the girl climbing the stairs beside him.

"What is it?" she asked in a low voice. "Do you need—"

"What?" He blinked at her, startled. Oh, she was so much above his touch, the season's Incomparable, who could have any man with the snap of her finger. Could have had any man. That had changed. Still, it remained that he was only a second son, with no property to his name and a bitterness that ate away at his soul. Had eaten away, because somehow she had changed that, too. Oh, God, God. He loved Serena so much, and losing her would be far worse than losing Luz had been.

"The way you're touching your chin," she went on, breaking through the haze of his thoughts. "You need a shave."

He touched his chin again. "Yes, I do." He forced himself to smile at her. "Another reason we were abed."

She leaned forward. "I seem to remember that Lady Markham has a beard."

He wanted to laugh. "She's elderly and not masquerading," he said when he could.

"The way she rules Lord Markham, one does wonder."

Again he held back laughter. "High time we were abed," he said, and instantly regretted his choice of words. They brought with them unwelcome images. There was, after all, still the remainder of the dangerous journey ahead.

"Yes, Ma."

He watched her swagger up the stairs, and his mouth went dry. No one from the taproom watching her now would have any doubts as to her gender. Or, for that matter, his attempt to appear as a female. He would have to be doubly alert.

Thus it was with considerable caution that he slipped out to the necessary, leaving Serena to perform her ablutions in their tiny room under a sloping roof. When he at last returned, it was to find her already abed, her back to him, with a single candle burning. A pallet lay neatly on the floor. The hunch of her shoulders, however, told him she was awake. Quickly he shaved and then blew out the candle, before stretching out on the pallet. He closed his eyes, forcing himself to take deep breaths, willing himself to relax. It was only a room, after all, no matter how small, and they had slept only feet from each other while on the road. This was different, though—far more intimate, far more dangerous.

"Oh, this is silly," Serena said suddenly, startling him. "It isn't as if we haven't slept together before."

Charles shut his eyes at that. "Not as mother and son," he said, desperately trying to distract himself.

"You know quite well what I mean. The nights we spent together—"

"Oh, Lord God above."

"What?" she said in confusion.

"Serena, you do realize we really have no choice but to marry after this?"

He heard the bedclothes rustle, and guessed that she had sat up. "Do you intend that we begin now?"

"No!"

"Pity," she said into the darkness.

He nearly jumped off the pallet. "What!"

"I always have wondered what it's like, you know. And since we are supposedly going to marry—"

"I believe I'll take myself off to the barn to sleep," he said conversationally. *Oh, Lord God above.*

"Don't be silly. You can't possibly wish to do that."

"It would be a deal more comfortable than staying here."

"I've embarrassed you, haven't I?"

"Not quite." He sat up, trying to control his racing pulse. "Do you finally admit, then, that we have to marry?"

"No."

"Serena—"

"But I do admit that society will think we should."

"At the least."

"I never understood that."

"Princess, think," he said patiently. "We've been alone in each other's company for days now."

"But we've not done anything," she protested.

"That won't matter worth a jot. You've heard gossip about girls who are ruined. What do you think that meant?"

"Well, I don't know. Which is why I asked what I did. I've always wondered about it."

He swore. "Serena, will you stop saying that?"

"If it had to be with anyone, I'd rather it were you."

He was quiet a minute. "I'm not sure if that's a compliment or not."

"Oh, by all means. But, Charles." Her voice was gentle. "I won't marry you."

"I'm not such a bad catch, princess," he shot back, completely forgetting his gloomy self-assessment. "Or is it that you meant to aim higher?"

She gasped. "That is a terrible thing to say!"

"But true?"

"No! My sister did, and—"

"And?" he prompted when she didn't go on.

" 'Tis like any other *ton* marriage, I suppose," she said, so offhandedly that he was instantly on guard.

"Is that your objection, princess? That you don't wish to be trapped in a *ton* marriage? Mayhap I don't wish it, either."

"I didn't say I didn't want it," she said in a small voice.

"Ah, princess." In the darkness he reached out his hand to her, though he knew she couldn't see. "I didn't mean it. But we are in a damnable situation."

"So we are." She sounded unutterably weary, and he suspected it wasn't from the rigors of traveling. "We can sort it out another time."

"Will you ever tell me why you object so strongly?"

Again she paused. "Mayhap."

"You owe me that at least, princess. Your reputation's not the only one which will be soiled."

"I suppose I do. Please, could we talk it over some other time?"

"I suppose we can," he said, his voice coming out more grudging than he would have liked. But, damn, he was going to find out the reasons behind her reluctance. He was going to convince her to marry him, or he would lose the best thing he had ever had in his life. "Good night, princess," he said, and rolled away from her, again willing himself to relax, though he felt the awareness of her through his entire body. He loved her, God help him, and it could only bring him pain.

The morning sun, however, slanting through the trees, brought cheerfulness and ease with it. True, Serena didn't love him, and Charles wasn't foolish enough to believe he could make her do so. True, that would make marriage to her difficult, and yet he thought they could manage it if they tried. No *ton* marriage for them, he thought. They got on well enough together, after all. All one had to do was to consider the days of strain and worry, now fortunately in the past. A brief day's journey, and they would be in London. It was true that they'd face difficulties there, but they'd weather it together. They'd been through worse.

The attack came unexpectedly. Only a scuffling sound, a sunlit glint on steel, gave Charles any warning. Ordinarily his instinct for danger was lightning-quick, something he felt without knowing quite why, as he had over the past day or so. The apparent lack of pursuit, however, had lulled him. Taken by surprise, off balance from the skirts of his gown, he whirled, just a fraction of time too late to avoid the blow to his right shoulder. Still, he was a fighter, and he fell into the fighter's crouch he'd never learned at Gentleman Jackson's Academy. He used his hand in a way that Jackson would never have approved, battering into his opponent's stomach. His assailant let out a "woof!" of air, but he was a fighter, too. A moment later, Charles felt another blow, this one to the back of his neck. An all-too-familiar blackness danced at the edge of his vision, but he knew he didn't dare give in to it. Instead, he managed to land his own blow, again into the man's stomach. And though he was struck again in the shoulder, though this time the pain screamed in his injured arm, he recovered, using now the skills he had learned from Jackson to dance back. *Garnett? What the hell?* he thought, seeing the man for the first time, before bringing his fist up and landing a hard, jarring blow on Garnett's jaw, and then falling to his knees.

That fast, it was over. Garnett, knocked unconscious by the force of the blow, lay sprawled on the ground, while Charles, arms wrapped around his midsection, bent forward, gasping for breath. "Eh, Captain, you're hurt," a voice said above him.

"Major," Charles gasped out automatically. "And I damned well know I'm hurt. A war injury."

"Not that, Major." The man, whoever he was, laid the gentlest of touches on Charles's right shoulder, making Charles breathe in sharply. "He has a wicked way with a blade."

Charles stared blankly at the hand he had pressed against his shoulder, stunned by the blood there, aware for the first time of the throbbing pain. "My God. He cut me."

"So he did, Major. Knew you were military," he added inconsequentially. "Best get you inside."

"No!" Charles said sharply. "If you could just get Ser—my son—"

"That don't fadge, Major." The man was kneeling beside him, binding Charles's wound with a capacious handkerchief. A merciful numbness had spread

throughout Charles's arm, and the glittering darkness
at the edge of his vision had returned. "That 'un's a
lady if ever I saw one."

"Damn." Charles gritted his teeth against the pain.
"How did you know?"

"The hands, Major. Always look at the hands."

"Damn," Charles said again. So simple a thing, and
so easily overlooked. Neither of them had given a
thought to Serena's long, slender fingers, or their del-
icacy of movement. Or, for that matter, his own square
ones. "If he's here—"

"He can't hurt her now," the man assured him.

"Not—him. The other one."

"Eh, there's another?"

"Yes." The thought of Alf, and of what he could be
doing to Serena at that very moment, was enough to
pull Charles upright. "Can't let him get to her. Got to—
get her."

"Major, I'll see to her—"

Gritting his teeth again, Charles rose to one leg.
"Can't let another one go. Not her. Can't—"

"I'll see to her," the man repeated, his voice stern
now.

"No." Charles braced his arm on his knee, and pain
shot through him. "Damn," he said, and succumbed to
the darkness.

ELEVEN

Another day of traveling. Serena finished plaiting her hair, stuffed it up under the boy's cap she'd worn yesterday, and made a face at her reflection in the tiny mirror. It seemed as if she'd been on the road forever. With luck, though, she and Charles would reach London by afternoon, and their adventure would be over.

She sighed and turned away from the mirror, wondering why she felt so curiously low. Certainly she wished to reach safety again, if such a thing truly existed in this world. Charles would get her there, she knew. Her faith in him was absolute. Marriage was something she'd never wanted for herself, however, and did not at all want now. Marriage to a man who was so capable, while she had never before faced anything more complicated than deciding what gown to wear to a ball. Marriage to a man who had been a soldier and still bore a soldier's scars, who could only view her world with contempt. Marriage to a man who didn't love her.

Fresh pain stabbed her. Before today she'd never known that love could hurt like this. Love, she'd thought, must be a wonderful feeling, joyous, easy, natural. There was nothing easy about this, not when she would have to work both for it and against it. If she were to gain any happiness for herself, she had to fight for his love. If he never did come to care as she did, she would then have to fight against her own feelings, and let him go. It would be the hardest thing she had ever done. No, she corrected herself. The hardest part would be to fight against bitterness and resentment. To fight against—oh, dear God—hatred.

Absently, Serena trailed over to the small attic window. Charles had been gone longer than she had expected, and they needed to be on their way soon to make the coach to London. It was a lovely day, with the sun all golden and mellow, on the fully leafed trees, and in the garden below. . . .

Serena's gaze sharpened, and she let out a gasp. The next moment she was flying out of the room and down the stairs, not caring who noticed her or what they would think. Bursting out from the inn's back door into the garden, she ran faster than she had ever thought she could. "Oh, God!" She fell onto her knees beside Charles's sprawled body. "Charles, oh, God—he's not dead?" she implored the man standing above her.

"Bloody hell, Serena, of course I'm not dead," Charles said, and the familiar irritation in his voice set her back onto her heels. If he could talk so, surely he wasn't badly hurt.

She looked up at the man again, and though he was little more than a silhouette against the morning sun, she recognized him. "Mr. Lamb, is he all right?"

"Fainted a bit, lass, but he's come 'round right and tight. But I don't like the look of that arm."

"Merciful heavens!" Serena reached out instinctively to touch the inadequately bandaged wound, and as quickly drew her hand back. "He can never travel like that."

"I told you I'm not dead," Charles snapped. "You could talk to me, Serena."

"How bad is it?" She bent her head to his, which was pale and sweaty, though the air was pleasantly cool.

"Bad enough. We're in trouble, princess. Damn." This, as he tried to move again.

"Best lay down, Major," Lamb said. "Do you know this man, miss?"

"Who?" Serena stared blankly for a moment at the figure lying prone in the grass, and then gasped. "Garnett!"

"Lass? Be ye well?"

"Yes." Serena shook her head, dispelling the brief feeling that now she might be the one to faint, and met Charles's fathomless eyes. "Is he dead?"

"Nay, lass. Hit with as good a facer as I've ever seen, but he'll be coming 'round right enough."

"Then we must be away! Charles, if he's here—"

"I know." Charles had managed to get one foot up again. "Is there any sign of Alf?"

"No, not that I've seen, but you know that doesn't mean anything."

"I know." He raised his head. "That sounds like the stage," he added, as the distinctive sound of the yard of tin reached them. "I can't travel like this, princess."

"Oh." It was a long exhalation. "Oh, Mr. Lamb." She looked up at him. "We are in such trouble."

"Someone's after ye, then?"

"After me, mostly, but I've put Major Kirk—"

"Serena," Charles said warningly.

"We have to trust him, Charles. Major Kirk is in danger because of me."

"Utter rot," Charles muttered.

"Well, you are! Do you know someone who will help us?"

"Eh, lass, ye insult me, that ye do." Lamb crouched down, near the shoulder which had once been Charles's injured one, but now was the healthier. "Here, I'll give you an arm up. Think I wouldn't help someone who's fought Boney? Nay, ye insult me."

"Not Boney personally." Charles's attempt at humor failed dismally. He grimaced as Lamb set his beefy arm under Charles's shoulder. "Though I dashed well tried."

"Good enough for me, Major. That's my cart, over behind the inn, with the milk. Think ye can walk there if I help?"

"But we haven't paid for our room," Serena protested, remembering for the first time the practical demands of their journey. Realizing, too, that until this time Charles had taken full responsibility for them.

"The innkeep's my cousin," Lamb called back, as he and Charles made halting progress toward the cart. "I live up Singleton way. Doubt you know it, but it's far enough from here, and quiet."

"But—"

"Just you go get your things, and I'll see to aught else. Well, lass?" he said, as Serena hesitated. "And what are you waiting for?"

"Yes," Serena said and, hardly knowing what she was doing, whirled around and retraced her steps. This time she was all too aware of the people who saw her passing: the cook, the maids, several of the inn's customers. The innkeeper might be Lamb's cousin and so might be trustworthy, but one wrong word from any of these people and she and Charles would be betrayed. It occurred to her, as she ran up the stairs, that just a few days ago she would never have thought in such a way. Yet, what other choice had she? Dashing back down the stairs, carrying their hastily bundled possessions, she prayed that they could get away before fresh disaster befell them.

Charles was already settled onto the matted straw in the back of the cart, his face bleached of color. Lamb boosted Serena up before, with amazing lightness for one of his size, he climbed onto the bench seat and took up his reins. Charles's lips, already set, pressed even more tightly together at the jolting, swaying movement.

"Hold on." Serena grasped his left hand and felt relief

when he gripped back. "We'll get through this. You'll be safe."

"Safe!" His laugh was harsh. "Did I not promise to keep *you* safe? There's no such thing, princess. One can be anywhere—traveling, in a house, in an inn garden, for God's sake—and run into disaster. No, princess." He turned his head away. "There's no such thing as safety."

"Someone hurt you. Very badly, I think."

"Hurt me?" The eyes he turned to her were blazing, and not entirely with anger. Dismayed, she put her hand to his cheek. Not very warm, but . . . "And will you stop that?" He batted her hand away. "Who the devil could have hurt me?"

"Luz," she said, very quietly.

Charles glared at her for a moment before turning his head away and closing his eyes. Leaning back against the side of the swaying cart, holding onto its side, she considered their situation. "We don't have a plan this time, do we?"

Charles didn't answer, but then she hadn't expected him to.

Wearily, Serena pulled herself from her bed in the Lambs' comfortable farmhouse that night, though she didn't strictly have to. Someone else would relieve whoever had been sitting with Charles all night. The Lambs, their family, and their servants had all drawn her and Charles into warmth and comfort that she had almost forgotten existed. From the man who served as butler to the lowliest kitchen maid, from the head groom and gardener and herdsman down, all conspired to keep their unexpected guests' presence secret. The loss of the Lambs' son had been recent, and the fact that Charles had been in the army was reason enough. It didn't hurt that, in spite of her

background and her obvious prettiness, Serena was
willing to work. Nor did Charles's chiseled good looks
do him any harm in the maids' eyes.

For all that, Serena, hastily donning the gown lent
her by the Lambs' eldest daughter, was worried. No
one else in the neighborhood could be entirely trusted
with their secret. Word of it was bound to get out, and
they wouldn't be able to escape this time. Charles was
too sick.

Already, as they had traveled from the inn, the damage from the injury was all too obvious. There was little
comfort to be had in the back of the cart, even for
someone who was healthy. For Charles, being knocked
about as he was as they jounced over the ruts and
slopes of the South Downs, it must have been agony.
He didn't protest her suggestion that he lie down, and
he put his left hand over his eyes in a gesture of weari-
ness, or illness. Yet he retained enough humor to jest
about his maidenly modesty when Serena tore his pet-
ticoats to use as bandages.

It was only when she had carefully untied the hap-
hazard bandage Mr. Lamb had wrapped on the wound
and eased back the torn edges of the cloth, which was
stuck to his skin, that both gasped, he with pain, she
with horror. Though she knew that the amount of
bloodstained skin made matters appear worse than
they were, still the jagged knife cut was long and appeared deep. Hands shaking, Serena steeled herself to
pad the wound and then wrap it more securely. When
she was done, Charles exhaled a long breath of air, but
he kept his forearm over his face.

By the time they reached the Lambs' farm, Charles's
face was almost as dismaying a sight as his wound. His
eyes were dull, and his arm was so obviously useless that
he had to be lifted down from the cart. Not until afterwards, when she'd seen Charles past the hurdle of

getting within doors, did she realize how strange the two of them must appear to the servants and grooms who gathered around and gawked at them. Even to her, their story sounded preposterous.

"How is he?" she asked softly, looking down at Charles, lying flat on his back in bed. His eyes were closed and deep-circled; his cheeks were stubbled and gaunt. Even in a fever, though, and perhaps a stupor, he was magnificently, splendidly male. His face was taut with suffering, but nothing could disguise its fine bone structure: the broad brow, sculpted cheekbones, firm chin, and arrogant nose. And then there were the bedclothes, pulled down to his waist to allow air to move freely over his wound. Serena was still dubious about that, though Mrs. Lamb assured her that she'd nursed any number of people and found this to be effective. Besides, she added, any attention from the local doctor would be disastrous. His tendency to be in his cups not only made him incompetent, but also untrustworthy.

"He's been that restless, miss." The maid who had been sitting with Charles rose and bobbed a little curtsy. "Seems as if his fever's rising." She looked down at him. "I think as he should be bled."

Serena sighed. "For now, I'll trust to what Mrs. Lamb says."

"If you say so, miss." The maid looked doubtfully down at Charles. "If he was my man, I wouldn't take no chances." She sighed, just as Serena had. "He's a fine-looking one, ain't he?"

Sudden rage filled Serena. From the beginning the maids had vied with each other for the privilege of caring for him. Only good manners kept her from striking out with jealousy and dismay. This was what she would have to face when—if—they married. There would always be women casting out lures for him.

How she managed to sound normal when she finally

spoke, she didn't know. "I'll sit with him," she said again, and the maid, who looked tired, at last left the room.

She studied him in the dim light, not knowing how much longer she'd have him. She'd been firm in her refusal to marry him, and he'd been equally determined that she would. Not for the first time, she wondered why, when he still obviously loved another woman. If anything, she would have thought he'd be eager to be rid of her.

A slight moan made her focus on him again. He was tossing restlessly, twisting the sheet around him. "Oh, Charles," she said, reaching out to untangle the sheet, and encountering bare skin. A nightshirt would only hamper their efforts to tend his wound, Mrs. Lamb had explained with a smile, by being in the way and by causing him unnecessary pain when it was moved. Thus he wore only his smallclothes. Until now, Serena had never been so aware of him as a man, but then, until this she had never seen him without a sheet covering him. Now, with that sheet pulled down to his waist, she couldn't help seeing his bare torso, even in the dim light. How different his body was from hers, she marveled. Though modesty always prevented her from looking at her own reflection, even when she wore a shift, she knew that her body was round and soft. In contrast, his was as lean and hard-muscled and sculpted as his face, with angles and planes that fascinated her. A scar snaked down his left side, while there were signs of his shoulder injury that she might have missed. Mrs. Lamb had pointed out a knob on his collarbone that had not knitted together as it should. There were other smaller, white marks, on his arms and body and hands, the signs of war. Poor man, she thought, stroking his hair back from his brow. Both were damp with sweat, though the night was cool. Even his chest gleamed with perspiration.

Abruptly the meaning of that struck her. His fever had broken. "Oh, dear God," she whispered, in prayer or relief or some other emotion she couldn't name. Fever, his greatest enemy, had been vanquished. He was going to live.

Mrs. Lamb would have to be told. Charles needed to be sponged down, as well as having a new dressing applied. As an unmarried lady, she couldn't do such things. Of course he'd be more comfortable, she thought, but only with reluctance did she start to pull back.

Of a sudden, a hand shot out and caught her wrist, holding her clamped in position. Serena gasped and looked down into his eyes, dark and fathomless with suffering. "You're well," he said, his voice hoarse.

She smiled and tried to pull free. "Of course I am. Did you think I wouldn't be?"

"I so feared . . ."

"You've kept me safe, Charles."

"Safe." He laughed bitterly. "Safe? I've put you in danger from Captain Garnett."

She frowned at that. "No, you fought him, and well. Don't you remember?"

"I remember only how scared I was."

Scared? "Charles, do let me go. I must fetch Mrs. Lamb—"

"Not yet." His gaze held hers, forceful, commanding. "No, not yet," he repeated, and with one tug pulled her down to him.

There was only possession in his kiss this time, not gentleness. Possession and passion and need. His mouth angled against hers again and again, hard, demanding; his lips coaxed hers apart, and his tongue danced with hers. Oh, she shouldn't let him do such things, not when he was injured, Serena thought, and yet her fingers tangled in his hair; yet she marveled at the feeling of that hard, chiseled chest against hers. At some point he had released her hand. Now she rested it on his shoulder, her fingers opening and closing compulsively on him. "Mine," he muttered between kisses, his hand clamping her neck as tightly as it had her wrist. "Mine."

"Yes, Charles," she gasped. He loved her! she thought jubilantly. He loved her. It didn't matter why, or how, or that his earlier insistence on marrying had had far more to do with reputation than with desire. It mattered not that she had never wished to marry, that she had always distrusted love matches. He loved her. "Yours."

"Yes. Oh, Luz."

It took a moment for that to penetrate through her love-dazed mind. Then comprehension struck. "Let me go!" she exclaimed, finding enough strength from anger and shock to wrench her head away. "I am not Luz!"

The body under hers went completely still. "What?"

"Luz. I am not Luz."

He gazed up at her blankly, and then groaned. "Oh, Lord, Serena," he said, and seemed to realize for the first time that he was holding her. "No, did I really call you that?"

"You were kissing Luz, Charles, not me," she accused him.

"I knew it was you," he insisted. "I did. I just—"

"You thought I was Luz," she went on implacably, so angry that she wanted to strike him. Never mind all that they'd gone through together. Never mind the times he'd saved her. She had poured all her heart, all of her soul into that kiss, and he had rejected it. "You have to tell me about her."

"Oh, God, no."

"After that, you owe it to me, Charles. I've respected your pain. I've felt it but I haven't asked you before this."

"Serena—"

"I'm demanding it now. You have no right. No right, Charles!" Her eyes filled with tears, and she hastily blinked them back. Oh, she loved this man, and he had hurt her to her soul. "No right," she said again, this time in a whisper.

"No. I haven't." He stared up at the ceiling, his expression bleak. " 'Tis not something I care to remember. But I do. All the time."

He looked so alone that she wanted to pillow his head against her breast. Instead, she took his hand. "How could Luz have hurt you so?"

He turned toward her. "Luz is dead."

"No! Oh, I'm sorry, Charles," she said frantically. "I'm sorry, I'm sorry. Don't talk about it. Oh, please, not if you don't want to."

"You've pushed me this far, Serena. You're going to hear it."

She took a deep breath. He was right. She had pushed him to it. "Tell me," she said, again in a whisper.

He looked at her hand as if seeing it for the first time, raised it to his lips, and then carefully laid it down on her lap. "Do you know about the retreat to Corunna?"

"Yes, a bit. Sir John Moore died there, didn't he?"

"Yes, I'll get to that. That damned march." His gaze was distant. "A forced march, no food, no rest, just plodding on over this damned mountain pass. Men fell everywhere, just dropping by the side of the road, and no one could stop to help them. And the women, Serena. God, the women." His eyes beseeched hers. "Every army has its camp followers, wives of soldiers, maybe, but usually—something else."

She took his hand again. She had to keep him steady.

She had to keep him linked to the present, rather than the horrific past. "How did they come to be with you?"

"Sometimes they had no choice," he said, his voice matter-of-fact. "We'd destroyed their homes, or the French had, and they'd nowhere else to go. Others—well, who knows why? Some of them were as strong as the men, maybe stronger. But, oh God, Serena, others fell. Others gave birth, and I don't know what happened to them. It haunts me, Serena. To this day, it haunts me."

She closed her eyes. "And you saw all this?"

"Afterwards, mostly. After most had happened."

"Where were you?"

"Rearguard, 95th Rifles. Someone had to protect the rear, keep the French from catching up with us. There was an infantry unit there, too, good fighters, good marksmen. Could I have some water?"

"Yes, of course." She went to the bureau and filled a tumbler. His eyes were so filled with pain that the best thing for him was sleep, though she doubted he would. Not yet, now that she'd started this. Mayhap it was just as well. "I can't do this without hurting you, Charles."

"Just do it, Serena." His lips went white as she slipped her arm under what had been his wounded shoulder, but he parted them to take a sip. "Ah." He leaned his head against her, as she'd wanted him to earlier. "That is good."

"Rest, Charles," she said in spite of herself, as she gently helped him back down onto the bed. "Else you'll get fevered again."

"I can't." Again his eyes beseeched hers. "I keep seeing it in my dreams,"

"Yes, I know. Rest anyway, Charles. Don't talk any more."

"I have to. I still live it, all the time. 'Tis time someone knows what 'tis like, fighting a war. Geoffrey doesn't. No one in town does. Although I sometimes wonder about Adam . . ."

"Adam?"

"Lord Adam Burnet."

"But he's never been in the army," she said in surprise.

"No, but sometimes there's a certain look. Ah, well." He sighed. "All the *ton* sees are those splendid uniforms and young men going off to fight as a lark. But it's no lark. We learn how to fight. We learn too damned well. Our uniforms get muddy and ripped— so much for looking splendid. We sweat and we fire our guns until the smoke is so dense we no longer know who we're firing at, and if we have to, we use our bayonets or our bare hands—"

"Stop!" she cried. "Oh, please stop."

"There it is, Serena," he said quietly, "and that's not a fraction of what it's like. Not even an idea of what it was like to cross those mountains for days, Serena, days. Our uniforms in rags, most of us without shoes, hungry, tired. You cannot know."

She blinked back tears, fiercely. He was right. Too few people in London did give thought to the war raging so far away. Too few people had any idea of what the soldiers faced. But she did. "I do know, Charles."

He looked up, and this time his eyes focused on her, not on some distant battlefield. "Ah, Serena." he said as quietly as she had, and stroked her cheek with the back of his fingers. "You do, don't you? You see hell, too."

She looked away, so that he wouldn't see that her tears had brimmed over. "Yes," she said when she could control her voice, and wiped carefully at her lower lids. Any time a strange man came near her, she tensed. She wondered if it would always be so. "I do."

"I'm sorry. You shouldn't have ever had to—"

"Yes, I should!" She rounded on him. "I could wish it

hadn't happened as it did, but I'm glad I know. Someone has to."

"The Incomparable."

She gestured impatiently. " 'Tis just a name, something someone gave to me and others decided to pick up. I'm not incomparable, Charles. I'm just me."

"The daughter of a wealthy earl," he pointed out.

Serena flinched. "Yes, so I am. But people will look at me differently when I return home. My father will look at me differently."

"What will he do?" he asked, as he had once before.

"I don't know. I really don't know." She took a deep breath. "Tell me the rest, Charles. I think you need to," she said as he turned his head away. "I need to hear it. Not because of Luz, or what you still feel for her—"

"Serena—"

"But because of Captain Garnett. He's chasing you as much as he is me. I saw what happened in the inn's garden. He was grinning, just before he struck. Why, Charles? Please." She clutched at his hand. "Why?"

"Curse it." He gazed toward the wall. "He killed Luz."

TWELVE

Serena gasped. "No! Oh, no!"

"I've no proof, but I know it. He knows what I suspect. He laughs, Serena, but he'd get me if he could."

"Shouldn't he be brought up on charges?"

"How? As I told you, I've no proof."

"Did you see it happen?"

He took a deep breath. "No, but I was there."

She frowned. "Then—"

"Then how do I know? I know him." He looked at her. "There's something wrong with him, Serena. Something—"

"Evil," she said quietly, seeing in her mind a little hut on Charles's estate.

"Yes," he said, just as quietly. "You know."

"Yes." She bowed her head, again holding back tears. He had his own pain, outside and inner, to deal with.

"He tried to kill me first." His face was distant. "That march," he said again. "I told you we had my regiment and an infantry regiment with us during the retreat from Sahagun. But there were stragglers, too. The French were so close behind us, and the conditions were so bad—snow, cold as you've never known it, sheer falls sometimes on one side, other times narrow defiles. There were places where we could have defended ourselves, but orders were to keep on going.

Days, Serena. Days. The stragglers were men who had just refused to give up."

"Garnett was one of them."

"Yes." He looked up at her. "He's not giving up now, is he?"

"No." Even though the conditions were far different, somehow he still managed to find them. And threaten them.

"He already knew Luz. We both did."

"How?"

"Later." He tried to raise his hand and winced. "It would be my good arm, curse it. He wants to cripple me. Any roads, we both knew Luz. I loved her. He wanted her."

She drew in her breath. Having been with Charles these last weeks, she could imagine what that meant, even if Charles felt nothing for her beyond protective-ness and honor, and perhaps his own form of stubbornness. "But would that be reason enough for him to want to kill her?"

He was quiet a moment. "Yes."

"Charles!"

"I'll explain in a moment. He may have hated her. He certainly hated me. It happened when we were at one of the mountain passes, and the French were close behind."

"What did?"

"The smoke, Serena. So much smoke from firing, that sometimes it's hard to see where you're shooting. It does-n't help when it's snowing." He looked up. "Have you ever been in a snowstorm, a bad one, and then there's a moment when the snow clears, just a bit?"

"Yes."

"I was lying on my stomach—all of us were—firing my rifle. Something knocked my cap off. I ignored it, and kept on shooting. I don't know what made me look to the side." He pursed his lips. "There it was, one of the gaps in the snow. And there, not twenty feet distant, looking right at me with his musket raised, was—"

"Garnett," Serena said.

"Garnett," he agreed. "I wouldn't have thought much of it, Serena. I would have thought it just an accident of war, except for his look. He smirked, Serena. I couldn't go after him, of course, not with the fighting. It wasn't until we'd beaten off the French for the moment, and I searched about for my cap, that I saw it."

"What?"

"A neat little hole through the middle of my cap. An inch or so lower, and I'd have been dead." His face was grim. "There was no doubt after that that he wanted to kill me, was there?"

"No." He still did. She had no doubt that, should Garnett suddenly appear, Charles would fight him, injured or not.

"Well." He closed his eyes. Serena wondered if he realized that he was holding her hand. "We reached Corunna at last. Days and days in those mountains, with fewer than what we'd started with. The fleet was there to rescue us, but they didn't have the right wind to get in for us. It was frustrating, to see the ships, and know we couldn't reach them yet. So we had to rest at last, though we didn't know when the French would fire upon us, or the fleet. Most of us collapsed, but we always had our weapons at hand, just in case. I was cleaning mine when Garnett came over to me. He pretended to apologize for the, ah, mistake. I pretended to accept, all to be polite. We were officers, after all. We were also mortal enemies, from that day on."

A scraping noise at the door made them both tense, until Mrs. Lamb came in, her nightgown billowing about her like a frigate's sails. She crossed the room to place her hand on Charles's head. "Your fever's gone, Major."

"Yes, ma'am," he said gravely, looking up at her. "I am sorry if I've put you to any bother."

She waved that off. "I've taken care of a few boys and men in my time." She chuckled. "Sometimes I think they're one and the same. Now." She looked at them, her hands on her hips. "You need to rest, Major, not talk."

Charles's expression was meek. "Yes, ma'am."

Mrs. Lamb gave him a look that said she wasn't fooled in the least. "And you, miss, have to have yours."

"Yes, Mrs. Lamb," Serena said, as meekly as Charles.

"All very well, missy, but what good will you be to him, or yourself, if you wear yourself out?"

"We'll talk for only a bit longer," Serena promised her. "We need to discuss ways to get back to London."

"Not very soon, missy. 'Twill take time for that wound of his to heal."

"How long?" Charles put in sharply.

"All depends. Resting will help. I'll take over here, missy."

"No, not quite yet, please, Mrs. Lamb," Serena said. If she allowed herself to be bullied into going to bed, Charles would never open up again. It had taken injury and a dream, followed by her insistence, to make him do so. The poison caused by his experiences, as real as any physical poison, would fester until it destroyed him. "Just a few more minutes, I promise."

"Just a few," Charles echoed.

Mrs. Lamb looked from one to the other, and then shook her head. "Oh, aye. But no more than that, mind."

"No more than that," Serena promised. She looked down at Charles as the door closed behind Mrs. Lamb. His skin was gray and his eyes were closed. "Charles? Do you want to stop?"

He looked up. "I don't know, Serena." He took a deep breath. "But . . ."

"I think you need to go on." Her voice was gentle, and so were the fingers she reached out to stroke his cheek. He turned his head toward the caress, willing, waiting.

"I did know it was you I kissed," he said abruptly. "I did. That damn dream." He winced. "My apologies. I've just realized I've been swearing like a trooper."

"Well, you are one."

"Not anymore. I seem to have forgotten my manners."

"Pray don't refine upon it. Now." She frowned. "I can't quite remember. After Corunna, where did you go?"

"After battling the French again at Elvina, when Sir John Moore was killed, do you mean? We kept on fighting, Serena, until we drove them off long enough to get on the ships. We got away, finally, to Lisbon. Wellesley was giving the orders, so once we reached Lisbon we went on to Oporto. I made my great mistake in Lisbon."

"What?"

"I told Garnett that Luz was mine, and I'd not have him bothering her. Damn." Weak though he was, he pounded his fist on the bed, and flinched. "Why did I do that?"

"Because you loved her," she said gently.

"No. Yes, I loved her, but it wasn't about her anymore. God help me, but men can be so stupid."

"I don't think I understand."

"No, how could you? Women don't fight enemies to the death, simply to keep them from winning."

She gasped. "Charles!"

"I know." He gave her the wide, flashing grin she'd thought never to see again. "Men can be remarkably foolish." He grew serious. "Most of the time, that's what war is about."

"Oh. But why," she frowned, "would he want to kill Luz?"

"Because she rebuffed him. Because she preferred me, and not him. Reasons enough for someone like him."

"Then." She took a deep breath before going on. "Then do you think he'll kill me?"

"Oh, no, sweetheart!" He reached for her hand. "Of course not. I won't let him."

He might not have a choice, she thought, and shuddered. He really didn't know what it had been like in that little hut, with him and Alf prowling around. She had no doubt that they would have killed her had it become necessary, and not thought a thing about it. "How did it happen?" she asked quietly.

He put his arm over his eyes. "We crossed the Douro and sent the French into retreat. A total rout, Serena—"

"But I thought that was a loss."

He snorted. "So it was reported, but it was a great victory. The French in Oporto surrendered to us in any number, throwing down their arms, or just running. We sent some troops after them, but that wasn't successful. Which was the stupid thing that probably caused the whole affair to be presented wrong. In any event, Wellington decided to go himself."

His strength was so obviously waning. She didn't know how much longer he could do this, not when she suspected that the worst was yet to come. "Sleep, Charles," she heard herself saying. "You need it so."

His eyes were despairing. "I'll only dream—"

"Go to sleep, Charles, else you'll be fevered again. I'll be here." She took his hand. "I promise."

"Yes," he said, and with a little sigh let go, his hand still in hers, his grip more gentle now. Serena settled back, trying to find a more comfortable position in the hard chair, and failing. He needed her so. She wouldn't leave while he did.

She must have dozed. She started when she heard him mutter and groan. She thought she heard Luz's name, though she wasn't sure. Oh dear, another nightmare. She reached out to stroke his brow, and it seemed to calm him for a moment. But then his eyes shot open, their expression so vague that she wondered what he was seeing. "Charles," she murmured, and to her surprise, he lifted her hand and kissed it. It broke her heart. "'Tis me, Serena. All's well."

Quite suddenly, he came awake. A soldier's trick. She remembered thinking that when he fell asleep so quickly. "What time is it?" he asked.

"Early, I think. 'Tis not full bright out."

"Soon, though." He glanced toward the window, and then back at her. "You should be abed, Serena."

She smiled. "I will be, soon enough."

"I've kept you here, made you listen—"

"Shh." She placed her finger over his lips. "You know I don't mind."

"I do." His eyes sought hers. "I won't burden you anymore."

She looked down at their clasped hands. Whose hand had he kissed in his dream? "I wonder if maybe you should. I've heard most of it already."

His lips tightened. "There's not much more to tell."

"No?" She raised her head. "I know nothing about Luz. Tell me about her."

"You can't want to hear that."

"But I do." Who was she punishing, she wondered, him or herself? "How did you meet her? What was she like?"

"Pretty, of course," he said, as if surprised she didn't know. "Dark, thick hair, and the darkest eyes I've ever seen. Different from English girls. Exotic, almost."

"Oh." Inwardly she bristled. After all, was she not the Incomparable?

"I became friendly with a Portuguese officer in Oporto, when we first landed on the Peninsula. We were of an age. He, and most of the other Portuguese, were happy to see the British. One day we were walking when we came across this girl." The expression in his eyes was far away. "She was the most beautiful girl, but Joaquim wasn't pleased to see her. She was his sister, you see, walking with her duenna, and he didn't like it that she was out for everyone to see. Or so he told me. He actually didn't like introducing her to me."

"Because you weren't Portuguese?"

"No. The de Texeiras—her family—were old and wealthy. What we would consider gentry."

"But you're of the aristocracy!"

He shook his head. "I'm a second son. I'm sure they thought they could do better for her than a British officer."

"As if they could!"

"Why, thank you." He looked at Serena in surprise. "That's rather nice to hear."

"Don't become too puffed up in your own conse-quence," she said severely. "I presume she spoke English."

"No."

She blinked at that. "No?"

"And I have no Portuguese."

"But then, how—"

"Did we understand each other?" His smile was ten-der. "With our eyes. With smiles. Sometimes Joaquim came along and translated. Of course, we could only speak about the most ordinary things. The weather, how I was enjoying Portugal, and such. Even so, we managed to say other things with our eyes."

Hmph, she thought.

"Even when he wasn't there, I managed to meet her walking every day, though the duenna seemed not to like it." He grinned. "I think she was lax in her job, though. After a day or so, I could predict when they'd be walking, and where." His smile faded. "Unfortunately, so could Garnett."

"How did he meet her?"

He took a deep breath. "I introduced him to her."

"What?"

"Yes. Ironic, isn't it? I'd only met him once or twice, but I already knew he was a dirty dish. There'd been some talk of his cheating, though nothing was ever proven. I quite understand how Joaquim must have felt when he introduced her to me, but I had no choice."

"Did he bother her at all?"

"He must have, because Joaquim was furious at me. That was the end of Luz's walks, and I wasn't allowed to see her anymore. Neither," he said with relish, "was Garnett."

"Good."

"Unfortunately, he blamed me, said he'd get revenge. If I'd known him better . . ."

"How could you?"

He took a deep breath. "I should have. The officer who accused him of cheating was attacked with a knife one night while he was walking—yes, it sounds familiar, doesn't it? He had his sword and so he managed to beat back whoever it was, but he was injured. We never did find out who did it."

"Garnett."

"Yes. Garnett. He promised he would get revenge. No," he said, frowning. "That he would be avenged, I think." He looked up at her. "That's different, isn't it?"

"Yes."

"It explains what happened later better, though of course I couldn't guess what he meant."

"No, how could you?"

He shifted, and winced. "No, no, I'm well enough," he said, as Serena bent forward. "In any event, the rest of our troops had arrived. One could hardly expect a gently bred girl to walk abroad with soldiers all about, after all. So that," he said, "was that."

"How long did you have?"

"One week."

"What! All this time you've been mourning her, because of one week?" And yet, how long had it taken her to fall in love with him? Less than that.

"Sometimes 'tis enough, Serena. Remember, I was very young."

"Oh, yes. All of two years younger?"

"Yes, about. But I hadn't seen battle yet, either. A man grows up very quickly then."

"Yes," she said quietly. "I'd imagine so."

"Sometimes I wonder if I would care so much if I'd seen more of her. If we could actually have spoken to each other." He squeezed her hand. "Except that I can't forget how she died."

They were coming to it now. "Tell me," she said softly, knowing that now he'd started, he'd have to tell the rest.

"Oh, God, I don't want to." He gazed up at her, his eyes agonized. "I don't want to." His grip tightened on her hand, and he took a deep breath. "It was when we took Oporto the second time. I told you, we had the French on the run. We didn't have much time, a day or so, to chase them, so I received permission to visit Luz for a few minutes. I was on Wellesley's staff by then," he added glumly. "Apparently I'd been mentioned in some dispatches from Corunna."

"Oh, yes, such a terrible fate," she said facetiously.

"I'm a soldier, Serena. 'Twas how I was trained, and 'twas how I came to be mentioned in the dispatches.

And I was made a damned—excuse me, *cursed*—staff officer because of it. I wanted to rejoin my regiment." He grinned. "Granted, my uniform was green, not scarlet, but I think I'd acquit myself well at a ball."

"Oh, absurd."

"And then there was Garnett."

She held his hand, knowing that someone had to keep him steady. "What happened?"

"His regiment was there. Granted, I didn't see much of him, as I was on staff. Something else he held against me."

"He thought he should be, too?"

"He did fight well on the passes, Serena. I assume he did elsewhere. Whether it was because of that accusation of cheating, or something else, he never received any real notice. In any event," Charles squeezed his eyes shut, "I went to Luz's home. God, Serena. If only I hadn't."

"How were you to know—"

"I should have, damn it! With Garnett there, I should have. He must have had it all set up beforehand, damn his eyes." He paused. "I'm swearing again."

"Don't regard it. I don't."

"You should," he said severely, though his eyes implored hers. "Do I have to relive this, Serena?"

No, he didn't. He was tired and in pain and he didn't need to go through this again. Not with the worst of it coming. "Don't you always relive it?"

"Yes," he said slowly.

"Oh, Charles."

"War's not pretty, Serena. Real people get hurt. Real people die," he said harshly. "I was shown into a parlor. Joaquim and I hadn't seen each other for a time, and so we talked while we waited for Luz and her duenna to come downstairs." His breath was as hoarse as his earlier words had been. "She hadn't

made it that far when there was this great blast. I did-
n't even get to see her."

"Oh, God, Charles!"

"It knocked us both off our feet. My first thought was
that somehow the French had recovered and were
shelling us. Joaquim recovered first. He ran out, calling
for his family. I was right behind. Oh, Serena." He
turned his head, and the agony she'd seen in his eyes
earlier was as nothing to what was there now. "Dust was
everywhere, floating down, all over me, and pieces of
plaster, too. I thought I was hearing bells, until I realized my ears were ringing. They were like that for
several days." He paused, as though to gather strength.
"I knew the house had been hit. I couldn't breathe because of all the dust, but I didn't care. I ran out, too,
calling for Luz. A block hit me, here." Apparently forgetting his new injury, he reached his hand up to point
out the spot. Serena, reaching out to grasp his arm,
stopped him in time. "It knocked me down. The next
thing I knew, I heard this odd roaring sound, and I
thought that was my ears, too. The house was falling
down around me."

"Oh, God, Charles!"

"There were more pieces of plaster and masonry,
slabs of granite and marble. They told me later that the
only thing that saved me was that I was caught under a
lintel. Everyone else—" He stopped, swallowed, and
then went on. "Dead. All dead."

Serena's hands were over her face, and she was rock-
ing back and forth. "Oh, God, Charles. Oh, God."

"I was out for a bit," he said, sounding detached now.
"When I woke up, I was in a small space. There was air,
but dust, too, and so I put my handkerchief—amazing
that I could reach for it, all things considered—over my
face. My left arm was useless. I tried to shift some of the
blocks, but each time I did, the others above them

shifted, too. So I started yelling. Yelled myself hoarse. It seemed years I was in there. Years, but finally I heard voices." He paused. "Do you know, that was when I finally became afraid?"

"Why?" she asked, horrified as much by his calmness as by his narrative.

"I don't know, really." He paused. "Yes, I do. I was afraid something would go wrong and the whole house would come down around me. Someone called to me, finally, and told me they would get me out, and at one point someone else, I have no idea who, got me water. I was so thirsty."

Without being asked, Serena rose to get him another tumbler of water, blinking back her tears so that he wouldn't see. Again she went through the difficult process of helping him drink, and when he was done laid her hand on his arm. "But they got you out," she managed to say.

"Yes. It took hours, they told me afterwards." His face was stony; he didn't seem aware of her hand on him. "The surgeon wanted to take my arm."

"Off?" she asked in horror.

"Yes. It was the only way he thought he could deal with it. I suppose he was right in one way, but I fought them." He looked up at her. "Literally, Serena. I don't know where I got the strength. It took three men to hold me down. I think I hit someone, with my good hand. The one that's injured now," he said wryly. "And I tried to stand. Finally the surgeon gave up. He said I'd likely die."

"Charles," she began hesitantly, wiping her eyes with her fingers and lowering her hands. "The scar on your side?"

His smile was twisted. "I'd give you my handkerchief, princess, but I don't seem to have one."

Serena shook her head as she searched in the pocket

of her dressing gown, borrowed from one of the Lamb daughters and much too big for her. She wiped her eyes and blew her nose, but she didn't put the handkerchief away. It was likely she'd need it again. "The scar?" she repeated.

"Oh, that. An old childhood injury, when I fell from a tree." Again he smiled, but this one was softer. "I'd have been strapped for that, save for the wound."

The attempt at levity helped a little bit. She smiled back at him, a watery smile. "You're here, Charles," she said softly, reaching out to stroke his face again. "But, oh, God." Her hand flew back to her face. " 'Tis my fault you're hurt this time."

"Serena." He pulled her hand back to his. "It is not."

"If you weren't helping me—"

"Garnett and I are enemies. If you don't know that by now, you should." He gripped her hand a little tighter. "It will likely happen again."

She stared at him, horror welling up inside her. "You think he did it."

"Think, Serena," he said coolly. "Who else could it have been? The French were on the run."

"But—"

" 'Tis true that there could still have been one or two about. Joaquim was a captain by then, and so he was their enemy. It could have been a parting shot, as it were, but it wasn't." His face hardened. "It was Garnett."

"But he killed Luz!"

"Of course he did. Because she refused him. Because he wanted to get at me."

"Oh, God." Her horror had grown. "Then he could—"

"Use you. Yes. Oh, princess." He brought her hand to his lips, palm up. "Do you think I'll let him?"

She took a deep breath. "How," she said shakily, "do you know it was he? Was he seen?"

"Of course not. It seems there was a small pile of gunpowder behind the house. One of the men saw it and ran to report it. But before he could get back with help, it exploded. All hell broke loose, of course, so it wasn't until later that someone tried to find out what had happened. He found a long, burned rope leading to the house—or what had been the house. Someone had lit the other end."

"Where was Garnett?"

"Well in view when it happened. He actually helped search for bodies, if you can believe that."

"My God."

"I've no doubt that if he'd found me, a slab would conveniently have fallen upon me." He paused. "And all because of jealousy over a girl."

"He is evil, Charles."

He nodded. "I didn't know any of this at the time. I was quite sick—my arm hurt like the devil, and I began to wish I'd let the surgeon amputate—"

"No," she said firmly.

"No," he agreed. "But it never did heal correctly, Serena. I was under that house for too long without attention. Hours, Serena. It felt like days."

"How awful."

"Yes, wasn't it? But I was going to live, damn it. By God, I decided to get Garnett if it was the last thing I did, for what he did to Luz." He closed his eyes. "All dead. All dead."

Tears brimmed into her eyes. Everything fell into place now—his discomfort at being within doors; his driving compulsion to get her to safety. And all because of a twisted man's twisted desire for revenge. She rose to get him water again, though he hadn't asked. When she returned to help him drink, she had composed herself, at least on the outside.

Charles drank thirstily. "Ah, that is good." He looked up at her, smiled, and to her immense surprise, nestled his head against her breasts.

"Charles!"

"Marry me, Serena." He looked serious, almost anxious. "Please."

"No. Not when the only reason is fear for our reputations."

"To hell with that. You know that's not it anymore. Marry me."

"No," she said again, with remarkable steadiness, all things considered. The feeling of his head against her breasts was doing odd things to her. "You still love Luz."

"Serena, that's in the past—"

"No. How can it be, if you keep remembering her, dreaming about her? I won't marry a man who loves someone else," she went on, though he had opened his mouth to speak. "Though I can't quite understand why you do."

He stared at her. "What? Why?"

"You saw her for one week, and you couldn't talk to each other."

"There are other ways of communicating, Serena. You know that."

"Nevertheless. She was always chaperoned, and you couldn't say what you felt, even if you could speak the same language. And you didn't even see her on that last day. Yet it doesn't matter. You can't forget her."

"You're right, it doesn't matter," he said urgently. "Serena, I think we should marry."

"No. You don't love me," she said, fighting for composure. "You know I don't want to marry. I told you that."

He looked perplexed. "I never understood that."

"It matters not. If you don't love me, which doesn't

necessarily mean anything, give me one reason why we should."

"We want each other."

She pulled her head back, stunned. "That's not true," she said, not caring for once if she hurt him.

"Look at me, Serena." He caught her chin and forced her to face him. "Can you honestly tell me you don't desire me?"

"Yes."

"Liar."

"No, I'm not." She rose, her face stony. "You need sleep. So do I. I'll get Mrs. Lamb to sit with you," she said, and whisked herself out of the room.

In the silence left after her departure, Charles looked up at the ceiling, gradually lightening with the coming of day. He would survive the wound to his shoulder. He'd had worse. Oh, but he didn't know if he would survive losing Serena. It wasn't just desire he felt for her, that he knew. It was more complex than that. Sometimes it hurt like hell, knowing they'd go their separate ways when they reached London. Luz was truly in the past. He'd begun realizing that lately, and talking about her now had helped him put her there once and for all. His dreams weren't really about Luz anymore, but about those last few moments before the house collapsed, that brief eternity of time when he'd tried to save her, and failed. He would never forget that time. Never. He wondered now, though, if he had ever truly loved her. He wondered if she had been only a sweet memory amid the horror and chaos of war.

The door opened again and Mrs. Lamb came in, relentlessly cheerful. "My, and don't you look tired. What were you two prosing on about? Well, never mind," she went on. "You look that tired, and so does Lady Serena. Has she been crying?"

He shook his head, though the mere motion hurt. "No, ma'am."

"Tsk. You both need sleep, Major, and that's a fact."

"Yes, ma'am," he said, and closed his eyes, knowing he wouldn't really rest, not with all that swirled through his head. For if he had mourned Luz all this time, how long would he mourn Serena?

THIRTEEN

The trip to Guildford in Mr. Lamb's pony cart was quiet and uneventful. Over the back roads they traveled, meeting few people, which was a relief. Charles was concerned, though. Garnett had never been seen about the area asking questions. He hadn't hurt the man that badly, though he knew he'd landed a flush hit. No, something havey-cavey was about, and he was on edge.

Covertly he glanced at Serena, sitting quietly beside him and dressed in her own clothes again, just as he wore his. The Lambs had been kind to two strangers, and all because he had been in the army. He and Serena had been damned—*dashed* lucky to have met people who'd helped them along the way.

Dashed. He closed his eyes, deeply ashamed at the way he had sworn so much while telling Serena his tale. He was, if truth be told, ashamed to tell most people any of it. It was too personal, too emotional. Yet there he'd been, telling her not only about Luz, but of all that had happened later, and the disaster that would forever remain in his dreams. He would never forget what had happened to him in Oporto.

The Lambs' pony cart had no back, and so he couldn't lean his head back as he wished to. Again he found himself wondering if he'd ever truly loved Luz. Serena had pointed out with biting, devastating accuracy just how little he'd known the woman he'd once wanted as his wife. He'd seen her just over a week in all. One week, and never unchaperoned. The few words they'd exchanged, with Joaquim interpreting, had been mere polite commonplaces. Would his feelings for her ever have ripened into something more? He'd never know. All dead, all dead.

"We're coming up on Guildford," Mr. Lamb said.

Charles came back to himself. Lost in reverie as he had been, he hadn't noticed the increase in traffic, even here on the narrow road. "We'll make the stage on time, will we not?" he said, anxious more for Serena than for himself. He was a soldier, battle-hardened, able to take most of what came his way, except perhaps for the injuries to his shoulders. One was recent, one was older. Both needed to be avenged.

"Aye, that you will. 'Tis just after noon."

Serena smiled at that. "How amazing to be traveling at a decent hour. In London I would be rising at this time."

Mr. Lamb's gaze softened as he looked at Serena. "Aye. I doubt you'll do much of that now, missy."

"So do I." She slanted a glance at Charles. "We've traveled at some odd hours, have we not?"

He managed a grin. "And stayed in strange places."

"Have you a plan?" she teased, though he heard the strain behind it.

"Only to travel on the stagecoach, which sounds strange in itself. I wonder if Samson has been brought back to London."

"By your brother, do you mean?"

"Yes. Mr. Wills did say he'd send a letter to him."

"I wish we could have done so in Brighton," she said wistfully.

"You know that we couldn't, if they'd put our names about at the inns."

"I know. But then you wouldn't have been hurt."

"Don't you worry, missy. No one'll be expecting you here. How could they?"

Charles nodded, but his eyes were alert. In spite of the weeks spent at the Lambs' with no sign of Alf or Garnett, they could still be about. He had no doubt that Garnett had paid someone at the inn handsomely to learn their destination. The chances were high he was in Guildford, waiting. Fortunately, Charles still had his pistols, and Serena was competent at loading and firing.

"I'll stay with ye until the stage comes," Mr. Lamb said unexpectedly.

"Oh, Mr. Lamb, you don't have to do that," Serena said, just as Charles spoke.

"I'd appreciate that, sir."

Serena looked at him in surprise. "Surely you don't expect Garnett and Alf to attack us there?"

"I don't know what to expect from them." He looked at her, his face grim. "You know that."

She lowered her eyes, and he suspected that she knew quite well what he meant. What had begun as a chase to capture her had unexpectedly turned into a match between him and his adversary. Garnett would see Charles dead. They both knew that.

"Don't worry, princess," he said softly, laying his hand on hers. Her eyes flashed up to him, startled, and then her fingers turned, to clutch his. "I'll keep you safe." Even if Garnett did attack them in Guildford.

Quigley, however, had no intention of taking them in Guildford. What he had instead was a plan, and an unlikely partner.

Quigley had been there several weeks, waiting. He couldn't afford to put up at the Surrey Inn, or the Crown or the White Hart, for that matter. Instead he'd had to content himself with a third-rate inn, where the food was inedible and the state of the beds dubious, to say the least. Kirk would pay for that.

He had no doubt of his ability to take both Kirk and Lady Serena, elusive though they'd proved to be, or as deadly as Kirk was, with his astonishing ability to survive nearly anything. If the gunshot in the mountain passes during the retreat to Corunna hadn't killed him, the explosion of the house in Oporto certainly should have. So should the attack in the inn's garden in Chichester. It would have, too, if Kirk hadn't fought back so strongly, and if someone hadn't come along to help him.

A few coins passed about, and he'd learned Kirk's destination. A few more, this time given more grudgingly, and he had the name of Kirk's savior. Of course he'd gone by the Lambs' farm, but there were too many people at work near what had proved to be a substantial manor house, to prevent his doing anything. Thus he had gone to Guildford, and settled down to wait.

One afternoon, long after the coach had departed for that day, Quigley wandered uninterestedly about the town, which he already knew too well. It was market day, and the streets were crowded. At first he didn't recognize the figure mincing toward him, but then he'd dived quickly into a nearby alley. What the devil was Sir Osbert Hyatt doing here? he thought.

Self-preservation had brought Quigley this far in life, and he wasn't about to let it fail him now. If Hyatt were here, it meant two things. One was that he knew that Kirk and Lady Serena would come here. The other was more deadly, as he had immediately realized in Brighton. Hyatt had decided to act on his own, and keep everything for himself.

Hyatt, wearing a waistcoat stretched to button-straining point across his substantial stomach, came near, and, lightning-quick, Quigley made his decision. "Well met, Sir Osbert," he said, stepping out before the other man.

Hyatt stumbled back a few paces, fear flickering in his eyes. *Good*, Quigley thought. Fear would put Hyatt at a disadvantage immediately. "Wh-what are you d-doing here?" Hyatt stuttered.

Quigley leaned his shoulder against the wall of the nearby building, though his seemingly relaxed pose would fool no one who looked at him closely. He was ready to spring at a moment's time. "I might ask you the same thing." The smile that spread across his face was wolfish. "I don't have to, of course. I already know."

"You d-do?"

"Of course. The same reason I am."

Hyatt studied him warily. "What, you have acquaintances here?"

Quigley laughed derisively. "Cut line. I followed you to Brighton, and then again when you found Kirk. No, you didn't know that, did you?" he went on, at Hyatt's startled look. "Then you led me to Lady Serena." He snapped his fingers. "Simple."

Hyatt nervously licked his lips. "I say. What d-do you intend to do now?"

Quigley studied the other man, his gaze assessing, critical. "I'm not quite sure. Obviously you don't trust me."

"Should I?" Hyatt said, showing some spirit for the first time since their encounter had begun. "You and Connor went off together on your own, without telling me where you were. Of course I don't trust you." He glanced around, nervous again. "Where is Connor?"

Quigley again bared his teeth in that wolfish grin. "I took care of him in Brighton."

"Took care of—oh. I see." Hyatt returned Quigley's cool, assessing look, rising a few notches in Quigley's estimation. "It seems I underestimated you, Mr. Garnett."

Quigley nodded in acknowledgement. "I believe you did."

"But don't make the mistake, sir, of underestimating me." Hyatt straightened, and for the first time Quigley saw danger in this man. "I may not be quite as—crude, for lack of a better word—as you, but I have my ways." He leaned on his stick. "Yes. I have my ways."

"Ha. A foolish dandy like you?"

Hyatt's smile was superior. "Someone planned everything. *Id est,* Garnett, I did. I see you don't know what that means," he went on. "*Id est.* I.E. It means 'that is.' I gather you didn't pay much heed to your studies at Harrow. Or was it Eton? What is that you say?" Hyatt cupped his hand behind his ear. "You didn't attend Cambridge, either? Hm. I wonder why."

Quigley's nostrils flared with insult and humiliation. Hyatt might have begun this caper, but it was he, Quigley, who had planned the remainder, and quite brilliantly, considering Kirk's interference. He had no intention of telling Hyatt that his father had bought him his colors because of the trouble he'd supposedly caused in his neighborhood. Even now, the injustice of that made his temper rise. After all, everyone had known that the squire's daughter was a flirt, and a liar to boot. Quigley had done nothing she hadn't wanted. . . .

That was past, though. Dwelling upon it would further weaken his position, especially since he suspected that Hyatt knew about it, damn his eyes. "Yes?" he said, with feigned boredom. "You were about to say?"

"Who learned that Kirk and Lady Serena were heading west, not east, in Brighton?"

Quigley burst out laughing. "And who followed you again? I'd wager you didn't know about their disguises any more than I did. And," he said, knowing this would bring him on top again, "who struck at Kirk while you slept?"

Hyatt's eyes flickered. "You let him get away."

"So I did." Quigley smiled. "Who knows how badly I

crippled him, though? Who knows how much help he'll be to Lady Serena?"

Awareness dawned in Hyatt's eyes. "Indeed. He may not be."

"It may be that we can take him."

"Here?"

"Mm. I'm not sure. Of course, they must come through Guildford. I presume you learned that the same way as I?"

"By bribery? Of course."

"Of course," Quigley agreed, and in that moment made his decision. Better the devil one knew than the one one didn't. "I believe, sir, that we can work together, if we try . . ."

Now they sat at their usual table in the tavern across from the White Hart inn, as they had each day for over a week, waiting. Quigley's patience in such matters was absolute. Catching Lady Serena was no longer his primary goal, though he did want to punish her for all she'd put him through. No, it was Kirk he wanted. Kirk, who knew too much about him. Kirk, who'd eluded him once too often. Quigley didn't get angry; he got vengeance. In Kirk's case, he wanted vengeance, indeed.

"I doubt they're coming today, either," Hyatt said wearily. "You struck too deep a blow, Garnett."

"Not deep enough, else the man would be dead."

Hyatt studied him. "What have you against Kirk?"

Quigley shook his head. He was not about to tell Hyatt of Kirk's suspicions on the Peninsula—quite accurate ones, of course—not if he wanted to keep some balance in their precarious relationship. Just now each knew something potentially damaging about the other. Quigley wished it to stay that way.

"We'll wait until the coach departs," he said, as he had every afternoon since they joined forces. His contempt for the chubby man sitting across from him, devouring a large beefsteak, had grown every day. Hyatt might have planned this little escapade, but following it through was not his strength. He wasn't quick enough, or devious enough. He was, in short, a most unsatisfactory partner. When the time came, Quigley would deal with him in short order.

He was indulging in a pleasant daydream of what he would do once he caught his two adversaries, particularly to Lady Serena, when suddenly Hyatt, tubby and dandyish though he was, straightened. "I say!" he exclaimed.

Quigley took a sip of ale from a pewter tankard. "Someone you know?"

"They're here."

The tankard hit the table with a bang. "Where?" he demanded, though he was already looking across the street. There, at last, their quarry stood. Kirk and Lady Serena. *Damn.* He had been lulled, too, just as Hyatt had. That wasn't like him. "Well, I'll be damned," he muttered.

"That giant with him—is that Lamb?"

"Yes. I saw him talking with Kirk in the taproom at Chichester."

"Well." Hyatt looked across the table at him, and both of them grinned, the same feral, dangerous grin.

"Well, indeed." Now it would begin, Quigley thought. Kirk and Lady Serena hadn't a prayer.

The stage was just pulling up at the White Hart inn when Mr. Lamb at last turned his carriage into Guildford. Passengers alighted from it, some to greet waiting people and walk away, others to drag themselves into the inn in hopes of finding a meal. The driver himself stomped about impatiently as new horses were harnessed to the coach. He had thirty miles left to London, and he needed to be there by evening.

Serena closed her eyes, blocking out the sight of both the busy High Street, though the Guildhall was topped by an enormous clock that hung over the street, the huge, rambling Tudor inn with its walls whitewashed and crossed with beams, and, most especially, the coach. She had reached the last stage of her long, strange journey, and she should have been glad. She wasn't.

She slanted a glance at Charles, sitting quietly beside her. Since the day he had told her his long, agonized story, he seemed different, more relaxed, more at ease, not only with people, but with himself. There was tension in him, though, and soon she would add to it. The thought broke her heart.

As if he felt her glance, Charles turned to her. "End of the adventure, princess."

He hadn't called her that for a very long time. She forced a smile. "Thank heavens. No more of your plans."

"They worked. You must admit that."

"Yes, yes, so you keep reminding me." All they'd experienced seemed almost funny in retrospect, except that it never had been. Except that at any time she had feared being caught by Garnett again and brought to some distant building and . . .

"Princess." Charles's voice was gentle as he touched her arm. "It all worked out. We're here."

"Yes," she said, but her voice was shaky.

"And safe."

"Yes."

The look he gave her was troubled, and his arm shifted against hers. She wondered if, had they been alone, he would have put it around her. She wondered if she would nestle against him, feeling sheltered and safe from the world.

Mr. Lamb was looking at them. "You've had some adventures, haven't ye?"

Serena blocked out the images that had assailed her in the last few moments, of Garnett and what he could do to her, of Charles and what she wished he would do. "Yes, Mr. Lamb," she said mechanically.

"We have," Charles agreed. "I'm just as glad they're over."

"Oh, aye. I don't blame you for that. You were lucky to survive such things." He pulled up his cart before the White Hart, just in front of the coach. "I'll wait to see you safely off."

"Thank you, sir." Charles jumped off and held his hand up to Serena. "Well?"

"Thank you." Her legs were shaky as she rose and let him help her descend. Surely the danger was behind her, and yet she was so frightened. Surely Garnett and Alf weren't here.

"Shall we find out how long we have?" Charles asked, taking her arm.

"Yes." They strolled together toward the driver, who told them morosely that they still had nearly a quarter hour before the coach left. Counting them and their two inside tickets, the coach was full. Where they were going to sit was a problem.

"We'll manage," Charles said, and, without asking, pulled Serena away. "Let's walk a bit."

Something in his tone put Serena instantly on guard. "Do you think we should? If Alf and Hyatt are here, they might accost us—"

"Not on the High Street," he said, though she noted he was careful to steer clear of any alleys.

If anything, her tension increased. "It does seem like a quaint town. If we had time—"

"Cut line." His voice was a growl. "We're not here to see the sights, and well you know it."

"Well?" she said coolly, suddenly annoyed. "Why are we walking? Surely not just to take the air before we board the coach."

"No." He stopped and looked down at her. His hands were clenched and his knuckles were white. Poor man, he must dread the hours they would spend in the coach to London. "I need to know, Serena, once and for all. What do you have against marrying me?"

"Oh!" She huffed her breath out in exasperation. "I thought we'd settled that at the Lambs'."

"No," he said seriously. "Not for me. Not because you've been compromised," he went quickly on. "You know that. And not because of Luz."

"Yes, because of Luz."

"So you told me—a few weeks ago?"

"It seems like years," she said, and for a moment they smiled, in perfect amity with each other. "It is Luz, of course."

"You told me long ago," he pressed on, "that you were never going to marry. You'd seen too many unhappy marriages."

She looked down at her gloves and twisted one finger back and forth. "So I have," she said in a low voice. "Love matches, arranged marriages, *mariages de convenance*. Marriage of a person of Quality to a Cit, exchanging a title for money, female or male." She stopped and looked up at him, scowling, and pulled away. "Charles, you've seen such things yourself."

"Marriage can't be easy. Even love matches must be difficult at times."

She sighed. "I suppose they are. Sometimes love matches are really only infatuation, or passion."

"Passion?" he said, amused, as they walked on. "Since when have you learned anything of passion?"

Her gaze was unflinching. "Since you kissed me."

"Good God!"

"Exactly."

"Serena, are you saying that's all we have?"

This time she was the one to stop. "Can you honestly say you love me?"

"I . . ." he began, and paused, just a little too long.

She walked on, feeling as though her heart were breaking. No. Knowing it was. "You love Luz."

"I'm not sure."

"No?"

"No. That may have been infatuation."

"Oh, really? Think, Charles. What we've been through together has been intense. Any feelings we have must come from that."

"Are you saying you have feelings for me?"

"Do you have feelings for me?"

"There's something," he said cautiously. "Serena." He caught her arm. "If we feel the same in London—"

"Assuming I've not been sent to the country."

"May I call on you?"

She, too, paused a bit before answering. "No."

"Why not?" he demanded.

To her chagrin, tears filled her eyes and she turned back to him. "I'd fail, Charles," she said miserably. "You've been so good to me, and I'd fail."

"Serena—"

"Let me go, Charles. Please. Let me go."

"Not bother you anymore, do you mean?"

"Yes, that, but not that alone. Let me go."

She saw his eyes widen, saw the astonishment dawning there. "By yourself, do you mean? No."

"Alf and Garnett are long gone—"

"Are they?"

"They must be. I'll be safer on the stage with other people around. Who'd think to look for me there?"

Uneasy, Charles shifted from foot to foot. Those two villains could be waiting for her in London. They could be at any of the coaching inns along the way. They could even be here, in hiding. His neck prickled at the thought. "No."

"Yes."

Turning away from the street so that no one would see what he was doing, he pulled out one pistol and tucked it into her reticule.

"Charles," she said in astonishment, and handed it back to him, butt first. "No."

"Yes," he said, and thrust it at her again. "At least take that."

"You will let me go alone?"

"No!" he exclaimed, as they turned and walked back toward the coach. "Not until I leave you at your father's house."

She turned to him, her eyes kindling with anger and some other emotion he could not name. "I don't want you." Each word was bit off. "I don't need you. You were convenient."

"Convenient!"

"Convenient," she repeated. "You were a means to an end. I don't need you any more, Mr. Kirk. You may return to your life, whatever that is, and let me be."

Anger rose in him, as it never had before. "Are you saying you were using me?"

"Of course I was." Her voice was cool. "I'd have done anything to keep you with me, so I'd be safe." She paused. "I'd have slept with you, had I needed to."

"By God, Serena!"

"Now do you understand?"

"You're a whore," he said flatly.

"Maybe I am," she said, though she flinched.

He swung away from her, breathing hard, so angry that he wanted to hit someone. More hurt than he'd ever been in his life. "Very well, then," he said, wanting to hurt her back. "Go on to London. Use some other man and leave me be."

"I intend to, sir," she said, and climbed aboard the waiting stage, its bulk between them and the street.

Charles sketched her an ironic bow as the coach's door closed, before stepping back into the shadows of the coaching inn's arch. The driver climbed heavily onto the box and took up the reins. With a jolt, the coach drove off. Serena was gone, and he'd never felt so alone in his life.

Eventually, ignoring the traffic of a busy market town, ignoring the post chaise that swept out of the inn behind him, Charles trudged toward Mr. Lamb's carriage. "You let her go, man?" Mr. Lamb said incredulously.

"Yes." He wondered if he sounded as weary as he felt. "I had to."

"But why, sir? Why?"

"Because she didn't want me."

"Didn't want—sir, if I've ever seen a woman in love, that is one."

"Infatuation, Mr. Lamb." His anger rose again at the thought of what she'd revealed to him. He was convenient. She would have used her body if she had to. He took a deep breath. "As she said, we've been together in intense conditions, and—"

Mr. Lamb snorted. "Nonsense. If you could have seen her when you were sick, fighting for your life."

"Oh?" Charles said without interest. She would have slept with him. He felt soiled.

"Aye, lad. Talking to you, sponging you down—no missishness in her, sir! Forcing you to take water or broth. No, man, she fought for ye, and the only reason I can think for that is that she loves ye."

"No." Charles shook his head. "She was helping me, the way I helped her."

"She said she loved you," Mr. Lamb said quietly.

Charles glanced sharply up. "When?"

"Many times, Major. Told you not to give up because she loved ye, and she couldn't imagine life without ye."

"The devil she did!" he exclaimed, and a bolt of energy shot through him. "Then why did she make me stay behind?"

Mr. Lamb shrugged. "I don't know, lad. What did ye say to her?"

"To make her do it? I don't know." *I called her Luz while I kissed her. When I wanted her, not Luz, and needed her and loved her,* he thought, and then forced his mind to that last conversation. No, he hadn't said anything, until she'd started insulting him, started telling him all the reasons why marriage between them was impossible. Until she'd said . . . "Bedamned!"

"Major?"

"She said she'd fail."

"That your marriage would fail?"

"No. That she'd fail. Bedamned, Mr. Lamb, she was protecting me."

He frowned. "You?"

"From herself. But why?" he asked in bewilderment. "I don't quite understand that."

"She loves ye," Mr. Lamb said, "and—what is it, Major?"

Charles's eyes were fixed on the curricle that had just driven past them on the other side of Mr. Lamb's cart. "I could swear that was Hyatt in that curricle."

"Who?"

"Sir Osbert Hyatt." What was he doing in Guildford? What, for that matter, had he been doing in Brighton?

Suddenly he straightened, wishing he hadn't ignored his soldier's sense of danger. "Hyatt's in it."

Mr. Lamb's frown deepened. "In what, Major?"

"He has something to do with Serena's abduction. I don't know how, but he's in it. He was at Brighton," he explained as he looked about distractedly for a horse. "I thought nothing of that at the time, but he was heading toward the coaching inn. And there was a third man there the day we left. Bedamned. I need a horse."

"Take Nonnie," Mr. Lamb offered immediately, already reaching to undo the traces of the cart.

"No. No offense, sir, but Nonnie's not as fast as I'd like. No, I have just enough money to take a mount here."

"Then go." Mr. Lamb urged him toward the White Hart. "Lady Serena is in danger."

"Yes. Yes." He thrust out his hand. "Thank you for all you've done for us, sir. If I can ever do anything for you—"

"Enough of that, man! There's no time. Go."

"Yes," Charles said, and, very frightened, strode toward the inn. Why had he ever let Serena travel to London, alone and undefended? Bloody fool, he castigated himself, breaking into a run across the inn yard. For if she couldn't imagine a world without him in it, he couldn't imagine one without her.

FOURTEEN

It was a long, tiring journey to London. Serena was accustomed to traveling such a distance in a well-sprung coach, with padded seats and comfortable, overstuffed squabs. There was none of that on this coach. Instead, there were people. She had been unfortunate enough to have the center seat, and so was squashed and jostled. Sometimes she felt as if the other passengers might huddle together, forcing her to fall to the floor. To her one side was a pinch-faced woman who was knitting some indistinguishable object, and who glared at Serena if she so much as brushed against her. On her other side was a stout sleeping man whose stentorian snores filled the coach, annoying everyone. Serena was grateful that he tended to lean against the side of the coach, rather than on her shoulder.

Across from her was a minister sitting with a cowed-looking girl who appeared to be his daughter, exhorting her against various sins such as looking at any male too long, or not wearing a fichu around her neck to cover the scandalously low-cut gowns that fashion dictated. As he went on about that last for so long that Serena began to wonder if he'd ever seen such gowns, or only wished he had, the man sitting next to the girl slanted him a sardonic glance. His hair was dark, and so were his eyes; his clothes were well made, if worn. He smiled at her, silently asking her to share the joke with him, and there was such familiarity in that glance that Serena looked quickly away. She had had quite enough of being mauled and chased and threatened by men. If one more bothered her in such a way, she just might do him bodily injury.

In spite of the discomforts of the coach, though, she only descended from it once or twice, and that only when it was absolutely necessary. Her stomach felt queasy when she thought of what she had done to Charles today. Though she knew it was for the best, still she bitterly regretted having to hurt him. She loved him, she thought despairingly, enough to give him up.

There was also one other good, practical reason for not going outside. They were traveling on the Brighton road now, where Alf and Garnett had spread her description. No matter how long ago that had been, and how many people must have passed through the inns since then, some people were sharp-eyed. Some people had good memories. She had no wish to be caught, and held, by Garnett again.

The stage driver held to the road as a post chaise passed him, though a curricle overtook them so closely that the coach was forced onto the muddy verge. It took quite some time for the horses, with some of the passengers pushing from the back, to pull the coach back onto the road, but eventually, with the driver cursing the air blue, they returned to the road and drove on as quickly as the tired horses could.

The traffic increased as the coach neared London. Though Serena was facing backwards, the comments and talk of the other passengers were enough to tell her how close they were to their ultimate destination. London. She would face a world which had once hailed her as an Incomparable, and now would scorn her. She would face some unknown fate. Most of all, perhaps most frightening of all, was that she would have to face her father.

The coach turned at Hyde Park Corner onto Piccadilly. Serena looked longingly at Berkeley Street as they passed it, but of course she couldn't expect the coach to stop just for her. Instead, she looked hungrily at familiar landmarks: Green Park, Hatchard's, Saint James. Her world, or it had been. She didn't know if it ever would be again.

The guard on the back of the coach blew his yard of tin, the resounding blast signaling in no uncertain terms that the coach from Guildford had arrived. With a flourish it came to a jolting stop. The snoring man beside her came instantly awake; the pinch-faced woman put her knitting away in a capacious bag; the minister lectured his daughter one last time about the evils of London; and the youngish-looking man with the dissolute face and the worn beaver hat, looking at Serena in inquiry, invited her to share whatever conveyance he could find. She raised her head, ignoring them all as best she could. She was an earl's daughter, after all, and could rightfully call herself "lady," though she doubted anyone on this worn coach would believe her. She was the Incomparable until someone said otherwise, and she had, by God, survived experiences that would leave any Bond Street beau, including, she suspected, the bounder across from her, shaking in his boots. She was far stronger than she had ever known, and she could face anything. She had courage enough to deal with whatever lay ahead.

Stiff and aching in every muscle, Serena alighted from the coach in the inn yard of the Belle Sauvage in Ludgate, miles away in both distance and atmosphere from Berkeley Square. The sun was beginning to set, turning the whitewashed walls of the inn to a rosy pink. Though it likely dated from the same time period as the one in Guildford, it was much larger. Surely there were hacks to be found. "Lady Serena?" someone called, and she whipped her head around in astonishment, not best pleased that someone was bandying her identity about in such a place. She searched the inn yard and saw, to her surprise, the overdressed little figure of Sir Osbert Hyatt. "I thought it was you," he said, jumping down from his curricle and stepping with great care across the cobblestones toward her. "What, were you in that stagecoach?"

"What do you do here, in such a place?" she countered. "Thank you." This to the young man who had ridden atop the vehicle and now tossed down her bandbox. "I cannot imagine you in such a place."

"Business," he said vaguely, and she realized that he must have just come from the City. Instantly she understood. He was a fortune hunter, of course, prepared to trade his title for a good bit of gold, as she had described so scathingly to Charles—when? Only this afternoon, and yet it seemed like days ago.

"But what do you do here, arriving on a common stage?" he went on.

" 'Tis a long story," she said wearily.

"You have been missed, you know."

Serena nodded. "I'd imagine so."

"Lady Serena." His voice had lowered. "Some people believe you will be gone for some seven or eight months."

Serena stared at him in blank incomprehension, and then suddenly took his meaning. "Oh, nonsense!" she exclaimed sharply. "I most certainly am not with child."

"I didn't mean to imply you were, but—"

"Do you see any hacks here?" she interrupted him, tired of such inconsequence. And to think he had once proposed to her.

"Pray, don't be foolish. Let me take you up in my curricle," he said, gesturing across the inn yard. It looked well-sprung and comfortable, everything the stage had not been. It was also vaguely familiar, though she had no memory of having seen it before, and very, very tempting. " 'Tis not very distant, and you look burnt to the socket."

She *was* tired, she thought, to her very bones, to her soul. "Thank you, Sir Osbert. I believe I will."

The curricle's squabs felt luxuriously soft against Serena's back as they turned toward Mayfair. "What were you doing in the City?" she asked idly, and then clamped her hand over her mouth. "Excuse me. That was terribly impertinent of me."

He gave her a tight little smile, and she couldn't help comparing his teeth, some of them brown and crooked, to Charles's strong, white ones. "Why, to meet you, of course."

"Oh, of course," she said, with a tired attempt at banter.

"I am totally serious." He risked taking his eyes from the heavy traffic. "You see, I am abducting you."

"Oh, for heaven's sake!" she exclaimed, suddenly awake and aware. "This is all becoming rather tiresome. Do you know what I've gone through to escape being caught? And now it happens in London. London, of all places!" She glared at him. "So what is it *you* want?"

He stared at her, astonished. "You're supposed to b-be afraid!"

Serena had crossed her arms over her chest. "Well, I'm not," she said, disgruntled. "You odious little toad."

"You'll p-pay for that," he threatened, though there was little force in his voice.

"Oh, really? Who will make me do so? You?"

"Quigley Garnett."

Instantly her irritation turned to icy fear. Quigley

Garnett. Of course. It all fell into place now. "He hired you to get revenge against Mr. Kirk, didn't he?"

"Lud, no! I hired him."

"Then you made a mistake, sir." Her face was stony, but her hands gripped her reticule. There was something hard and bulky in there. Charles's pistol. "You may think you are in charge, but depend upon it. He has the upper hand."

"No, he hasn't. I won't let him," Hyatt said sulkily.

"It's no matter of what you'll allow, sir." She had shifted the reticule in her lap now, so that it faced upward. "He has quite taken any power you may have from you. Pray don't sulk, sir," she went on. "It is terribly unmanly of you. So." She settled back, gazing at him. *Careful, careful. Untie the strings of the reticule and don't let him see what you're doing.* "What was your plan?"

He turned down a street she hardly recognized, on the fringes of Mayfair. "The same as it is now. I intended for you to be compromised." The smile he gave her had regained some of its assurance. "You were to have disappeared. No one would have known where. Meeting up with Kirk as you did, and traveling together simply ruined your reputation further."

"Why in the world would you want that?" she asked, mystified. She had pulled the reticule open, and still he had not noticed. *Careful, careful.*

"Think, my dear. Who will marry you with so damaged a history? No one." He stroked a finger down her hand, and she stiffened, frightened that he would discover what she was doing. "Except me."

She stared at him for a moment and then started laughing, genuine, hearty laughter. "Oh, you're out of all reason foolish, if you think I'll marry you! 'Tis for the money, I presume."

"What choice do you have?" He gave her a superior smile. "Someone has to redeem you."

She laughed again. "Not you. So tell me, sir, where are you taking me?" She was reaching inside the reticule now, and her hand had closed over the barrel of the pistol.

He shot her a disgruntled look. "You'll change your mind by the time I'm done with you."

"Oh, really. So where are you taking me? Excuse me," she added, feigning a sneeze into the handkerchief she'd brought out. Now her hand was on the butt of the pistol.

"To a little place I keep to house my mistresses."

"No, you're not. Oh, dear. I'm going to sneeze again." There. She had it. "Take me to Harlow House instead."

His head whipped around. "What the devil? Harlow House?"

"Yes." The pistol was out now, in her lap, and still he had not noticed.

"No! In this, my dear, you really have no choice."

"But I do," she said, and aimed the pistol, concealed in her skirts so that no one else could see, at him.

Charles reached London after what seemed to him to be the longest journey of his life, spent worrying about Serena and cursing most of his mounts. He had little money, and that had to last until London, so that he could spare only a coin or two for each one. Unfortunately, such a small amount of money gained him only inferior mounts. The first was a plodding nag, who simply would not go fast, not if Charles dug in his heels, not if the reins were slapped smartly on his back. He was relieved to exchange him, at long last, at the George Inn in the town of Cobham. Yes, the stage to London had already come in, the groom who was stabling a new horse for him said, though that had been a considerable time ago. Yes, there had been a man matching Hyatt's description driving what the groom enthusiastically described as a bang-up rig, before that. Of Alf and Garnett, however, there had been no sign. Somehow Charles found that more ominous than their being seen would have been.

His second mount was far more to Charles's taste, quick and responsive; that he was skittish was no problem. Charles knew well how to control a horse. Unfortunately, though, this mount, too, proved to be a disappointment, pulling up lame just outside a small village. Fortunately, there was an inn there. The innkeeper's son was only too happy to drive Charles to the next coaching inn—for a fee, of course. "We see that with that one all the time," he said as he drove the rickety cart, so cheerfully that Charles was instantly suspicious. Of course, the two inns were in collusion with each other, he thought, though he'd never be able to prove it.

The grooms at the third inn seemed pleased, too, even though he glowered at them, and tossed them another few precious coins. And, yes, the stage to London had come through quite a time back, though no one could remember a curricle such as he described, or a man such as he described. It was all discouraging and dispiriting, and terrifying. God knew what Serena, his dear love, might be feeling right now.

And so it went that entire nightmarish afternoon, with one inadequate horse exchanged for another, while the stage seemed impossibly far ahead, and London appeared to be receding from him, not growing closer. Serena was there by now. Alone and unprotected, not expecting trouble, she was likely to be in the hands of those villains. The thought made him grit his teeth, and turned his insides to water.

At the inn in Wandsworth, however, Charles had his

first piece of luck. Glumly expecting to mount yet another nag, he didn't so much as glance at the groom who ran to hold the horse's head. "I need a fast mount," he said, gambling the remainder of his money on the slim chance that he would reach London in time. "And has the London stage from Guildford come through yet?"

"Not half an hour since, Major Kirk," the groom said.

Charles whirled around. For the life of him, he couldn't place the man, though his face seemed familiar. Then it came to him. "Private Reardon," he said, striding forward with hand outstretched. "What are you doing here?"

"I can't shake your hand, Major. 'Twouldn't be right."

"Of course it would. We're not in the army now. How did you get out—oh." He gazed at the private's left arm, with its empty sleeve tacked up to his elbow. "I didn't know," he said quietly.

"Same arm as you, Major," Reardon said cheerfully, as he moved to unsaddle the horse, more competently than Charles would have expected. "Thought you knew about it."

"Corunna?" he asked.

"Sahagun. Heard I was fortunate to miss the retreat."

"Yes," Charles said, ashamed that he hadn't known that a man from one of his battalions had been so seriously wounded, when he had always made it a point to learn all that happened to his men. That cursed forced march over the mountain passes to Corunna, when he, and everyone else, had been concerned only with his own survival. "I'm sorry."

"Oh, don't be, Major. My brother owns the inn and he found work for me, once I was fit. And I've always been good with horses." He frowned. "But what are you doing with this bonesetter? Where's Samson?"

" 'Tis a long story, Reardon. Can you help me?"

"That I can, Major. I can give you that prime bit o' blood over there."

Charles glanced at the stall Reardon had indicated, and raised his eyebrows in surprise. The horse Reardon was leading out was as fine as any Charles had ever seen, with a long neck, large eyes, and a good-sized chest. "I can't afford a prime goer like that," he protested.

"M'brother won't mind." Reardon was competently putting the saddle on the horse's back. "Not for you, Major."

"But—"

"I'll stand bail for you. Proper proud of anyone who served in the army, sir, my brother is."

Charles let out his breath and decided not to protest further. It would do no good. Besides, he thought, checking the fit of the girth, he did need a good mount if he were to catch up to the stagecoach. "Did you say the stage came through here a half-hour ago?" he said, straightening in surprise.

"Aye, and proper mad the driver was." Reardon grinned. "Cursing more than any trooper I've ever heard."

"What held them up?"

"They had an accident some miles back. Not a bad one," he said when Charles took an involuntary step forward. "No one hurt, more shaken."

"What happened?"

"You know that bend past Kingston? Some fool of a driver in a curricle came too close, forced them off the road."

"Good God!"

"Aye. Not off all the way, mind, just onto the verge."

"Then what held them up?"

He grinned. "Mud."

"Mud?"

"Aye. They got stuck in mud. Took all the horses and most of the men to get it on the road again."

Charles closed his eyes in thanksgiving. Serena was still unharmed, and the stage had been delayed enough for him to catch it. "Did the curricle come by here?" he asked suddenly.

"Maybe, from what the driver said. A flashy thing, wheels picked out in yellow, and a flash horse. Go in him, but no stamina."

It sounded like Hyatt's rig. The thought chilled him. If he'd somehow pushed the stage off the road deliberately, he'd got ahead of it. *Damn.* Serena was unaware of his possible involvement in the plot against her.

It spurred him to action. Without further thought he mounted the horse and took up the reins. "I'm grateful to you, Reardon. I'll see he's returned to you safely."

"Happy to do it for you, Major. You should be able to catch the stage."

"How do you know—"

"The look on your face. They have more horses, but you have less weight. You'll do it."

Charles nodded his head. "Thank you," he said again, and, wheeling the horse about, set out from the inn yard. The horse had a nice, even gait, and it seemed so ready to shake out its fidgets that all Charles needed to do was give it its head. Mayhap he would catch the stage. He had better. If he didn't, God help Serena.

Hyatt looked at the pistol incredulously. "What the devil—"

" 'Tis a pistol, Sir Osbert."

"I know what it is. You can't use that."

"Oh, but I can. It is loaded, and, I assure you, I am a

fine shot. Hm." She studied Hyatt critically. "Of course, this close I could hardly miss."

"Now, now, Lady Serena, there's no need for violence—"

"Violence!" Her voice shook so much with anger that she had to force herself to be calm. She didn't dare lose control of herself, or he would have the advantage again. "I was manhandled at your orders. I was abducted when I was going about my own business, at your orders. I was held captive in a hut four days, tied down—did I tell you that Alf struck me once? Oh, dear, yes, I do believe violence may indeed be necessary." She studied Hyatt. "Will Alf and Garnett be awaiting us?"

"Alf? Oh, Connor. No. He's gone."

"Gone?" Serena asked, and then shivered as the implications of that struck her. "Where?"

"Garnett wouldn't say."

Garnett. Serena would have closed her eyes, except for her need to watch Hyatt carefully. For all of Alf's strength, Garnett was by far the more dangerous of the two. She had no doubt that he'd dealt with Alf most efficiently. She had no doubt he would do so with her, if he had to.

"Is Garnett at the house you were taking me to?"

"No." Hyatt smiled for the first time since Serena had brandished the pistol. "At Harlow House."

Charles's luck failed him again in London. The horse, so reliable on the open road, began to show a tendency to shy amid traffic that only grew worse as they neared town. Though he'd galloped out his energy, now he showed more and to share, sidestepping, tossing up his head, and balking at the least provocation. Only Charles's superb horsemanship kept him in check, though his arms ached with the effort. Finally, when the horse had balked for the third time, this time showing no indication that he would move, Charles conceded defeat. To the angry shouts of the drivers and riders behind him, he swung off the horse, took hold of the bridle, and tugged him to the side.

After he had rubbed the horse's nose for a moment or two and spoken softly to him, the horse consented to move another few yards. Gritting his teeth against frustration, against the pain, which seemed to have traveled up through his neck and into the back of his skull, Charles spent several more precious moments soothing him again. The coach had surely reached its destination by now, which meant that Serena could be facing any number of things. He had to reach her, if only he could get this damned nag to move. If only he could . . .

Find a place to stable him. He blew out his breath in relief. There, a few yards away, was an inn. He wasn't known there, and he had no money, but his calling card should suffice. Putting one last burst of energy into it, he coaxed the horse to the inn.

Inside the gate the horse, away from the busy traffic, stepped up his pace. *Of course,* Charles thought, before turning to the groom who ran forward. "Sir?"

"I need him stabled."

"Yes, sir. Talk to the innkeeper, and—"

"I haven't time," he said, thrusting out his calling card.

The groom stared at it blankly, making Charles smile to himself. Here was someone who didn't recognize him as a military man. "But—"

"Send to my brother. He'll stand bail for it."

"But, sir," the groom protested, as Charles ran toward the gate.

"Viscount Sherbourne," he called back. He'd forgotten that particular detail. "Sherbourne House."

"But—"

"He'll stand bail for it," he repeated, and was out onto the street again.

So little time, so little time, and so far yet to go. He'd never reach Ludgate on foot, no matter how fast he ran. *Fool,* he castigated himself, not for the first time. If he'd just taken the time, precious though it had been, to cash in the ticket for the stage, he would have been able to afford better mounts. Now he didn't think he could afford even to hire a hack. His lack of foresight, unusual in a man who had once been good at strategy, had, because of his emotions, tripped him up. It might prove to have dangerous consequences, indeed.

Short of breath, he slowed his pace, though he continued on. He was a soldier, he told himself. He had survived that hellish march over the mountains in Spain; he could keep on here. There was a chance he'd either find Serena at the inn, or learn that she'd got safe away in a hack. There was a better chance she hadn't.

Going in the opposite direction, a vehicle caught Charles's attention. A curricle, its wheels picked out in yellow, pulled by a showy, but lathered, chestnut. *Good God!* Charles pulled up. Sir Osbert Hyatt. And, sitting next to him was Serena.

Charles turned around immediately. There wasn't much he could do against a man in a vehicle, who could always drive away from him. Nor could he always see it, though the heavy traffic helped him keep close behind. At least he had his pistols, he thought, patting his pockets, and then frowned. There was only one— *oh, yes.* He'd given one to Serena in Guildford. Fortunately, both had forgotten she had it; with any luck she had remembered she had it by now. The remaining pistol held two shots. Luck might be turning for them at last.

The curricle turned off Piccadilly and into Mayfair,

where there were fewer carriages and carts, and still he had to keep behind. If it were easier for him to see the curricle, he was more visible, too, especially since he had no idea where it was going. For a moment it slowed, and then it picked up its pace, making him frown in bewilderment. It turned down Shepherd Market, made a sharp turn away, and then doubled back onto Hertford Street, making his frown deepen. Finally it turned, yet again, onto Curzon Street. Baffling though it might be, Charles suddenly knew Hyatt's destination. Harlow House. *What the devil?*

FIFTEEN

"Do you expect Garnett will be there now?" Serena asked, far more rattled than she let show.

"I don't know." The strain of driving with a pistol trained on him was beginning to show on Hyatt. "He was to stop at his rooms first to make himself more presentable. Then, I believe, he was to send a ransom note."

"Ransom!" Serena exclaimed as Hyatt stopped the curricle before Harlow House. "Oh, my poor father. He must be terribly worried."

"I doubt it," a voice said coolly. Serena looked down as Garnett stepped out from the shadows of the wall surrounding Harlow House. "The urchin I sent with the note returned with one to the effect that the earl would never pay such a thing."

"Oh, God," Serena said.

"Precisely." Garnett stepped toward the carriage, his own pistol trained on Serena. "Hello, my dear. You've led me a merry dance. I'll have your pistol now, please."

For one mutinous moment, Serena considered refusing. Garnett's pistol was steady on her, though. She remembered too well how dangerous he could be. "Oh, very well," she said, disgruntled and tired, and handed down the pistol. He pocketed it, grinning. "But you'll not get what you want."

"No? We shall see. Hyatt, help her down. Perhaps you can do something right. But then, never send a—"

"Toad?" Serena supplied, even though Hyatt, now on the pavement, held her wrists firmly behind her. She wanted to call out to the coachman of a carriage passing by, who was looking at them curiously, but she didn't dare. That she would be the *on-dit* at *ton* affairs tonight was the least of her worries.

"I congratulate you, Lady Serena. An apt choice of words. Never send a toad to do a man's job. I do believe, however, Hyatt, that you can still serve some purpose here." He eyed them both speculatively. "Of course. You have just returned from Brighton and wish to offer your concern to the earl. All the more convincing, as it won't be totally false."

"And then?" Hyatt said, eyeing Garnett's pistol warily.

"Why, then, you offer for her hand again to save her damaged reputation."

"My father won't agree," Serena said.

"With a pistol aimed at you? I believe he will." He prodded her in the back with it, and she stumbled forward. "Do be careful, my dear. We wouldn't want you to fall, would we?"

She must keep a cool head, she thought, and turned. "I fail to see how you will profit by this."

He smirked at her. "You will see, my dear. You will see. Now. We'll wait until Hyatt is received into the house. Ah. There. Into the drive with you, my lady. I believe we shall give him the time to make his offer. Yes. And then . . ."

She twisted her head to look at him. "I do believe you're making this up as you go along," she said, almost accusingly.

"Why, how very perceptive of you, Lady Serena. I do believe I underestimated you."

"I do believe you have." Serena's lips were set. Was there any escape from this? she wondered frantically. Garnett had two pistols, his own and Charles's, and even she knew, from a quick glance, that Charles's was superior. On the other hand, it was tucked into his pocket, and his left-hand one at that. Maybe . . .

"My lady?" someone said, sounding surprised, and she looked up to see the head groom. "Are you truly back?"

"Yes, Perry." She was appalled to hear her voice shake. "But—"

"Do stay back," Garnett said urbanely. "I have a pistol, you see."

Perry took an involuntary step back. "I'll just get help, then—"

"No!" Serena exclaimed. "He's dangerous. There's no telling what he'll do."

"Ah, now you understand," Garnett said. "Upstairs, now. That's it. Use the knocker. Good."

The door opened before Serena could even raise her hand, and Fletcher, the butler, stood in the doorway. "Lady Serena! We saw through the window—"

"Where is my father?" she interrupted him.

"In the library, my lady. With"—his nostrils pinched—"Sir Osbert."

"Good. The library, Serena?" Garnett said, prodding her back again.

"Just one thing." Again she twisted her head to look at him. "Charles told me about what he thinks happened in Oporto. Is he correct?"

Garnett laughed, loud and long. "Let me just say that he may not be wrong."

Anger filled her, healing, energizing. "If a Mr. Kirk calls, admit him," she called back to Fletcher.

"Damn you," Garnett hissed, and pushed the pistol fiercely against her again. "You'll pay for that."

She would have closed her eyes, had she not needed to be alert. She had to try something. "Yes."

"The library, now. No more delays."

"Yes."

"Tell your butler to admit us."

"Do so, please," she said, as Fletcher hesitated.

"But do not announce us," Garnett told him.

Fletcher looked from her to Garnett. "My lady?"

"Do so, Fletcher," she repeated. At that moment, Serena gave up. So this was where it ended. She was so tired. She had been running so long, had been frightened for so long. She knew Charles had seen her with Hyatt, but he was on foot. He would never be in time to help her. The long chase was over.

"Very well, my lady," Fletcher said after a long moment and, after knocking on the library door, after receiving the earl's permission to enter, opened the door.

Charles pounded along the cobbled pavement, along dark alleys, through lanes the *ton* rarely frequented. The curricle might have been ahead of him, but he knew the lay of the land. This was his territory. He'd mapped it thoroughly as a boy. It might appear twisting and tortuous to one who didn't know it as he did. Because of this route he would be close behind the curricle when it reached Harlow House, or perhaps even with it.

He was out of breath when he at last burst out onto Charles Street, just one house down from the Harlow mansion. The curricle was nowhere in sight, which meant that Serena and Hyatt had already reached their destination. The question now was, how long ago?

Speed was still important, but so, now, was stamina. Charles forced himself to slow to a walk to regain the strength he would need, should there be a confrontation of some kind. He had little doubt there would be.

Several grooms were staring at the façade of Harlow House when Charles turned in at the drive. The curricle was already there, standing untended. "You, there," he called to one of the grooms. "Has Lady Serena arrived?"

The groom nearest to the front door stepped forward. "Yes, sir, but—"

He strode toward the house. "Good."

"But, sir, you can't go in there—"

"Major Kirk," he called curtly over his shoulder, and then stopped. "Was she alone?"

"No, sir, there were two men with her." He cleared his throat. "One had a pistol."

"A small man, rather fat?"

"No, sir. A tall, darkish man."

"Thank you," he said, and ran toward the stairs of the house. *Garnett.* It had to be, he thought, holding back the curses that came to his lips. He would have to proceed very carefully.

The massive front door opened even before he had a chance to lift the knocker. "Mr. Kirk?" said the man who stood before him.

"Yes," Charles said, startled.

"Lady Serena said to admit you."

"Where are they?"

"This way, sir. One of them was holding a gun on her."

Garnett. Again he bit back an oath. "Was she all right?"

"She looked so, sir. Frightened, I believe."

"As well she might be."

"If I may ask, what is going on, sir?"

Charles shook his head. "It would take too long to explain just now." He stopped behind the butler, near a paneled door set into an embrasure. "Is that where they are?" he asked, instinctively lowering his voice.

"Yes, sir." The butler nodded, his own voice hushed. "The library."

"What would you suggest? No." He straightened. "Is there another way in?"

"Yes, sir, through the salon."

"Then let's go that way."

"Very good, sir," the butler said, new respect in his voice, and led him through another room farther down the hall.

Charles moved quietly across to the door that connected the salon to the library. "Are the hinges kept oiled?"

"Of course they are, sir!" the butler whispered reprovingly.

"Then the door should open quietly."

He hesitated. "It does have one peculiarity, sir."

"Which is?"

"It needs to be pulled this way first before the knob will turn. It also opens this way."

Charles nodded. It was the best he could hope for, all things considered. "Thank you. You'd best stay back when I open the door."

"Yes, sir. Good luck, sir."

Charles nodded again, and reached for the knob. It turned silently under his hand, and the door opened inward with nary a creak. Taking a deep breath, he stepped into the library.

"And so, you see, my lord," Garnett was saying pleasantly to the earl, who was staring at him in disbelief and horror as Charles slipped within, "it truly is in your best interest to do as I ask."

"It is not," the earl proclaimed, and his eyes shifted toward Charles. Immediately Charles put his finger to his lips, and then surveyed the room, again learning the lay of the land. Hyatt, he saw to his relief, stood by the other door, staring at the earl. With any luck he would not be a factor in whatever was about to happen. Across the room from him, apparently caught by surprise by the unexpected turn of events in his life, sat the earl, an opened book lying face down and unheeded on the floor beside him. He shouldn't be a factor, either. At least, Charles hoped not.

And then there was Garnett, the deadliest of them all. He stood nearer, his pistol drawn and trained at Serena. Charles went cold at the sight, and at her stance, limp, slumped. *Ah, Serena,* he thought, forgetting for the moment that he didn't dare indulge in sympathy. She'd lost the will to fight. She wouldn't be a factor, either, and for the life of him he didn't know if that was good or bad. He studied the room some more, and then went cold. Garnett's arm was about Serena's waist, and his pistol was aimed at her side. *Dear God.*

Stop it, he admonished himself. *You're a soldier. Act like one.* To his left was a wall of bookcases. It covered his movements for a moment, before he had to leave its protection. He managed to move halfway across it, and then trouble struck.

"Garnett!" Hyatt cried, and Garnett, distracted, looked at him. Only for a moment, though, because of Hyatt's shaking hand, pointing toward Charles. "It's Kirk!"

As quickly as that, Garnett whirled, with Serena suddenly grasped to his waist, and his pistol at her throat. "Well, well," he said mockingly. "Kirk. I was wondering when you'd show your face."

"Major Kirk, Father," Serena said, to Charles's surprise. "I told you about him."

"Be quiet." Garnett pressed the pistol harder against Serena's throat. "Well, Kirk. I don't believe you'll elude me this time."

"He did kill Luz," Serena called.

"Perhaps I will," Charles said calmly. He forced himself to ignore Serena for the moment, though the anger within him now burned at fever pitch as he was quickly studying the room. Chairs stood at Garnett's side, blocking his way. A direct assault would not work in this situation, not with Serena seriously threatened. He'd have to try something else, improvise something. Unfortunately, he could not think of a thing.

Unexpectedly, Serena's eyes darted to the left, and her left eye blinked, while her head shifted a tiny bit in that direction. She was going to try something, he realized, and it terrified him. He couldn't stop her.

"So," Charles said pleasantly, hoping to lull Garnett, hoping he'd lessen his grip on Serena's waist. "What is your plan?"

"Why, to get money, of course. What do you think?"

Charles leaned back just a tiny bit, let his pistol lower just a tiny bit, though he was as alert as ever he'd been. "And how do you plan to escape?"

"I'll have a hostage, of course. I don't believe you'll care for that, Kirk. Sorry, old boy," he called over to Hyatt, who was standing as tall as he could, enraged and totally ineffective, with no pistols and no fighting skills. "I never did intend for you to have her. I will."

"To the contrary, Garnett," Charles said. "You're welcome to her."

"I beg your pardon?"

Charles leaned back even farther. "She's been naught but trouble to me. Complaining about the food, about walking so much—hell, even about our hiding places."

Serena smiled briefly, and then raised her eyebrow in inquiry. A quick glance showed him that Garnett's arm had indeed loosened. Taking a deep breath, he nodded very slightly, and prayed that whatever she had planned would work.

Without any warning, even to Charles, Serena stomped on Garnett's instep and then spun, her nails raking down his face. Instinctively he tossed her aside. "You little hellcat—"

It was Charles's chance. He leaned forward, pistol

aimed. "This is for Luz," he said and shot Garnett neatly just below his left collarbone. "And this," he took aim again and fired into Garnett's right shoulder, "is for Serena."

Garnett's pistol discharged harmlessly at the ceiling, making some plaster rain down on them. Then, trying without success to clutch his shoulder, he fell to the floor.

As quickly as that, it was over. Charles fairly bounded over the chair nearest him toward Serena, lying in a heap on the floor. "Oh, my dear!" He drew in his breath as she raised her head, her eyes dazed. "Oh, my dear," he said again, and grasped her shoulders. "Are you all right? Did they hurt you?"

"N-no. But, oh, Charles!" She launched herself at him. "Oh, I was so scared."

"I know. I know." He held her close with arms that shook. "So was I. But it's over, dear." He glanced up to see Hyatt, though struggling, held in the grasp of two strong footmen. "It's truly over."

"Ahem." Someone nearby cleared his throat, and they looked up to see the earl. "Would someone care to explain to me what this was all about?"

Charles glanced at Garnett, who was trying to hold both his wounds, pushed the gun farther from his reach, and then rose, his arm about Serena's waist. "My lord, I am Major Kirk—"

"So I gathered." He looked coolly at Serena. "Well, Serena?"

Serena glanced quickly at Charles and took one step, as brave as ever Charles had seen her. "Daddy?" she said uncertainly.

That did it. The earl opened his arms to her, and she stumbled into them. "Oh, my little girl," he said, holding her convulsively. "My little girl."

"Daddy," Serena said again, and broke down. She had done that only once during their long, perilous journey, Charles thought, feeling very much out of place and no longer needed. Without calling attention to himself, he turned toward the door.

"Kirk," the earl called over Serena's head, his eyes hard. "I wish to have a word with you."

"Certainly, my lord. If you will allow me to inform my family that I'm safe, and change out of all my dirt first?"

The earl inclined his head. "Yes. And then I expect you back here."

"Yes, my lord," Charles said, trying not to be annoyed at the earl's imperious tone, and left, feeling peculiarly flat. Their adventure was over.

Somewhat later, with Geoffrey having clapped him on the back in relief, with Ariel, emotional from the effects of her pregnancy, having cried over him, after his mother had fussed over him and his grandmother had scolded, Charles was again admitted to Harlow House, this time with Fletcher grinning at him. He was his own neat, precise self. His valet had trimmed and combed his hair, he had been shaved to within an inch of his life, and his coat of blue superfine was cut along severe, almost military lines. Though he was shown into an anteroom, it was only a moment or so before Fletcher returned to usher him into the earl's study. "Lady Serena?" he asked without preamble.

"Resting in her room, I believe, sir. As you might understand, she was quite tired."

Charles nodded. That Serena was exhausted he could well understand, indeed. If he, who had become hardened to such confrontations, had found it difficult, how must a gently bred young lady feel? "I'm not surprised," he said, and paused. "What sort of mood is the earl in, Fletcher?"

Fletcher shook his head. "It's hard to tell, sir."

Again Charles nodded. He remembered Serena telling him the same thing, though clearly the earl had been overjoyed and overcome with relief to see her. How he would feel about the man who had been with her for so long and had so clearly compromised her was another matter.

"Enter," the earl called when Fletcher knocked on the study door.

Charles went in. He thought he heard Fletcher whisper, "Good luck," but he wasn't certain. "Good evening, my lord," he said, and executed a neat bow.

To his surprise, the earl came out from behind his desk, his hand outstretched. "And good evening to you. Please, sit. I understand you were hurt recently?"

"Nothing life-threatening, my lord, and I am recovered from it."

"Please, call me Harlow. I'm sorry to call you out so late in the evening, but you can understand my concern. May I offer you something to drink, by the by?"

"A whiskey would not come amiss, my—Harlow," he said, his bafflement growing. Harlow was behaving as if this were a normal social call, when it was anything but.

"Good. Here, sir," the earl said, and settled across from Charles in a leather wing chair, his eyes so keen, so assessing, that Charles quickly revised his opinion. This man was awake upon all suits.

"Thank you. Your butler tells me Lady Serena is well."

"Yes. Apparently I have you to thank for that? Although," he went on before Charles could say anything, "she did tell me some odd sort of story about hiding in bushes and wearing boy's clothes?"

In spite of everything, Charles smiled. "We did agree some time back that the entire thing sounded preposterous. Shall I tell you, sir?"

"If you would," Harlow said, as if they were discussing something so mundane as the weather.

And so Charles told the story, from beginning to end, leaving nothing out. Both were quiet when he had finished. "It does sound preposterous," the earl said. "You were, indeed, with her for all save four days?"

"Yes, sir." He paused. "Has she told you what she feared would happen had she stayed Garnett's captive much longer?"

Harlow turned away. "She didn't need to," he said in a low voice. "I must thank you for rescuing her from that."

"They were resourceful, sir," he said frankly. "There were times I thought we'd not escape them."

"And then, God help her." He straightened. "They'll go before the magistrates, of course, and 'tis likely they'll be transported. There'll be the devil of a scandal about it, but my daughter is safe. I'm grateful to you. However." His lean face, so unlike Serena's, turned stern. "The fact remains that you compromised her."

"I'm well aware of that, sir."

"What do you intend to do about it?"

"Marry her, of course," he said promptly.

Harlow's brow furrowed. "She said you wouldn't."

"Pardon me, sir, but I asked her many a time," he corrected firmly. "Did she say instead that we wouldn't?"

"Yes," the earl said, after a moment.

"She agreed with me quite early that she had been compromised," Charles went on. "But she never once agreed that we should marry."

"Hm."

"She told me she never wished to marry, and that was early along, too. She did the same thing in Guildford." He paused. "It seems like years since we were at Guildford."

"And?"

"She said something curious there. She said she'd fail me. No." He looked at the earl. "Not that. That she would fail."

Harlow didn't speak right away. "Do you love her?"

"Of course I love her."

"Do you know if she loves you?"

"I've no idea, sir. If she does, she never said so."

"Of course she wouldn't," the earl said in exasperation. "Clearly you know little about women."

"I thought I did, my lord."

"Call me Harlow," he repeated. "And no, you don't. A woman will not declare herself until a man does."

"Why not, sir?"

"Think, man. If a woman loves a man—and I don't think much of these modern marriages made for what passes as love—and she declares that love, it scares him. He may back off, and what happens to her then? Or if he doesn't," he said slowly, "he has her in his power. Where, if 'tis the other way around—"

"She holds him in *her* power," Charles said quietly.

"Not in the same way, and well you know it, sir. Not when a man may do with his wife as he wishes."

"I would never hurt Serena."

"Unless you didn't love her."

"But I do, sir." Charles leaned forward, his expression earnest. "Of course I do."

"Because she is the daughter of a wealthy earl? Because she is the Incomparable? Or because—"

"She *is* incomparable, Harlow," Charles interrupted, with the icy voice he'd once used to control his troops. "Unlike anyone I've ever known. Managing, maddening, obstinate—"

"High praise indeed, sir."

Charles grinned. "Also brave, funny, and quite beautiful, even when dusty and a little bit untidy. But, sir, surely you can't want a viscount's second son for your daughter?" he said seriously.

"Who will have her else, to be frank? Hyatt was correct

on that, damn his eyes." Harlow looked away, his jaw clenched. "Her reputation has been ruined."

"When all she did was try to survive," Charles said, quiet again.

"As I'm aware." He, too, fell silent, and then sighed. "Would you have her, if she wished it?"

"In a minute, sir, though I doubt she does." He frowned. "Why did she say she'd fail?"

The earl looked at him assessingly. "What did she tell you of me?"

"Very little, except for one thing." Charles paused, and then forged ahead. "She believes you wished for a son."

"A son!" Harlow said, startled. "She must know I love her."

"No, sir. She's not sure of that at all."

"A son," he repeated, and then jumped to his feet, paced to the drinks table, and replenished his brandy. "Damn her."

"Serena?" Charles said, startled.

"No. My late, unlamented wife." He sat down and downed half his brandy in one swallow. "Shall I tell you something about Serena?"

Mystified, Charles nodded. "Yes, sir."

"We married for love, my wife and I. Yes, I know what I said a moment ago. It was an arranged marriage originally, of course. Early on, though, we fell in love."

"I see," Charles said.

"No, you don't," Harlow said emphatically. "When what we thought was love wore off, we had nothing to hold us together. We were only infatuated, but we had been too young to know it. By then, though, it was too late for our girls." He drank the remainder of his brandy. "My wife was sulky and discontented, and I withdrew into this room, or into the library. The family became divided."

Charles frowned. "I don't get your drift, sir."

" 'Tis like this." Harlow shifted in his chair, and finally looked at Charles. "Sometimes families divide. Sometimes one parent will cling to a particular child, leaving the other child to the other parent."

"Your family, sir?"

"Yes, my family. My wife barely knew Serena was there. By God, man!" He stabbed at the air. "Serena is my daughter. I love her."

"Yet your wife told her—"

"No. My wife didn't tell Serena that because she believed it. She said it as a weapon against me."

"But Serena believed it," he said, stunned.

"My wife died when Serena was eight. How old could she have been when she was told it? Of course she believed it. She still does, from what you've told me." His eyes were bleak. "A powerful weapon indeed, to strike me from the grave."

"No, sir," Charles said quietly. "It struck Serena instead."

"Serena was simply a tool for her. She saw an unhappy marriage," he explained, almost gently. "She saw what was supposedly a love match, when it was anything but, and she was too young to know it. And now she's seen arranged marriages—"

"And marriages of convenience, and marriages to Cits for money in exchange for a title. Yes, sir, she told me that. And she hadn't a good example, had she? No offense, sir."

Harlow waved that off. "No, Kirk. I understand it now. Serena believes she was the cause of the failure, because she wasn't a son and I blamed my wife. Damn her eyes," he added, and this time Charles knew he was referring to his wife.

"You never wished she was a son?"

"No."

"Not even when she was born?"

"Not even before she was born."

"She needs to hear that from you, sir, if I may say so," Charles said.

"I intend to—"

"No." Charles was frowning, remembering things Serena had said throughout their long escape, remembering how she had acted. "There's more, sir. I can't quite put it into words. She needs something from you, but damned if I know what it is."

The earl was watching him, his gaze inscrutable. "Do you wish to see her?"

"She is still awake?" Charles said in surprise. "Fletcher told me she was resting."

The earl shook his head. "I had it from her maid, just before you came in. Apparently she can't sleep." He paused. "You see, she needs something from you, too."

Charles rose. He had a strong suspicion he knew what the earl meant. "May I have your permission to court her, sir?"

The earl waved him away. "Don't be foolish. I believe you earned that right at Oakhurst."

Earned, not owed. Charles smiled and held out his hand as the other man rose. "Then I'll go to see her, sir."

"She is in the drawing room. Fletcher will lead you there." They made their bows to each other, until Harlow crossed the room and rang for the butler.

Charles followed Fletcher up the wide, shallow stairs that led to the drawing room. Her father was a complex man, Serena had told him. The earl's study was plain, and yet there was such opulence in the public areas in the house, with the marble stairway, the plush carpeting, and the great chandelier that hung from the ceiling above to the U of the double staircase. It was brilliant with candles, as if there were a ball or rout being held there. Fletcher noticed the direction of

Charles's gaze, and smiled. "In celebration of Lady Serena's return, sir," he explained.

"As well it should be," he said, and stood to the side as Fletcher knocked lightly on the drawing room door, announced Charles's name, and then withdrew. He and Serena were left alone.

She stood at a window, holding back a drape and looking out, as if it were daytime and there was something to see. She was dressed as he'd never seen her, in light green silk that fell in soft folds from her breasts and gently outlined her hips. Her hair was dressed simply, too, in a coil at the back of her head, with only a few wisps left to curl about her face. Such simplicity was costly, but then, the earl was wealthy. The effect was worth it. He guessed that she looked beautiful. But then, she always had to him.

Serena turned at his entrance. The silence between them was awkward, as it never had been on the road. "The garden is lovely out there at this time of year," she said finally.

"I imagine it is," he said, and at last came farther into the room. "You are well?"

"Of course." She sounded surprised. "Why should I not be?"

"After today . . ."

She smiled. "After everything."

It came to him, then, what she needed from her father. Forgiveness. Absolution for having to flee on the road. Absolution for having been abducted in the first place. Absolution for what she might have suffered at Garnett's hands. For all of it. "I think you need to talk to your father," he said,

"Why?" she asked, watching him warily as he paced toward her.

"He'll tell you. Now." He stopped so that his gaze could take her in. She was all woman, and she was his.

She simply didn't know it yet. "Not at all like what you wore in Brighton."

She laughed, and it broke any restraint remaining between them. "I could say the same for you, Mr. Kirk. That is a fine coat. Weston?"

"Mr. Kirk!" His eyebrows rose. "Serena, after being together for so long, you call me that?"

"But we are not on the road anymore, sir."

"So we aren't," he said, and at last possessed her hands. "No, don't pull away, Serena. Look at me. Look at me, dear."

Her face rose at the unexpected endearment. "I— you shouldn't call me such."

"No? Why not?"

"Because you feel you must." She pulled free at last and went again to the window. Her shoulders were very straight, and yet he could feel the despair emanating from her, the strain. "Because you feel you compromised me."

"No. Because we had fun together."

She whirled. "Fun!"

"Yes. Because we stole horses and rode down roads we didn't know. You enjoyed that. So did I." His grin widened. "Sidesaddle, my dear, with no riding habit. You have very nice ankles, you know."

"Oh, stop! Please stop!" she said despairingly.

"Slender, well-turned—hm. I wonder what your legs are like."

"Stop it!"

"That terrible inn in Brighton. Do you remember?"

"That little maworm of an innkeeper? Of course I do."

"We went around in disguise and I tried to teach you how to walk as a boy," he went on.

She gave him a little, unwilling smile. "You were an unlikely farm woman."

"And you, a boy. Too many curves, my dear," he said, and winked.

"Charles!"

"Ah, my name, at last. A barmaid tried to seduce you . . ."

"Charles!" she repeated.

"And we toured that odd building in Chichester's market square, and were thoroughly bored with everything else."

"And then you were hurt. Oh, Charles!" Her face crumpled. "I thought you would die. I thought I would lose you."

He was across the room in two strides, holding her close against him. "But you didn't, dear. You didn't. If anything, you brought me back to life."

She pulled away from him. He pulled out his handkerchief and gently mopped her face. "H-how?"

"I'd never told anyone about Luz."

Her eyes flew to his. "I know. I know how you need her."

"Silly girl. I need you."

"But—"

He lightly touched her nose with his fingertip. "I love you."

She pulled completely away at that, crushing his handkerchief in her hand. "But you love Luz!"

"Do I? I saw her for less than a fortnight," he said, paraphrasing her words. "She looked different from English girls. I knew no Portuguese, she knew no English. When we were together, we had her duenna with us, or her brother, who disapproved but translated what we said. About the weather, about how different I found the country and the food, that I enjoyed my stay. Less than a fortnight." He paused to take a deep breath. "And then that last day, I didn't see her at all."

Serena looked over her shoulder at him. "All dead," she whispered.

"But I lived." He turned her to face him. "I lived, and I can't believe there wasn't a reason for it. Maybe the reason was you."

For the first time, he saw hope dawning in her eyes. "To rescue me?"

"No. For you to rescue *me*." He searched her face. "Luz was a dream when I needed a dream, far from home in a strange country. She was my . . ." He searched for a word and then found it. "She was my Dulcinea."

"Oh," she breathed, and he could see by her face that she understood the reference to *Don Quixote*.

"But you, Serena," he went on, before she could fully assimilate what he had just said, before she could believe he was still obsessed by that dream, "you are—"

"Aldonza?" she supplied helpfully.

"No!" It came out as a great gust of laughter. "Not quite that earthy, my love. But you are here, real and solid and alive. Luz gave me a dream. You gave me my life back." He steeled himself and took the risk. "I love you, Serena."

She was crying again, but they were different tears, tears of hope. "But if I fail you—"

"Life is a risk, Serena. Marriage is a risk. We'll argue and disagree, like anyone. But," he said portentously, "I have a plan."

That did it. She laughed and went into his arms, rubbing her face against his shoulder. "Oh, Charles, I love you so much, but I thought it was hopeless. That's why I said what I did in Guildford. I needed to drive you away from me. No, I did, Charles!" she said, as if he'd been about to protest. "I needed to do it then, so I wouldn't hurt you worse later. So you wouldn't feel obliged."

He snorted. "Obliged. I've never felt obliged."

"But—"

"I wanted to marry you from the beginning, of course. You look so very fetching with twigs in your hair."

"Do be serious," she said, though she shook with laughter.

"Why? I've been so for too long."

"I wanted to marry you, too," she confessed. "You were my hero."

He snorted again. "A most reluctant one."

"Reluctant? I don't believe so."

He rested his forehead against hers. "Not for my princess. Never for that."

"Am I your princess?"

"Yes," he said, and waited. "And I am?" he finally prompted.

"Incomparable," she said, and went into his arms.

AUTHOR'S NOTE

Researching this book was a royal pain. Since I do my best work in bed (no comments, please), it was there that I did my research. Most of the time I was surrounded by maps, both recent and contemporaneous, guidebooks, literary works, a thesaurus, the invaluable magazine *Realm*, the equally invaluable reprint in facsimile of the 1829 edition of *Paterson's Roads*, and the totally useless, but highly entertaining, facsimile reprint of the 1892 guidebook, *Belgravia and Mayfair*. With the aid of a magnifying glass I spent so many hours poring over the Victorian reprints of the 1805 ordnance maps of England, trying, often in vain, to collate place names against those found in *Paterson's*, that I often despaired of actually writing the book. Charles' and Serena's adventures took me all over England, in more ways than one.

Serious students of history will have noticed that I've taken a few liberties. I tried to be as accurate as possible with the larger picture of the early days of the Peninsular War; I may possibly have failed. I don't know of any building that exploded in Oporto, since those French who hadn't already fled practically begged to surrender. However, it's possible that some building somewhere on the Peninsula was rigged to explode.

Those who know their literature are also no doubt gnashing their teeth over what must seem to be a glaring mistake. "*She Walks In Beauty* wasn't published until 1815," I can hear them muttering. "What's it doing in a book set in 1809?" Providing the author fun, of course. It was just too appropriate to pass up.

If I appear to complain in this afterword, I'm really not. I hope you've had as much fun reading Charles's and Serena's story as I had writing it. I'm also not really complaining about the research. I love doing it

I'm grateful to Helen Woolverton of Odd Facts

Unearthed, for her reprints of *Paterson's Roads* and that absurd guide to Belgravia and Mayfair; to Anne Woodley for the basic information found on her website on the Peninsular War; and the online Regency group, for their help. I'm not sure, though, that I'm grateful to Jeanne Goldrick for introducing me to those 1805 ordnance maps. Oh, how I'd like to have my eyes back. . . .